The Pariah Child: Sarafina's Return

OTHER BOOKS BY NATASHA D. LANE

The Woman in the Tree
The Pariah Child & the Ever-Giving Stone

THE PARIAH CHILD:
SARAFINA'S RETURN

By Natasha D. Lane

PROLOGUE

Sarah's cheek was cool against the well's stone wall. She pressed closer to the structure, enjoying the contrast in temperature. While her front was cooled from shade and stone, her back was warmed by the morning sun.

She felt steady.

Sarah wrapped her arms around the well as far as they could go. She chuckled when they didn't even make it halfway.

Though her mother Lucille had told her to sleep in, Sarah had woken up with the sunrise. After tossing under her blanket for some time, she decided a walk in the woods would rest her. And it had, especially now that the woods were safe again. No wolves, dragons, or Lyrican faeries. Just all the creatures who had been there before.

No Serwa or Alexander either. No Jacob.

The well's cold suddenly felt dampening. Sarah moved away from it, standing up to head home. She walked slowly from an exhaustion that tugged at her, as well as the thoughts which drowned her mind.

Maybe she'd be able to go back again one day.

When her home came into view, Sarah took a single deep breath, then marched inside. To her surprise, the house was quiet. There were no bacon or flapjacks on the stove. Apparently, her parents were sleeping in, too.

Her heart swelled. They deserved it after spending a year searching for her. She had never meant to be gone that long. How could time in Lyrica be so different? But Serwa had warned Sarah. She just didn't want to think it would happen to her.

Closing her bedroom door quietly, Sarah fell onto her bed. She stretched out over her comforter, before pulling the blanket to her chin and propping *Peter & Wendy* on her chest.

Since Sarah returned from Lyrica—or ran away, which was her mother's only reasonable explanation—every day had been easier than before she left. Her mother still kept a wary eye on her, yet she was kinder, gentler with Sarah. And her father Paul had gotten into the habit of checking Sarah's bedroom each evening and morning.

There was a peace.

Sarah wiggled her toes while she read the last page and turned to the back of the book. There, on the inside of the back cover, was a promise Sarah's younger self had scribbled down so many years ago.

"I promise that one day I'm going to go on an adventure, just like Wendy and Peter. And we're going to beat all the bad men and save the day."

-Sarafina L. Wickeson"

Sarah smiled. She traced her hands over her oath and on the last word, a strange tingling began in her finger. Golden spirals of dust appeared. There was a light "poof" before the dust vanished, leaving behind an imprint.

Sarah looked between her tingling finger and the back cover.

At the end of her oath there was a box with a golden check mark.

CHAPTER 1

(Two Years Later)

Sarah's hair spread over the water like wildfire, consuming her body, hiding the pale skin and freckles as she sunk. She took a deep breath before submerging herself, leaving only her blue eyes to stare at the vastness in front of her. She closed them and imagined her skin burning as it had done several years ago. But now she was consumed by water and water would quench the fire.

She leaned her head back. All sounds became hollow; all movement was a vibration.

Her skin had burned, her skin was burning, but she was not afraid for she was consumed by water.

"Sarafina!" Lucille banged on the bathroom door. "Sarafina!"

Sarah shot up in the tub, taking in a sharp breath. Her long hair was plastered against her back and her skin was covered in goosebumps.

"Did you turn into a fish in there, girl?"

Sarah's hand shook as she gripped the rim of the tub and tried to steady herself. Her mind had sent her wandering again.

"Hurry up and get dressed," Lucille called. "We're waiting downstairs with dinner."

"Yes, Mama."

Sarah waited until she heard retreating footsteps, then stumbled from the tub and grabbed her towel. She went to wipe the steam off the mirror but realized there was none.

Did I fall asleep again?

Sarah rubbed her eyes. The tips of her fingers looked like prunes.

She sighed. "I'm surprised I haven't drowned yet."

Sarah rung out her hair and headed to her room. She pulled a dress over top her head, not bothering with the buttons. She knew her mother's patience was thinning.

"Sarafina!"

From her bedroom, she tottered down the hall, tucking her necklace into her dress as she reached the stairwell. Just as her mother placed her right foot on the bottom step, Sarah appeared at the top of the stairs.

Sarah smiled at her mother. Lucille shook her head and returned to the table.

"Hey, there, water bug!" Her father Paul greeted her with a grin as she took her seat.

"Very funny, Daddy," she replied, starting to fill her plate.

"Not before we pray, young lady." Lucille held out her hands to Paul and Sarah. The three clasped palms and bowed their heads.

"Dear Heavenly Father, thank you for this food you have blessed us with and the company you have blessed us with, Lord. We hope that we may continue to serve you on this earth for many days to come. Amen."

"That was beautiful, Lucille." Paul gave his wife's hand a squeeze.

"Thank you." She smiled. "Someone has to keep this family's souls intact."

Paul slathered his cornbread in butter and stuffed it in his mouth. "I think our souls are doing just fine, dear."

Watching him from the corner of her eye, Lucille stuck up her nose. "Well, you did miss church last Sunday, Paul."

"Yes, because I had to work."

"Working on your soul is more important," she retorted.

"It was *your* decision we should start going to church in town," he huffed. "I was happy with the evening sermon you held for Sarah and I once I got home."

Lucille shook her head, gathering some peas on her plate. "It's better to attend church with our neighbors. We can't always stay out here. We need to get to know people, Paul."

"Oh, so now they'll call us 'friend' when they gossip about us. I guess it'll help ease the guilt."

Lucille glared at him.

Sarah stuffed a piece of chicken in her mouth, preventing her laughter. Since Sarah had last *disappeared*, as her mother liked to describe it, Lucille had made it her mission to become an honorable town member. Along with going to church, Lucille attended any community event and even ran for official office. Of course, no one voted for her but that didn't stop her from walking around with a smile plastered on her face.

"Sarah?"

"Huh?" Her mother's voice pulled Sarah from her thoughts.

Lucille frowned. "The proper response is 'yes,' Sarah. 'Huh' is what low-class folks use. God, we need to get you some etiquette courses."

Paul scoffed. "Is she auditioning to be the Queen of England?"

Sarah took another big bite of chicken. The laughter was brewing in her throat.

"It's small differences like 'yes' and 'huh' that'll get a girl a husband, Paul. Actually, I found out some news today." She gave them a pointed look before taking her time spreading a slather of butter on her cornbread.

Neither Paul or Sarah responded.

Lucille continued. "Little Elaine, the one with the blonde curls and pretty eyes? Well, from what the ladies told me she may be married after graduation."

"Married? How old's that girl?"

"Fifteen, Paul. Same age as Sarah." Lucille looked at her daughter. Sarah averted her gaze to her plate.

Paul shrugged. "I guess it seems about the right age for her. She'll be fully grown by time she graduates, ripe for marrying. Who's the lucky boy?"

"You know, Thomas Lanston? His father owns the shoe repair store and his mother runs the new bakery."

Paul nodded. "Well, they seem like they'll make a fine couple. Give her family my congratulations if you see them."

Lucille turned to Sarah. She watched her daughter for a few moments, then moved back to her husband.

"The news got me thinking." Lucille scooted the food around on her plate.

A shiver ran up Sarah's spine.

Paul was pulling off the last bit of meat from a chicken bone when he raised his brow and met Lucille's eyes.

Sarah's heart had started racing. She wiggled her toes beneath the table as a sudden urge to leave the room, as well as the conversation overtook her.

Lucille gave a shaky smile. "Sarah and Elaine are the same age. We need to start thinking about—"

"Nope." He tossed the cleaned bone on his plate.

Sarah gawked at her mother. Had she really been suggesting it was time to marry her off?

"Why is it fine and well for Elaine but not for Sarah?"

The young woman blinked rapidly to ensure it was actually her mother in front of her speaking. They had never discussed marriage. She wasn't even sure she wanted to get married though she doubted there'd be a line of suitors at her door.

Missing for a year? Town crazy? Not very appealing to her male peers.

If Sarah was being honest, however, they weren't very appealing to her either.

"Sarah is my daughter. Elaine ain't," he said. "She just needs to focus on school and being a kid."

Lucille dropped her fork, narrowing her eyes. "You ever think maybe she spends too much time worrying about school? She has perfect scores and spends all her time alone."

"I don't like the kids at school," Sarah replied, finally breaking her silence. Dozens of retorts, much better than what she had said, raced through her mind. Each response hoped to make it first to the tip of her tongue. She could feel the air heating in her chest while she debated how best to continue.

Paul added, "And I don't want any boys barking around my daughter."

Thank God for dads. Sarah sent her father the most thankful grin.

Lucille threw her hands up. "Is she going to spend the rest of her life alone?"

"Mama, I'll be fine." She pressed her forehead into the palm of her hand. "I don't mind being alone. Other people are troublesome."

Lucille leaned across the table with widening eyes, forcing Sarah to meet them. She hesitated.

"You don't even know what that means, Sarafina," she said. "To be alone…"

Paul placed a hand on Lucille's shoulder. "Honey—"

She shrugged him off and turned back to her food. "You'll be an old maid, young lady."

Paul's blue eyes twinkled. He tossed his fork onto his plate, the metal clattering breaking the moment. He glanced between his wife and daughter before placing two old, wrinkled hands on his full belly.

"Oh, you don't gotta worry about her being an old maid, honey," he said. "I heard they have the most fun."

He winked at Sarah and this time she giggled right through the chicken.

Lucille snatched her plate from the table and tossed it into the sink, where she began scrubbing the dish like it was a skunked dog.

Paul pursed his lips and nodded toward the stairs. Sarah quickly finished her food before moving from the table. A quick peck on her mother's cheek and Sarah was up the stairs. She didn't have the strength to hold against her mother's approaching storm.

The door clicked shut. Relief washed over Sarah. Alone in her room, she could breathe. She stood on her tippy-toes and stretched her arms up high. Her muscles ached from working on the farm and her bones cracked from sitting in school all day.

Sarah found her way to her bed and fell across it, her feet hanging off the side. She heard some muttering downstairs but pushed her mind from the hushed voices. It would do her no good to listen to their arguing.

Instead, she pulled out *Peter & Wendy* from under her bed. She flipped to the back cover. The golden checkmark still glittered.

"It's kind of like it was only yesterday, not nearly three years ago."

She traced her fingers over the rest of the unchecked cover.

"What about the rest of my adventures?" she asked. "Will I have a chance to finish them, too?"

Sarah waited a moment, hoping the tingling would return to her fingers and another golden checkmark would appear.

None did. She pressed the book to her chest, her eyes burning some. Images of Lyrica raced through her mind. So much of the experience was still fresh but several memories were fading, slipping through her fingers when she tried to grasp them.

What color were Abelard's eyes again? Green or blue?

And what flowers did Serwa have painted on her cottage walls?

What did Gan like to call her?

A knot built in her stomach.

Sarah untucked the necklace she wore and grasped its trinkets. Alex's ruby and Nettle's small sword always brought her comfort. They were hers and hers alone. Reminders that she hadn't imagined the entire thing.

"Will I ever get to see them again?" She turned to the book once more.

It held no answer.

CHAPTER 2

Sarah tucked her shirt in and tiptoed down the stairs. The first plank of wood creaked beneath her weight, causing her to pause before the next step. Knowing the third step was the loudest, Sarah took a breath and jumped. She landed on the fourth step, making sure to hold herself straight by the end of her toes.

The house remained silent. She looked behind her, adjusting her bow and arrow as she peered into the darkness. No lights flashed and there was no movement.

With a precise grace, Sarah zig-zag jumped down the stairs, until she landed on the floor of her kitchen. She tugged her weapon around her and headed outside to the stables.

The stars were bright in the mid-spring sky, spread across the dark cover of night like a jeweled blanket. Sarah took in a deep breath. She enjoyed the freedom the early morning provided her. The quiet and peace it gave her soul.

In the stables, Nancy was already up and stomping her hooves in her stall, while the cows slept away. She housed the same fiery spirit as her mother Nelly.

Sarah's chest constricted a bit at the thought. If only she had returned from Lyrica a bit sooner...

She shook herself. Nancy's neighs were growing louder, so Sarah opened the stall and mounted her. She was a young horse but strong. Her muscles were solid under Sarah's weight and she carried the girl like she was nothing.

Sarah balled her hands into Nancy's mane. She kicked her sides and they started toward the forest. When they had crossed the first line of trees, Sarah urged her forward and suddenly Nancy was off. The banging of her hooves broke the early morning silence. Aside from the strands Sarah held, Nancy's mane swung wildly around her, bouncing along with Sarah's red curls.

Sarah rested low on Nancy. She arched her back and narrowed her eyes, which were watering thanks to the wind. She could feel Nancy's muscles tightening and loosening as her legs kicked up dust from the ground. She could feel the horse's heart beat quicken, right along with her own.

A smile spread across Sarah's face as she imagined how she and Nancy would look to someone else. Two heroes in the night racing on to another adventure, one black, one red. Fire and darkness. Her mind whirled with a tale.

Gradually, Nancy's gallop slowed until they came to a halt.

Sarah eyed the quiet forest surrounding her.

"It is when things are most quiet one must be most cautious."

Alex.

Sarah inhaled and steadied herself, using Nancy as support. She sat back from the horse, so she was sitting upright. She was silent but her eyes still scanned the forest. Slowly, she reached behind her and drew an arrow.

Snap!

Her bow was at the ready.

"They're coming," Sarah whispered.

She turned to the left and aimed upward. Releasing the arrow, it landed in the center of her stuffed target.

Satisfaction washed over her.

"You'll have to do better than that!" she screamed and reached for another arrow.

Once Sarah had returned from Lyrica, Ethlen and Franklin, along with the other creatures she had played with in the forest as a child, had helped her turn the woods into a training ground. Though she found herself mostly on her back at the start, their strategies were becoming predictable. And she had become stronger.

She grinned.

There was a chill from behind. Sarah dropped forward and tucked her head beside Nancy's while the air shifted above her. Sarah shot up and readied her bow. As the stuffed target swung backwards, Sarah released her arrow, piercing its head.

The target fell to the ground. Sarah already had another arrow mounted. She kicked Nancy in her sides and the horse ran farther into the forest. Targets fell down from the trees, surrounding her like the cursed wolves had done once before.

The arrows were light in her hands, almost weightless with how fast they left her; one after the other, flying through the sky and puncturing her stuffed enemies. Sarah did not count how many targets had appeared. At the slightest sound, there was the quickest flash of a color and an arrow was already soaring through the air. She only stopped when her arrows were gone and her hands were grasping nothing.

Now they'll wait until—

There was a noise to her left. The target flew straight at her, knocking Sarah to the ground, shoulder first. She balled her fists at the sudden pain but kept quiet. A branch above her creaked. She pulled her daddy's knife from her ankle and jumped to her feet, then charged toward the target. With the knife raised, Sarah leapt and pushed the blade into the target's throat. They dropped to the ground.

Her knees crashed into the earth yet she didn't have a moment to feel them.

"Nancy!" She raced toward the horse who had been standing in the trees several yards away. At the sight of Sarah running, her horse galloped in her direction. When there was less than a yard separating them, Sarah pushed herself off the ground and reached for Nancy's neck. Once her arm was wrapped around the horse's neck, she pulled herself onto the animal's back. Nancy didn't hesitate at the sudden weight.

"Alright, so they changed things up. We can still finish!"

Together, they raced deeper into the trees. Sarah braced herself. Her hands were sweating and her breathing was becoming rapid.

"Here it comes," she said.

A low hanging branch appeared in the distance. Sarah locked her eyes on it. They grew closer.

"Now!" With Nancy still galloping, Sarah moved, so she was squatting on the horse's back. She kept low and stretched her arms out, until she could press the tips of her fingers into Nancy's neck.

There was only a short distance. Keeping steady, Sarah rose on the horse's back. She did a few quick steps, then jumped. What felt like several minutes passed before the bark scraped against her palms.

Sarah tightened her hold, waiting for Nancy to turn around but the branch grew limp.

It snapped.

Crossing her arms in preparation for the impact, Sarah sailed to the forest floor. She slammed against the earth and tumbled over three times, before landing by Mother Tree.

She groaned. Nancy nuzzled Sarah.

"I'm okay, Nancy." She reached up and stroked the horse's nose. "I'm just a little sore is all."

Sarah sat up, her back cracking as she did so. She stretched her arms out, then leaned against Mother Tree with Nancy standing beside her. She looked up at what was left of the broken branch.

"I really need to work on that. My flimsy arms don't have any strength in them, though. Doesn't help much."

Nancy clomped her hooves and blew from her nose.

"Yes, I know it's not all about physical strength. Still, it can't hurt, Nancy."

Sarah placed her palm flat against Mother Tree. She inhaled the scent of the forest, allowing the calm to take her. Their energies flowed in and out of one another, moving across the woods.

Mother Tree was old. Her spirit was strong.

Nancy grunted and Sarah opened her eyes, pulling herself back into the real world. The horse looked to the sky which had turned a lighter blue.

It was time for school.

Sighing, Sarah picked herself off the ground and rubbed her aching shoulder.

"Ready to ride?" She smiled at Nancy, then jumped up while grabbing a hold of the horse's mane. A sharp pain shot through her shoulder and her grip loosened. Nancy moved in the direction Sarah pulled her, spinning the young woman in a circle.

Unable to find a good hold, Sarah was tossed from Nancy's side. Her head slammed against Mother Tree's trunk, making first impact. All the air left her body. She slumped downward until the stars rested above her vision. They seemed shinier. Brighter.

Sarah attempted to move but her body refused. There was only the pain in her head anchoring her to the ground.

The stars dulled. The sky faded and lovely blue took its place.

It had been a long time since Sarah felt this freedom. All around her there was nothing but space, space she was rooted in. She stretched and it felt like she had many arms that were touching everywhere. She knew this feeling. She had been here before.

"Sarah? Sarah?"

Who was calling her?

"Sarah!"

"Yes? Who are you?"

It was like a light switch was slowly turning off. Darkness creeped from the edges of the blue, overtaking it until only a small area remained. That was where the voice called her from.

Sarah followed the voice. She peered through the circle of blue, not certain if she wanted to see what was on the other side.

There was an elderly woman. Her image was unsteady but she was looking up at Sarah.

"It is dangerous here," the woman stated. "They lied, Sarah."

Sarah squinted and peered through the little blue.

"If you can hear me, please, come back."

The woman was hunched over with a long braid that hung down her back. Her face was covered in wrinkles, especially laugh lines.

"I know her."

Everything began shaking. Sarah fought to remain stable; the woman seemed so familiar.

"Please, Chosen One."

"Gan?"

The world became tremors and then nothing.

Sarah rested her head against Nancy's side as they made their way home. The sky was still a shaded blue above them.

When she awoke from her dream, she could move again. She had a nice sized lump on her head but there was no blood. No need to waste money on a doctor.

Considering the odd dream she had though, maybe Sarah hit her head just a little too hard. Or was it a memory? Gan had reached out to her the firt stime in the blue world, hadn't she?

Sarah shook herself. All the memories were blurring together as time went on.

The house came into view. Sarah crossed her fingers as she carefully stepped onto the porch. There was no noise from the kitchen and all the rooms remained dark. Opening the screen door, she paused.

"No need for sneaking, Sarah. I've been waiting since dawn." Lucille's voice sent shivers down Sarah's spine like a wet blanket in the winter.

She suppressed a groan and stepped inside the kitchen. "Hi, Mama."

Lucille was leaning against the sink. Her hair was unkempt, there were dark circles under her eyes, and she was still in her nightgown. Apparently, she had been up much earlier than dawn.

Sarah cast her eyes to the floor and rubbed her arm. "I was going to go and...school's starting, so—"

"I thought you said you would stop this, Sarafina."

"Mama, I said I would try."

"Well, you ain't trying hard enough, are you?" Lucille had her arms crossed. Veins protruded along her fists.

She stood from the sink and placed her hand on its rim. Sarah stared up at her. There was an exhaustion in her mother's eyes that was more apparent than the dark circles.

"Sarah, I have asked you not to go frolicking in the woods. It's dangerous and what if one of the neighbors saw you?" The scowl on her mother's face also coated her words.

Sarah bit her tongue. "Mama, I'd have to travel miles to get to the closest neighbor," she replied. "No one is going to see me."

"It's still not acceptable, Sarah," her mother snapped, slamming her hand against the sink. "You aren't some wild child. You're supposed to be a young lady."

"Why can't I just be Sarah?" she shouted. "Wouldn't that be okay?"

Lucille was silent.

"I like it out in the woods," Sarah continued. "It's...where I feel at peace."

Lucille slouched over and shook her head. The veins in her hands shrunk, no longer ready to burst at the seams.

Finally, she turned her head up again and looked at her

daughter.

"You are such a disappointment, Sarafina."

Sarah's throat tightened as she took in a sharp breath. Her mother's words were wrapping around her neck like a python, causing her lips to purse as the pain swelled inside her.

"I should beat you. I would if I thought it would do any good," Lucille said.

Sarah turned away, trying to control the temper in her voice. "Mama, stop."

"There is something very wrong with you, girl," she continued. "What type of child runs away? Disappears for a year, leaving her parents worried sick? Only you. You!"

Sarah spun back around and charged forward, her blue eyes bright with anger. "The kind who has you for a mother," she snapped. "You can beat me all you like but I will never make you happy. You know that. I know it and I don't care."

Lucille paled. Her lips became thin pink lines, while her eyes doubled in size. She took several steps away from her daughter, until she was pressed against the wall.

Sarah raised a brow. "Mama?"

"I see you now," Lucille whispered. She was shaking. "I see you, Devil Child."

"I am not a devil child!" Sarah screamed. The house creaked around them.

"See?" Lucille said. "I always knew it, just didn't want to believe it because I'm your mama. I...I birthed you but I knew." She pointed a trembling finger at Sarah. "You were always an odd baby. No one even knows where you got that red hair from. It's a sign. You—"

"Lucille!"

Lucille and Sarah turned to the stairs. Paul was standing on the third step staring down at them.

"Sarah, go get ready for school," he commanded. "Lucille, start cooking breakfast."

"Paul, she—"

"I said, *cook breakfast.*"

Sarah looked between her parents. Lucille did not move but the veins in her hands were ready to burst again.

Paul shook his head and moved to sit at the table where he

stared at his wife. He turned, reached over, and squeezed her hand. She looked down at him.

"Make breakfast, Lucille."

She paused, gave him a short nod, and turned to the sink.

Sarah didn't wait a moment longer. She darted up the stairs and into the bathroom. Quickly, she undressed and washed up. She tried to find comfort in the warm water that soothed her aches, but her mind remained focused on what her mother had said.

She shivered. Each word felt like it was laced in venom. Yet one hurt more than the others.

Devil Child.

CHAPTER 3

Several hours had passed since Sarah's shouting match with her mother. She had tip-toed between her bedroom and bathroom while she prepared for school. Now standing in the bathroom, Sarah realized the residual rage from their argument had her on edge, including a few strands of her wild hair.

For the most part, Sarah's curly red hair was tamed into one long braid. It fell past her shoulders and a bit before the mid of her back. She smoothed her hands over the braid in an attempt to conceal any untamed curls. The effort was futile. She would tuck one curl away, only for another to spring to life.

Sarah placed her hands on her hips and sighed.

"What's the point?" she asked her reflection. She gazed over her bright red hair, noting how it was starting to take on an orange tint now that summer wasn't too far away. She shook her head.

With her index finger, Sarah took her rebellious curls and twirled them, so they hung free around her.

She looked at her reflection in the mirror and shrugged.

Guess fitting in isn't part of the plan.

Sarah grabbed her bookbag before heading down the stairs. Her father had left already and Lucille was sitting in the kitchen picking at her food. She looked up, but Sarah averted her gaze. She was nearly running to the door when her mother finally spoke.

"Sarah?"

Her name suddenly felt like a curse.

"Yes?" She kept her eyes forward, focused on the woods beyond her home.

"Uh...have a good day in school, okay?" Lucille's voice was shaky, almost forcefully sweet.

"I will." Sarah shot from the kitchen like she was running for the last piece of Huckleberry pie. She kept pumping her legs until she was deep in the forest.

Once her heart had settled and her lungs could take in the air with ease, Sarah felt safer in her home away from home. Flowers were blooming all across the forest, decorating the woods. Birds chirped, bees buzzed, and there was a nice breeze every now-and-again. Spring was alive and kicking.

Sarah hopped over logs and skipped over rocks, making her way to school. Hidden and alone in the woods, Sarah felt more secure than she ever did in the old schoolhouse. The kids hadn't been any kinder once she returned after "missing" for a year.

Everyone wanted to know where she had gone, what she had done, and, of course, why she had left in the first place. Sarah dreamed of telling her father the truth, telling him the whole crazy adventure. She wanted to tell him how much she had missed him and how she had had nightmares about never seeing him again.

She wanted to but Sarah was no fool. If her mother heard her breathe a word of the truth, she would be ready with the straight jacket.

No, Sarah had to keep the truth to herself, no matter how lonely it could be.

The school bell rang. Sarah picked up her dress and raced down the path that brought her to the back door. The school halls were already flooded with her peers who were bunched into various groups along the hallway. Sarah made eye contact with no one. She tugged her bag tight on her shoulder and marched down the hall toward her classroom.

Elaine and her flock had already occupied the space. They were perched on their desks squawking loudly with Elaine at the center: beautiful blonde hair, light blue eyes, cross-legged, and wearing an ear-to-ear smile.

"It's the most wonderful thing I've ever seen, Elaine, really!"

"Thomas is such a gentleman. You're so lucky!"

"Oh, I can't wait to see you in a wedding dress, Elaine. We all know he's going to ask."

The girls were oh-ing over her like she was the prize cattle at the State Fair.

Sarah entered the room without notice and took her seat in the last row. She pulled her long braid to the side and stared out the window. No matter how badly she wanted to tune Elaine's flock out, each time they mentioned Thomas, her ears leaned in for more.

Sarah had been the first to know about Thomas and Elaine, though not intentionally. One day, she'd stayed late after school, working on a project. When she was done, Sarah left through the back door to cut through the woods. That's when she saw them.

They'd been attempting to hide behind the stack of firewood but Sarah had seen them clear as day. Elaine was wearing her prettiest blue dress, the one with the nice lace trim. Thomas wore a green cuffed shirt that complemented his dark brown hair. And they were together. Their hands and lips were clasped together like they never had plans of parting.

Sarah had stayed hidden in the school until she heard them leave. She'd walked home that day in a daze. Yes, Thomas and Elaine were both well to do. Yes, Elaine was pretty and Thomas was as handsome as they come. It only made sense they would court.

Still, Sarah had hoped Thomas, with his gentle smile and dimpled cheeks, would want more than popularity or beauty. She had hoped he'd want her...

The final bell rang and the classroom filled with students. The teacher, Mr. Greensburg, came in for the first lesson of the day: Arithmetic.

"Good morning, class. I hope you all are prepared for today's lesson," he said, his mustache twitching with each word. "We're continuing on with last week's lesson and practicing our equations."

He spun on his heels, grabbed a piece of chalk, and began writing lists of equations on the board.

Sarah grabbed a pencil from her desk and some paper. Her fingers were like dragonflies, zooming across the page in an attempt to keep up with Mr. Greensburg. He would stop every now-and-then to lecture about one equation before turning toward the blackboard again. Sarah listened while writing and wrote while listening until her fingers grew slack.

She tried writing faster yet her hand would not budge. She lifted her head from her papers. It felt as heavy as a three gallons of milk. The class blackboard was blurry. It had become nothing but lines of black and white that couldn't stay in one place.

Sarah took a deep breath. She blinked rapidly, trying to gain focus again. The equations were falling off the blackboard and onto the classroom floor. Nothing was making sense.

She tried to grasp her pencil. Her hand remained stagnant, and then everything became light. Her vision was coated in that lovely blue again but this time there was no Gan, no trees, no Lyrica. Instead, Sarah heard wings flapping. The sound grew louder the longer she stayed in the blue until...

Sarah jumped in her seat just as the bell rang. She gasped, taking in air, coming back from wherever she had been. The blue was gone and she was left with the lifeless colors of her classroom.

She peered around, expecting all eyes to be on her.

Instead, her peers were chatting loudly with the school bell as they left the room. She turned her attention to the front. Mr. Greensburg was gone, as well as his lists of equations. Instead, Ms. Carr stood at the chalkboard, eraser in hand, removing the lines of a sonnet.

Where had Mr. Greensburg gone?

Sarah stared down at her notebook. The pages were full from the day's subjects but she couldn't even remember Mr. Greensburg leaving. Her stomach churned.

"Sarafina, are you alright?" Ms. Carr was now standing by Sarah's desk, her almond brown hair tucked into a perfectly round bun. Her lips thinned as her eyes roamed over Sarah.

"You look pale as a ghost."

Sarah shook her head and tried to smile. "I'm fine."

"Are you sure?"

"Yes, ma'am. The fresh air from my walk home will help me," she replied. "Have a nice day." Sarah got up to leave, though her body now seemed ignorant to the action, and she fell back into her seat.

Ms. Carr smiled and stood faithfully by Sarah's desk.

"Is there something wrong, ma'am?"

Ms. Carr shook her head. "No, not at all. The opposite actually."

She walked around the desk and took the seat beside Sarah. "I want to talk to you about something, Sarafina."

"Uh...okay." Sarah backed into her seat. "Have I done something wrong?"

"What? Oh, no, not at all." Ms. Carr smiled. "I want to ask you a question, actually. Have you considered further schooling?"

Sarah frowned. "My family wouldn't have enough to send me to college, even if I were a boy."

"College is expensive but there are ways around it," said Ms. Carr.

"I'm not sure if—"

"You are smart enough, Sarafina," she corrected. "The smartest in this school, exceeding your peers in all grade levels."

Sarah gawked. Blinking, she leaned closer to her teacher, trying to ensure she had heard her right.

"Really?"

The smile on Ms. Carr's face grew to her ears. "Yes, which is why I think you should be the first young woman from our small school to attend college. You don't want to spend all your life here, do you?"

Sarah pulled her hair over her shoulder. She played with the end of her braid, not really looking at Ms. Carr but past her.

What would it be like if I could leave here? If I could go somewhere where no one knew anything about the crazy, poor girl named Sarah? The Devil Child...

An image of her mother flashed in her mind. Suddenly, the idea of leaving seemed like the only option.

"Just imagine New York, Sarafina. Some of the tallest buildings in the world. The brightest lights." Ms. Carr sighed and sloped back in her chair, her eyes beaming.

Sarah watched her curiously. Flashes of emotions darted across Ms. Carr's face.

"Where have you traveled, Ms. Carr?" Sarah moved forward in her seat, tapping her fingers on her knees.

The woman grinned. She sat forward as well, and placed her face in her hand.

"I saved up enough to spend one summer in England. It was wonderful."

"England! What was it like? Do you still have friends there?'

She nodded. "I miss it very much. It's like once you get a taste of the world, you can't help but wish for more."

"Well, why did you return then?" Sarah clamped a hand over her mouth. She sat back. "I'm sorry. I didn't mean to sass."

Ms. Carr shrunk in her seat and looked up at Sarah. "It is a valid question, especially since I'm encouraging you to depart, as well."

"Still, I shouldn't have—"

"I'm not really sure why I came back, Sarafina. One day I had this sudden urge to return. Have you ever had that feeling?" she asked. "A sudden desire to return to something familiar."

Sarah thought of Lyrica. "Very much lately."

"The funny thing is once you return, you want to go back to the place you had been before."

"You can never have both?" Sarah asked.

"Doesn't seem like it." Ms. Carr tapped her chin. "But, you know, if there's anyone smart enough to figure it out, it's you, Sarafina."

"Thank you, Ms. Carr." Sarah didn't want to smile yet she found her lips curving up. She didn't receive compliments often.

"No need to thank me. It's a fact, not baseless praise. Will you think about what I told you?"

Sarah nodded.

"I'm glad. I will see you tomorrow for last period?"

"Yes, ma'am."

"Good."

Sarah gave Ms. Carr a quick smile, before grabbing her things and leaving the school house. She walked toward the path home when the wind picked up. The books she held tumbled from her hands. Sarah bent down to gather them but froze with her hand on the spine of her English text.

What are you doing here?

He stood on the other side of the road, a casual look on his face, his eyes focused on Sarah. Her heart shook and she wanted to kill the bit of joy she felt from seeing him. But she couldn't and her eyes were locked on him as his were on her.

Then, he smiled. Sarah shook herself, before closing her eyes. She had to be hallucinating. The visions and sounds were from her head injury. That was all.

When she opened her eyes once more, Jacob was gone. The road across from her was empty.

CHAPTER 4

"Where are you, you little snake?" Sarah's eyes were narrowed, her brow slanted, and her lips sore from chewing on them. She had brought a book for company but found she couldn't pretend to read. Her eyes were glued to the road, waiting for Jacob to return.

A week had passed since her sighting of him. She had stayed late each day, waiting for him to appear again with nothing to show for her efforts. Now, perched out front on the school steps, she was spending her Saturday doing the same thing.

Sarah rubbed the book's spine. "Am I wasting my time here?"

The spring sun cast the trees' long shadows down the dirt road, and the wooden steps were warm beneath Sarah. Leaning forward, she peered into the trees, hoping to see him hiding among their shadows.

There was laughter. Sarah shot from her seat.

Rustling came from the woods across the road. Sarah moved down one step. She imagined her hair standing up on her head like a cat with its claws out. The rustling grew louder. She took another step down, ready to chase Jacob if he ran.

She could see a figure, the sun moving their shadow alongside the trees.

"Tom, come on!" said one voice.

"My grandmother moves faster than you," said another.

"I'm coming. I'm coming."

Sarah plopped back in her seat just as Thomas and three other town boys broke through the woods and started down the road. Each boy dusted himself off when he emerged into sight. Thomas brought up the rear.

They laughed and pushed each other around until they caught

sight of Sarah.

She snatched her book and flipped to a random page, keeping her head down but her eyes up. The boys spent a few seconds eyeing her, before continuing their march up the road. There was no friendly greeting, verbal or otherwise. It was almost like she wasn't there. Like these boys hadn't known her since they were toddlers.

When Thomas looked in her direction, Sarah turned her eyes downward and prayed.

"Hey, there, Sarah!"

She looked up. Thomas had the biggest smile on his face as he waved his hand wildly.

Blood rushed to Sarah's cheeks. "H-hi, Thomas."

His friends glanced back at him and walked a little faster.

"How are you this afternoon?" He stuck his hands in his pocket and strolled.

"I'm fine." She chuckled. "Just doing some reading for English. And you? Enjoying the spring weather?"

He nodded. "A lot of bugs. Otherwise it's good. I'll see you in school?"

"Yup. See ya then, Thomas." Sarah waved, wondering if she looked like a grinning idiot.

He gave her another wave before catching up with his friends.

Sarah watched them until they had vanished around a bend. Then, she fell back onto the school porch, sprawling out. She released the breath she had been holding. It was like someone had put a rope around her heart and wouldn't stop pulling until the boys were gone.

Stretching her legs out, she could feel the sun touch her skin. Tingles of warmth wrapped around her legs and moved up her body. She breathed and let the feeling move over her.

The sun was as warm as it had been on Lyrica. Its rays were like individual spotlights, shining down on each person, giving them their own little bit of comfort. But Sarah was greedy. She wanted it all. She wanted to feel all the heat, all the light, and forget about all the times she had only felt darkness.

An intense heat spread over Sarah's hands. She opened her eyes only to see small flames dancing in her palms.

"Crap!"

She blew on her hands and smashed her palms on the porch,

extinguishing the flames.

Sarah looked all around her, her neck cracking with the force of each movement.

But there was no one. She was alone.

She shook her head and ran her fingers through her hair. "Control, Sarah," she said. "Control."

She took a long breath before staring across the road. Everything was quiet. There was only an emptiness in front of her.

"I'm not wasting any more time on you, Jacob." Sarah grabbed her book and walked down the stairs to the road.

The dirt road was a longer distance to home. But the longer she took to get home, the more time she could spend away from her mother. The tension hadn't eased between them over the last few days. She could see through her mother's forced kindness.

Sarah hummed while she walked, kicking at stray rocks. Though Lucille preferred Sarah's hair braided, the young woman had left the house with her tresses out in all their red, curly glory.

Moving along the road, Sarah's hair bounced around her. She pictured Thomas walking at her side. He was taller than her and his hair much more tamed. He would smile down at Sarah, his green eyes so beautiful they made her mouth go dry. Then, he'd grab her hand and they'd talk about everything. It'd be just like before he got better, when she had been tutoring him despite his being a grade above her. Thomas was...

A chill crawled up her spine.

"Sarah?"

Thomas was...

"Sarah!"

A hand touched her shoulder.

"Jacob?" Sarah glanced behind her.

There was no one there.

Suddenly, she stumbled off the road and down the bank into the trees. She got to her knees just as a truck sped by, nearly knocking her down again.

Sarah remained crouched by the side of the road, taking in several breaths. She hadn't seen the truck, hadn't heard it, but it had been close enough to touch her.

"Maybe Mama's right. My daydreaming is going to kill me."

She stood up, then peered down the road. It was as empty as it had been when she left the schoolhouse.

Reaching a hand back, she touched her shoulder. Someone had stood behind her. Someone had pushed her off the road.

Jacob.

Sarah squeezed her shoulder and looked skyward, then turned away from the road and headed into the woods.

"The road may take longer," she said, "but apparently the woods are safer."

Dusting her dress off, Sarah started her way home in the opposite direction. She peered up at the woods around her, then down at her shadow. She turned her head from side-to-side and stuck out her left arm, moving it around and watching her shadow reflect each action. She did the same with her right arm and legs.

"You're much taller, Sarah," she said, examining her frame with a small grin. "Much taller than you were two years ago. I wonder if Alex would even recognize me?"

Sarah ran her fingers over the top of her head. She imagined they were Alex's fingers ruffling her hair like he always did. Serwa would snap at him, tell him to stop coddling her. Then, after a short spat between the two, they'd all cuddle up by the campfire and sleep.

Here heart warmed.

Wherever you two are, I hope you're happy.

Footsteps crunched on sticks behind her.

Sarah spun around and planted her feet firmly into the ground. Her eyes shifted around the forest, but she saw no one.

"They're coming. They're coming!" a voice murmured frantically.

"Hide!"

"Run. Run, now."

There were voices all around her, yet Sarah was alone. A gust of wind blew in and the leaves rustled like they were trying to speak with her.

"Shh, shh, quiet."

"Don't let them hear."

"Axel, no!"

The wind blew, picking up fallen leaves and blowing them in

spirals that danced on the forest floor. In the spiral a light green mist formed that danced around itself, taking shape.

The breeze came to a halt, the mist faded, and the leaves fell. In their place stood a little boy. He was no more than three feet tall with scrawny shoulders and a short haircut. And he was translucent.

Sarah looked him up and down, opening and closing her eyes. She was sure all the color had drained from her face and if she looked down, she'd find it all in a puddle at her feet.

But as much as she was staring at the boy, he hadn't even glanced at her. While Sarah looked at him from the south, he was gazing west. His shoulders were rising and falling at a quick pace. With every inhalation, his stomach sunk and his ribs protruded.

Then, he ran.

He darted right past Sarah and deeper into the woods. Without thinking, she followed and struggled to keep up. The boy was fast. Almost as if he were walking on air.

He was panting in front of her, his body shuddering with every breath.

Sarah waved her hands and screamed behind him. "Hey! W-wait, why are you running? I...I can help you. Just stop—"

Suddenly, he stopped running. He glanced from left to right. Finally, he turned forward, keeping his eyes low. His body quivered like a baby bird who had fallen from the nest.

The boy leapt and turned his eyes upward. Tears fell down his cheeks and he clutched at whatever was behind him.

The same mist that had created the boy formed again. Strands twisted and turned around each other repeatedly until a man stood in front of the child.

He was dressed in bright silver armor with a carved, painted symbol on his back. The symbol was in the shape of two cupped hands holding a flame. On either hand there was a bright blue arrow pointing up.

The man was about six feet tall with shoulder length brown hair, but that was all Sarah could see.

He took one step toward the boy, who cringed and sunk to the ground. Then, he raised his hand and a dagger formed.

"No!" Sarah screamed. She lunged toward them.

He brought the dagger down and they faded into nothing.

Tremors ran through Sarah's own body now. She reached for the earth around her, searching for a trail of the boy and man, any sign of where they'd gone.

And then there was a torrent of screams.

Sarah fell to the ground, clutching at her ears.

Translucent children formed all around her. They ran in every direction with armored men chasing behind them. And the more children appeared, the more the screaming in her head grew louder.

"Stop, stop, stop," Sarah whispered. "Please. I can't."

"*Why won't it work?*"

"What?"

"*Why won't it work? Stupid spellbook. Open!*"

The screams became a hollow dinging in her head with only one voice breaking through.

"*I did everything they said. Everything!*"

Sarah opened her eyes. There was a girl kneeling on the ground, no more than a yard away from her. She had puffy hair in tight curls with dark tan skin, and she wore a long purple dress. She was holding something in her hand and banging it against the ground.

"*You stupid thing. Work, work now.*"

A door creaked.

The girl froze.

"*No,*" she whispered and then she vanished.

CHAPTER 5

Sarah wasn't certain how long she had been awake. She woke up around midnight and had been falling in and out of sleep ever since. Every time her mind relaxed and her body eased into a slumber, the horrified face of the little boy appeared.

His eyes wide in fear, his shoulders small and shaking, his lungs gasping for air, while his ribs pushed at his skin...who was he and what had happened to him?

Sarah wiped the sweat from her brow. She had heard her mother get up for breakfast hours ago, yet Lucille hadn't barged into her room to wake her. It was a weekend but there was always work to be done on the farm and assistance need in the house upkeep. Sleeping in was not a privilege farm girls received.

Still, Sarah was going to take advantage of it while she could.

She tucked her blanket close around her and grasped the necklace she wore. Hanging from its chain was the jewel Alex had given her as a farewell gift, as well as Nettle's tiny sword. She hummed and rubbed her fingers over their edges, pulling her knees to her chest.

Muffled voices traveled up the stairs. Her father had left for the day, and her mother hadn't told her to expect any company.

Sarah scooted out of bed and made her way down the stairs. Paul and Lucille both sat at the kitchen table, surrounded by empty plates with smiles on their faces.

"Daddy?"

Paul turned in his chair and smiled at his daughter.

"Hey, there. Glad to see you're finally up."

"I...uh, I'm sorry," she stumbled. "I'll finish my chores. I wasn't feeling well."

Paul pushed his chair out. He stood up, still towering over Sarah even though she had grown several feet in the last year.

"Don't worry about it," he said, patting her head. "Your Mama checked on you this morning while you we're sleep. Said you were sweating like a Christmas ham."

Sarah stared past her father. Lucille was placing their dishes in the sink, her focus unmoving from the soapy water.

Sarah returned her eyes. "I was having some trouble sleeping."

He placed a hand on her forehead. "Seems like your fever went down, too. You sure you're feeling better?" He tilted her head upward so her blue eyes reflected into his own.

Sarah gave him a weak smile and nodded. "Yes, I feel much better."

"Good," he said and patted her head again. "Can't be working knowing my baby's sick."

Sarah looked outside. It had to be nearly noon. "Daddy, aren't you late?"

"Naw. One of the young boys needed me to switch shifts with him," he said, grabbing his coat. "His wife's due to pop any minute and he's helping her during the day, then working while she sleeps. I'll start my normal schedule again in a few weeks."

"Make sure to tell him I said 'congratulations,' Paul."

He gave Lucille a quick peck on the cheek. "I will," he replied, giving Sarah a wink. "Mama made your favorite, by the way. I'll see you later tonight."

Paul left from the screen door and jumped into their little pickup. The engine sputtered a few times before roaring to life.

Sarah watched him drive away from the farm toward the mountains. Once he was gone, she moved to the steps, ready to return to her room and try to get some sleep.

"Not hungry?" Lucille asked.

Sarah looked at her. Her mother wore an uneasy smile and had that same exhaustion in her eyes from a few weeks ago.

"I've got flapjacks cooked in bacon grease." There was persistence in her voice.

Sarah stared at the plate of food beyond Lucille. Though Sarah wasn't sure if she would be able to keep it down, her stomach had other plans.

It growled and she took a seat at the table while her mother prepared her plate. Lucille placed five flapjacks in front of Sarah along with a container of warm syrup.

Sarah quickly doused the fried dough and tore into the flapjacks like she hadn't eaten in days.

Lucille busied herself around the kitchen. Sarah could feel her eyes on her.

"Are they good?" Lucille asked.

"Mhm," Sarah replied as her mouth was consumed by the sugary syrup.

"They were always your favorite. Even when you were a baby."

Lucille turned to Sarah. The young woman looked away. She began moving the remaining pancake slices around her plate. Most of the syrup was gone now, absorbed by the fluffy dough, but a few drops lingered.

Sarah wiped up the drops one by one with her finger before licking it clean. Her eyes remained on the plate.

"I guess it's just 'cause they're always good." She swiped her finger across the plate again.

Lucille let out a little laugh that shook her mommy belly. She smiled at Sarah.

"You know...I do love you, Sarafina."

The words rang true, yet sounded odd coming from her mother's mouth. Sarah's lips moved to respond on instinct but froze when Sarah realized she did not know what to say. If it had been before, when she was young and eager to please, the words "I love you, too, Mama" would have rolled off her tongue with no restraint. But she was no longer a child, framed by the ideologies of her parents, obsessed with making them proud; and so, she stared at her mother.

With one sharp inhale, it seemed Lucille had taken all the air in the room. She grabbed Sarah's hands, her own having become shivers and trembles. Sarah didn't want to look at her but Lucille's firm grip forced her to do so.

Eyes overflowing with sadness.

Lucille bit her lip.

"I know what I said...I should have never said it, but I-I don't understand you, Sarah."

"Ma—"

"The things you do, the things you say, I-I can't get my head around it all," Lucille said. "I've tried and my mind always comes back to that one answer."

"I'm some demon, Mama!" Sarah snatched her hand away.

"No," Lucille stammered, still grasping the air where Sarah's hand had been. "But you are my child and you're not right. You're not."

"Why do always do this?" Sarah felt like her blood was running with fire.

"And I will love you..."

"Just stop."

"No matter what."

"Stop!" Sarah stomped her foot. Water gushed out of the kitchen sink, immediately spilling over onto the floor while the knobs spun in circles.

Lucille gasped and ran over to stop the water. Sarah rushed from the kitchen door to the stables. She leapt over the stall doors and hopped on Nancy's back. In one swift move, she unlocked the door and they were off into the woods.

"Faster, Nancy. Faster! You know where to go," Sarah screamed into the horse's ear. The wind made her eyes water. Still, Sarah kept them open. She needed to lie to herself about why she was crying.

Suddenly, Nancy came to a halt. Sarah rested against the horse, their hearts beating in sync, before finally catching her breath. She climbed to the ground and approached the well.

Once there, Sarah lowered the bucket into the water like she had done so many times before. She dumped the water over herself and the cool was refreshing to her burning skin.

Sarah was soaked from head to toe but the sudden chill was good. It stopped her; made her heart and mind pause for a moment when everything inside her told for her to run and never look back.

Sarah turned to Nancy. The horse's eyes were jet black. To Sarah, they seemed more human than her mother's. Behind all of Lucille's sadness, there was nothing but accusations and disappointment.

Sarah's eyes burned. "I don't want to be here, anymore, Nancy," she said. "Not like this. I can't be here like this."

Nancy stomped her hooves and neighed.

"But where am I supposed to run to?" Sarah asked. "Where am I...what the—"

It was like the world exploded. The earth trembled and the trees shook. Everything was moving at the same time and Sarah found herself on the ground trying to stay steady.

Nancy moved from left to right, kicking her hooves in the air, unsure of which direction to run for safety. Sarah tried to stand and calm her friend, yet balance evaded her. While clutching onto the earth, on all fours, Sarah turned her head up and looked toward the mountains.

"No!" she shouted, though the sound of crumbling rocks drowned out all noise. Dust filled the sky above the mountain, permeating the light blue with a blackness that reached out to the town.

A chill ran over Sarah. Something had happened.

"Nancy!" She found her footing and wobbled over to the horse. Indulging no pretense of grace, Sarah climbed on and ushered Nancy forward. The horse sped off in the direction of the mountains, Sarah nearly hanging off the side, her red hair almost sweeping the ground.

Sarah fixated her eyes on the black cloud of dust, watching to see if it would disappear and she would wake up from a horrible dream. But the cloud remained.

"Please," she whispered into Nancy's mane. "Please be okay."

The horse picked up speed as they reached the mountain. She turned around the curves of the path like a professional. She was fast but steady as not to lean over too far and stumble. Sarah moved with her, keeping her body at a similar angle to Nancy's as they charged higher up the mountain.

Slowly, the sky began disappearing. Soon black overtook the blue sky and the blue became an occasional occurrence. The air grew thin, yet it was filled with particles of coal.

Sarah leaned her hand out. In no time it was covered with dark specks, which she wiped onto her dress, leaving streaks of black.

The path grew steep. Nancy's gallop turned into a slow trudge.

"You can do it, girl, come on." Sarah patted Nancy's head and stroked her mane. "Just this hill and then we'll be there."

The dirt was loose and gravelly. Nancy would slide back two steps before taking three forward. Sarah could see the top of the hill in front of them. She could hear meshed voices in the distance, making her heart burn with the strongest desire to see what was over the hilltop.

"I'm coming, Daddy," she said, her hands balled into fists.

Nancy slid back, her hooves leaving trails in the earth. Sarah kicked her sides, encouraging her to go on.

"We can do this!"

The horse turned skyward and neighed. She snorted, puffs of mist coming from her nose, then leapt forward, over the hill. They remained perched at the top. Nancy dug her hooves into the ground and pulled them ahead, before they could slide backwards.

Once again on a flat path, Nancy shook herself and leapt into a gallop toward the mines.

The meshed voices became clearer. The black cloud faded. There was nothing stopping them from being consumed by the chaos.

The cuts of wood that had once marked the mine entrance were now snapped into pieces. Rocks were scattered everywhere but the largest of them had fallen into one pile in front of the mine, blocking any possible exit. The earth above the entrance had sunk in like it had been split in half.

Sarah jumped from Nancy's back and raced toward the cave-in. She pulled at the rocks, though her moist hands slipped off the smooth surfaces, and she fell to the ground. Again Sarah stood up and grabbed at the rocks, ignoring the pain in her shoulders as she tried to pull them free.

She clawed at the pile of stone and contorted her hands to move around the rubble for a better grip but found none. The pile would not move.

If everyone could just leave, I could move the rocks and get Daddy out.

She cursed the people around her, wishing they would disappear.

Sarah was getting to her feet again to try to free her father when a calloused hand wrapped around her arm.

"What are you doing?"

"My daddy's in there!" she screamed and wrenched her arm free.

The man scowled at her with a raised brow, a mixture of hate and pity in his eyes.

She ignored his gaze and moved to step around him. He mimicked her movements, effectively blocking her way.

"I've got men coming with tools to break through the pile-up. You need to go home to your mama until then."

"We can't wait for your men," Sarah shouted so loudly that shock replaced the man's look of hate. Apparently he hadn't expected much of a fight.

She tried to calm her voice, tried to stop her chest from rising and falling so quickly, but she knew every moment she stalled was one less moment for her father.

"Listen," Sarah said, hands shaking, "there have to be some planks of wood around. If we can all get together and—"

He grabbed her hand and twisted it hard. Sarah hissed in pain as he pulled her away from the cave-in, firming his grip with each step.

Sarah dug her heels into the earth and pulled away from him. "No! I'm not leaving. I'm not leaving."

He reached for Sarah's other arm, but she was moving it so wildly he couldn't find a grip. "You're as stubborn as a mule. Come on, girl."

Sarah waved her arm through the air, averting his grip when someone grabbed her free arm from behind. There was another man with a hold on her now.

"She's just as crazy as they say, Jim. Better watch out." The men laughed and began dragging her away.

Sarah thrashed and twisted under their holds, hoping to set herself free. They continued to pull her.

"Daddy!" she shouted, knowing her voice would never find him through the rubble. "Daddy!"

She pushed and moved against the men but their grip only tightened.

She yelled, the thought of never seeing her father again filling her with a hollow anguish in her chest. The further they dragged her, the bigger the hole grew, emptiness replacing the spot reserved for her daddy.

Through a mess of curly red hair, Sarah watched the mine entrance fade into the distance. The only evidence she had ever been there, even attempted to save her father, were the drag trails she left as the two men forced her away.

Sarah's eyes stung while tears washed over her face.

"Daddy..."

Her gaze fell to the ground. The drag trails grew longer. And then, her eyes widened.

"Stupid girl." She could hear Serwa's voice cursing her. How could she have been so silly?

Sarah took a deep breath. She tightened her arms and stepped forward, slamming her foot against the land.

Her body pulsed, the earth shook, and the rocks blocking the entrance to the mine were blown outward. Screams rose into the sky as the families of the miners fell to the ground.

The men holding Sarah released her, and while the rocks poured over the mountain, Sarah ran for the entrance. Dust surrounded her again, falling from the mine like rain.

"Daddy, Daddy..." She moved through the mines blind, stretching her arms out toward an unknown. She could hear heavy breathing.

"He—" Sarah stumbled. She quickly moved to the side, searching for a wall, and reached out to identify who she had fallen over.

"Daddy? Are you there?"

A sharp intake. "Sarah?"

Her hands finally stopped shaking. Her stomach untangled itself and her lungs allowed her to take in more than a pinch of air. He was alright.

"I've got you now. Just lean on me a bit, okay?"

Her father did not respond but Sarah lifted him up anyway. He leaned against the wall while she heaved him along.

"We're almost there," she said as the first sign of light appeared.

Paul fell forward. Sarah attempted to lift him but his body had grown completely limp. The panic that had fled clawed at her again.

Sarah grabbed her father's arms and pulled him toward the exit. He was taller than her and heavier. Still, Sarah was moving him through the mine like he was a newborn.

Once they had made it out, Sarah kept going, pulling him several more feet, afraid the mine would somehow swallow him again.

When they were far enough away, Sarah dropped his arm. She reached down and tried to wake him. He did not stir.

She shook him and patted his cheeks, praying for any sign of movement.

He gave none.

"No...no." She cupped his face in her hands and sobbed like she was a child lost in the woods again. Except, this time her father would not be able to save her.

CHAPTER 6

One. Two. Three.

The sound of strangled air and gravel.

Sarah sat with her back to the door, her eyes watery and staring at the ceiling. There was a hollow exhale.

One. Two. Three...three?

Sarah turned her body forward and pressed her ear against the door. There was nothing. The sound of her father's breathing did not greet her.

She didn't feel the coldness of the metal knob as she swung the door open, or the pain of her knee crashing to the floor when she stumbled. Sarah recovered, pulled herself up, and raced toward her father.

She had left their door open, despite her mother's warnings. Now she flung it wide, slid to the floor, and placed her ear on his chest. Then, she heard it. The coal dust grinding inside her father's chest as he inhaled.

Sarah's heart relaxed and the water finally spilled from her eyes. She clutched at the bedsheets that covered her father and buried her face into his soft abdomen.

When she was younger and just taller than his waist, her father would hold her to him. If she were upset, her childhood tears would soak his belly that had come from too many years of pancakes and bacon.

Clutching onto him now, she knew she'd give anything for him to hold her once more.

"Don't leave me, Daddy," she whispered, forcing a sob down her throat. "Don't leave me."

The moon illuminated the dark night outside. Sarah glanced

between her father and the evening outside her parent's bedroom window. She wondered if the creeping darkness she felt surrounding her was comparable to the darkness in the sky.

It felt so permanent.

There was a creak from behind her.

Sarah spun around. Her mother stood in the doorway, eyes red and puffy, a bowl of soup in her hand. Her lips trembled. She did not meet Sarah's gaze.

"Your supper's on the table. Go eat, Sarah."

She glanced at her father.

The doctor had visited the day of the accident but without much to say. He didn't know how long her father would be unconscious. It had already been three days.

"Sarah—"

"Mama, could I eat with Daddy tonight?"

"No."

Sarah stared up at her mother. Her arm rested protectively over her father. "Please, Mama. I...I just want to be here when he wakes up."

Her mother closed her eyes. The grip she had on the bowl tightened. She exhaled.

"I said 'no,' Sarafina." She looked straight ahead, past Sarah and out the window. "Your father has enough to worry about with all that dirt and earth in his chest."

Earth.

Sarah glanced between her hands and her father's chest. She smiled.

"Foolish girl." Serwa's words filled her mind again.

"Wipe that grin off your face!" Her mother had stormed past her. She slammed the bowl on a nightstand and glared at her daughter. "What are you smiling for, huh?"

Sarah turned away. She pulled her arm away from her father and brought her hands to her lap.

"Nothing, Mama."

There was a sharp intake of air. Glancing up from under her eyelids, Sarah saw her mother's face fill with red. But not from anger.

The steady, hard line that was Lucille's mouth began to

tremble. The gloss from her eyes spilled down her cheeks and the woman fell to her knees. She covered her face with her hands as if they could hide from Sarah the fact her mother was weeping.

Sarah reached for Lucille but her arms stopped short. She looked toward her father.

If she could only be alone with him for a moment...

A large sob escaped her mother and the woman fell forward onto Sarah. Her nails dug into her daughter's thighs.

"Mama, that hurts." She tried adjusting under her mother's hold.

Lucille dug her nails deeper."What did you do at the mines, Sarah?"

Sarah closed her eyes and silently cursed all her neighbors. Why couldn't they ever keep their mouths shut? Or at least this one time.

She released a silent breath.

"N-nothing. I was trying to get Daddy out but...but the rocks were too big—"

"The whole town was there. They all saw what you did." Her mother turned her head up, staring into Sarah's face. More tears spilled.

"Are you the reason?" her mother asked with brown eyes that appeared the darkest they had ever been. "Is this our punishment for you?"

Sarah's stomach clenched. The hands in her lap turned into fists and she moved away from her mother.

Lucille stared, eyes still wary on her daughter.

Sarah stepped back, giving one last glance toward her father before closing the door and moving down the hall. Her mother's wails quickly followed her retreat. Sarah's own eyes burned with fresh tears. But it wasn't her job to comfort Lucille.

She moved down the stairs and into the kitchen, where she grabbed her boots from their place by the door. Her bowl of soup rested at the edge of the table. Sarah hadn't had much of an appetite since bringing her father back.

She scoffed at the word. Had he really come back? Did he still count as living if he was not conscious?

Sinking to the kitchen floor, Sarah pressed her eyes against her knees. Her jaw trembled and she bit her lip to keep it steady.

"I did the best I could," she said, fighting back the tears. "I saved Daddy. Not Mama, not the miners, not anyone in this damn town!" The rage bolted through her like a spike. She had saved him, along with the other trapped miners, and she was being treated like a villain?

Sarah wiped her tears away and got to her feet. She couldn't cry. Not too much. Because no matter what anyone said about her, she was going to save her father.

Sarah was considering sneaking back into her house. She had pretended to leave for school hours ago in the hopes of being alone with her father while her mother went into town. For some reason, her mother was taking her good time.

Sarah rolled her eyes. The one time the woman decided not to be punctual.

Finally, her house's screen door creaked and her mother stepped outside. The roar of her father's pickup followed.

Sarah sighed, pushed herself up, and started jogging toward her home. When she arrived at the forest's edge, the pale blue pickup was disappearing behind a cloud of dust. It had to be her mother. Her father still hadn't woken up.

This was her chance. Likely her only chance considering Lucille had been very particular about Sarah being left alone with her father. So particular, Sarah had to lie and skip school to have this moment with him.

Her fingertips tingled and the smell of burning wood greeted her nose.

Frantically removing her hold from the tree she was leaning on, Sarah stepped back and shook her hands out.

"I cannot start burning things every time I get upset. Come on now, Sarah!"

Once the engine's roar was mute, Sarah stepped from the trees and into her house. If her mother was taking the truck, that meant she was heading into town. They had gone shopping already, which actually meant Lucille was going to see her "friends."

Sarah rolled her eyes.

She moved up the stairs, then down the hall to her parents' door. Her father's gravelly breathing no longer surprised her. It had become background noise to her dreams.

Her mother had done a good job of keeping him presentable. He was shaved, his hair combed, and clothes changed. If Sarah didn't know better, she would have thought he was resting after returning from work.

But he wasn't.

She kneeled by his bedside and clasped his hands in hers. Her blue eyes poured over his face. The wrinkles, the sunspots, and the laugh lines. Now all she needed was to see his eyes—the same blue as her own—open again.

"I'm going to bring you back, Daddy. Just hold on."

Sarah sat back on her legs and placed her hands on her thighs. Staring at her father, she reached out with her magic. She wanted earth, so she pictured it in her mind.

Dirt beneath their house, mud after a rainstorm, fresh soil for their farm...

Sarah could feel the element strongly. It was in the cracks of the room walls, the floorboards, and moving along the window's edge with the wind. But she needed the earth, the coal, inside her father.

Sarah placed a hand on his chest. She focused her energy there, letting it spread over him.

Where is it?

Then, she felt it. Just some of the coal, in his lungs. There was more between his ribs like little pebbles stuck between piano keys. The rest lined his windpipe.

She took a deep breath. "I can do this."

Sarah called to the earth, pulling it with her magic until it loosened from her father's chest.

She cupped her left hand. With her right, she made an arc motion, moving from his chest to his throat, and finally to her left palm. The bits of coal followed.

Again and again, she repeated the movements until she couldn't feel the coal in her father. Sarah placed a hand on his chest once more. She checked, then double checked.

Opening her eyes, Sarah pulled her magic inside herself. Her father's gravelly breathing had ceased. His chest moved with less effort. And in her left hand was a small, neat pile of coal dust.

Using the tips of her fingers, Sarah pinched the very top of the pile. The black smeared across her skin.

"So much trouble from something so tiny," she whispered,

before turning her gaze on her father. "You'll be okay now, Daddy."

The sound of their pickup truck made Sarah jump to her feet. The engine stopped and the rusty creak of the pickup door took its place.

Sarah pushed her parents' window open with her right hand and tossed the coal out. The dust disappeared and she squeezed the window shut before tip-toeing to her room. Quietly, she pushed her window open, flenching each time it squeaked.

Her house wasn't much in height but Sarah didn't want to take the chance. Her day wasn't over after all and dying would really ruin her to-do list.

She sighed, before calling to the wind. A gust of air shot diagonally across her house, tossing her curls around her. Sarah prayed, then she leapt from her window sill. The strong gust caught her and she went spiraling upward. Fear pulled at Sarah's heart as her magic moved her higher into the sky. She needed to remain calm if she wanted to feel solid ground again.

Sarah imagined herself landing safely on the ground and slowly her fear eased. As soon as her feet had touched the earth, she collapsed on all fours. Breathing heavily, she peered around to see if her mother had noticed a redheaded girl soaring through the air.

When Lucille didn't rush out the house, Sarah made her way to the forest. She kneeled by Mother Tree. Sweat had built on her brow.

Now onto her next task. She had never tried going to the blue herself. Hopefully, the first time was a charm.

"Come on, come on. Find it, Sarah," she whispered still resting by Mother Tree.

Her energy moved through the trees with no effort. She could feel their roots stretching beneath the earth and the branches reaching up to the sky. She could even stretch her senses across the forest floor. The only problem was what she sought was not within the forest.

Sarah fell back onto her legs and released a frustrated exhale. She had pushed herself a bit too hard, she knew that. But she also knew had to get back to the blue place where Gan had reached out to her. The question was how?

She groaned, before falling forward and placing her forehead against her thighs. "Think, think, think."

The blue place usually reflected parts of the real world. How could she get to the reflection of her forest?

Sarah gazed at the trees, partially hoping a blue portal would just appear and take her to Gan. She rolled her eyes. Locating or opening portals was not a skill she had picked up in Lyrica. Still, she couldn't quit. Gan had reached out to her. That along with the images of screaming children and knights had set her on edge. Something was wrong in Lyrica, and she had to figure out what.

She eyed the roots that moved outward from Mother Tree. They expelled and dived into the ground like waves.

She crossed her arms and tapped her fingers against her elbows.

"If the blue reflects the real world, then maybe roots are like the anchors? I can follow them and they'll lead me back."

She bobbed her head and grabbed the root nearest to her.

Once more, Sarah.

Pouring all she had into it, her magic moved along the root. Sarah could sense it, like an extra limb, curling and twisting through the earth. She could feel it. There was the dampness and chill of the soil, the scurrying jitters of life surrounding it, even the rough skin of other roots as she passed them.

Sarah could feel all of it. Everything. And it all ran deep, beyond Mother Tree.

Her body seemed to lift up in the air. The speed of her magic accelerated and the familiar blue encompassed all she saw.

Sarah took a deep breath. She pictured Gan, thought of their conversations, replayed how her old friend had come to her last. It couldn't have been a dream.

"Gan, I'm here. I'm here." Her magic slipped from every part of her, advancing over the blue landscape. "I got your message. Now see me. Please."

"Hello?"

Sarah spun around. A smile was already tugging at her lips, only to falter.

"Um...hi?" The young man standing in front of Sarah was not Gan. In fact, he had an entire foot on the old elf. His hair was straight and ear-length, which matched well with his pronounced features. Including his pointed ears.

"You're an elf."

The young man glanced around. "Well, last time I woke I was at least. But, where is—"

She squealed. "Yes! I did it. Oh, Serwa and Alex would be so proud."

"You know Serwa and Alex?"

Hearing their names spoken by another brought Sarah to a standstill. Her celebration ended, and she found herself examining the elf from head to toe.

"How do you know my friends?" Sarah asked.

He crossed his arms and arched an eyebrow. "Maybe you could answer my question first?"

The tips of Sarah's fingers tingled. An uneasiness settled into her stomach.

She had no way of knowing if the elf was friend or foe. Was he a member of Gan's tribe?

Turning to him, Sarah lifted her chin and hardened her energy in the space. He peered around at the sudden shift in atmosphere, but otherwise seemed unbothered.

"I know Serwa and Alex. They're friends of mine."

"Mine, as well." He narrowed his eyes. "Where are you from?"

"It's my turn to ask a question," she replied. "Do you know an elf named Gan? I need to speak with her."

He cocked his head to the side, an odd smile on his face. "What do you want with my grandmother?"

As Sarah prepared to respond, he closed the space between them. Being a foot taller than her, he tilted down until they were face-to-face. Sarah stumbled back but he grabbed her by the elbow, boring his eyes into her.

"Are you...are you from Earth?"

She nodded.

"And is your hair the color of fire?"

"Uh, red, yes. Who are you again?"

The young man smirked. "I'm Skuntz. It's nice to see you again, Sarafina."

Stepping away, he offered his hand. Sarah did not take it.

"Tell me who you really are. What have you done with Gan?"

"I have told you and I haven't done anything with my grandmother."

Sarah shook her head. "Skuntz was younger than me when we met. It's only been two years, so there's no way you can be him."

"I am who I say," he replied, an incredulous look on his face "And it hasn't been two years since you left. It's been twelve, at least in Lyrican time."

She blinked at him. "Lyrican time?"

She had completely forgotten. Time in Lyrica was either faster or slower than on Earth. Rarely did the two match. Serwa had told her that near the end of her first journey, which meant...

"I've been gone for twelve years?"

Skuntz scratched his head. "Listen, I'm sorry to give you more bad news. My grandmother isn't in our home and she won't be able to speak with you until she returns."

"Where is she?" Sarah asked, though the words sounded distant. Her ears were full of Skuntz's last comment.

Twelve years.

"Sarafina?" He was staring at her, a slight crevice between his brows.

"Uh, sorry." She shook herself. "Gan reached out to me and I need to know she's well."

"My grandmother is fine," he said. "She's left to help the wounded. I was praying by the Great Spirit. That would explain how I got called here."

"Who are the wounded? Is there another plague?"

Skuntz pinched his eyes and shook his head. "Of course, I'd have to tell you this, as well." He sighed. "Sarafina, Lyrica is at war."

"No. The stone is returned. Balance was restored."

"It's not the elementals. Lyrica isn't dying like before," he replied. "The humans never took the oath, they never agreed to peace. Now they're hunting."

"Hunting what?"

His image was starting to fade.

"Skuntz?"

"I can barely see you anymore. And I feel...tired?"

"What are they hunting?" she asked again.

"Everything that isn't human."

The young man blinked a few times before falling over. Sarah reached for him but his body had turned into mist.

"No, darn it!"

Sarah looked around her. Again, she was alone.

Sarah slammed her fists against the earth, then grasped the root which had lead her to the blue place. She traced her energy back. Slowly, slowly until the blue was gone and she had returned home.

CHAPTER 7

"Have you done your chores?" Her mother busied herself around the kitchen, keeping her back to Sarah.

"Uh, no. I'll go do them right now."

"It's half past four, Sarah. You should already have started. Get to it."

She paused. It had taken her nearly three hours to remove the coal.

"Did you hear me, girl?"

"Y-yes, Mama." Without another word, Sarah walked back to the stables. As soon as she was free from her mother's presence, the tension eased. She had managed to save her father without being caught, or at least she hoped she had. The doctor was scheduled to visit early next week. Then Sarah would know for sure.

Now there was only Lyrica.

She pushed the stable doors open, then immediately stumbled backwards and slapped a hand over her nose.

It seems I actually have two problems. Ugh. How did Daddy do this every day?

Holding her breath, Sarah pulled the wagon in from beside the stable. She tried inhaling as little as possible, while she filled the wagon with horse and cow dung. Once that was done, she moved it all into the manure spreader, rinsed Nancy's hooves clean, and hitched her up.

Nancy moved slowly across the fields while Sarah rode her. The spring sun blazed down on them. In the midst of the heat, Sarah reached up to adjust her straw hat only to touch air.

"I guess it'll be me and my sunburn tonight." She sighed, went to play with her hair, but realized her hands were filthy and placed them on Nancy's sides.

At the rate they were going, Sarah knew she had at least another hour before having to go into the house. A single hour to figure out how she could help Gan and everyone else in Lyrica.

Serwa had been right. She had warned Sarah, their entire group, about the human's failure to take the oath. Her warning was coming back to haunt them.

A hollow feeling opened inside Sarah. What did that mean for Serwa and Alexander? Had they been captured? And what about Solar and the other dragons? Nettle?

The feeling inside her deepened.

She gripped her thighs and released a breath. Her arms were shaking.

"So much can happen in twelve years. What if they're all..." She swallowed the word away. Nettle was still young for a fairy. She'd be alive for several more centuries. Even Serwa and Alexander had longer life spans. They wouldn't be killed easily either and Skuntz would have told her if they had passed.

She bobbed her head. "They're fine. They're alive and fine."

They had to be.

"But how am I going to get back?" she asked herself. "Will the well even work without Solar or Nettle?"

Sarah stared behind her into the forest.

Franklin and the other gnomes had been on Earth for years now. Ethlen and her fairies, too. It couldn't hurt to ask them though.

Nancy's steps halted. Sarah looked back at the now empty manure spreader.

She heaved a breath. The hardest task was complete.

Sarah walked Nancy to the stables, then completed her other chores. Once the animals had been fed, the fences checked, and the sky began to darken, it was time for dinner.

Heading into the house, she left her shoes on the porch, planning to give them a good cleaning the next day. Her mother sat at the kitchen table, a plate of food untouched in front of her.

Sarah wiped her dirty hands on her dress, watching her mother. She looked toward the stairs, then returned her gaze.

"Everything okay, Mama?"

"Hm." The woman stared straight ahead. "I'm not sure. How

was school today, Sarafina?"

Sarah stretched her smile wide across her face. "It was great! We started a new book with Ms. Carr."

"You did?"

She nodded.

"What about your science class?"

"We just learned more about photosynthesis," Sarah replied.

"Hm. And did you have any lessons with coal today? I found smudges of it all over the house, including my and your father's bedroom."

A cold fear spread from the bottom of Sarah's empty stomach. Her smile immediately left and her feet rooted to the kitchen floor.

Lucille used her fork to poke a potato on theplate. "Your father's breathing well today. Air's coming out easy."

Sarah wanted to nod. That was the normal thing to do. However, her entire being was rigid. Her muscles had become taut while she struggled between fight or flight.

Lucille stared at her daughter, except there was no conviction, accusation, or anger in her eyes.

She knows.

"Did you go to school today, Sarah?"

The words seemed distant in comparison to the thudding of her heart.

She knows.

Breathing was suddenly so much more difficult. Was this what it had felt like for her father?

When Sarah did not respond, Lucille stood. "Wash up. I'll leave your plate on the table."

Like a shock had been sent through her system, Sarah jolted to her bedroom, slamming the door shut. Memories of "Devil Child" uttered by her mother rushed forward along with the whispers of her peers. But no one really knew about her powers. Everything had been a rumor.

The scent of sun, sweat, and work clung to her clothes, yet Sarah dared not leave her room. After some time, she heard her mother's heavy footsteps climb the stairs and move down the hall. The bedroom door creaked closed.

But what Sarah knew she'd never forget was the sound of her

parents' door locking.

When she couldn't take the smell any longer and her stomach had grumbled enough, Sarah made her way to the kitchen. Her dinner plate remained on the table. Prefering to eat outside over chancing her mother coming down, Sarah started to make her way to the porch.

There was someone outside. She had felt them as soon as she grasped the door handle.

Why didn't I feel them before now?

She shook her head. Her lack of focus would get to her one day.

The outside screen door rattled as the surprise guest knocked on its old frame.

Sarah peered out the window. Thomas waved at her as he stood on her porch with a box in his hand. She pulled the curtain shut.

Suddenly, her entire house looked a wreck. Her new-to-her dress lacked the luster it'd had several weeks ago. She was certain her freckles had multiplied and spread over her entire body, as well.

And Thomas was right outside.

"Sarah?"

Covering her face, she shook her head. "So much for a walk."

"Is this a bad time?"

Sarah wiped her eyes for good measure. She pulled her mess of curls over one shoulder. Then, finally, she opened her house door.

"H-hi, Thomas. How are you? What...what brings you all the way out here?" She smiled and placed her shaking hands behind her back.

Thomas tried returning the favor. A small curve of his lips was all he gave.

"I wanted to check on you," he replied. "How ya holding up?" Thomas tried to broaden his smile, though his eyes would not meet Sarah's.

She stood on the threshold of her home, watching him, taking note of his body language. Thomas was always carefree, confident, and he was kind. But what if...

Reaching out with her magic, she asked, "Are you alone?"

His eyes finally met hers. He nodded. "It's just me. Is that alright? Your parents are home, aren't they? I can come back another time, maybe after school. Sarah?"

Only the animals and us.

She exhaled and placed a hand on her chest. Her traitorous tears finally fell.

"Oh, no, no. What's wrong, Sarah? I'm sorry if I upset you."

There was a wide grin on her lips. "No, not at all. These are what my mama calls happy tears."

He quirked a dark brow. " Alright, then. But, just in case..."

He held the box out to Sarah, which she accepted while she sniffed and sniveled. Splashes of her tears gave the box's top a speckled look. The bottom greeted her palms with a comforting warmth and the smell of sugary pecans permeated the space between the two friends.

Sarah looked at Thomas. The dimples were showing in his cheeks.

"My mom remembered it was your favorite. Honestly, I think she misses having a girl around the house." He chuckled and slipped his hands into his pockets.

Sarah wrapped her arms around the pie, pulling it close to her. The heat spread over her chest. She had the sudden urge to let that heat move through her, to cause spiral of flames to dance from her fingertips.

Instead, she excused herself to put the pie away, then took a seat on the porch beside Thomas.

"I'm sorry my parents can't come down. Mama's...busy and Daddy is...well, resting."

He nodded. "Is there any news from the doctor?"

"Not really. He thinks Daddy will get better. There's a lot of coal in his chest, he says."

"Hm. I'm sure you've already heard this but I'm sorry, Sarah." He ruffled his hair some, then turned to fully face her. "I truly am. I wish none of it had ever happened. Your family doesn't deserve any of this."

She sighed, looking over Thomas' handsome face. He was already a great friend. He would certainly make a wonderful husband. Elaine was lucky.

Sarah placed her chin in her hand. She stared out toward the forest, the last bit of sun casting a blue hue over it.

"I thought you had brought the others her to taunt me."

"What?"

"I thought that's why you were acting so strange. Silly of me, huh?"

"I wouldn't do that. We're friends. And, I know everyone isn't a fan of you or your family." He shrugged. "You've only ever been kind to me. How can I see you any different?"

"Thanks," she replied, tucking her hair behind her ears. "How are you feeling, by the way? The new medicine seems to be helping?"

"Sure is. The doctor doesn't think this winter will be as hard as the last for me."

"Hm." Sarah looked away from him.

I suppose that means he won't need any extra tutoring. Of course.

She cleared her throat and straightened. "How's school been? I haven't had a chance to ask you about your grades since you've come back."

"Much better thanks to your lessons. I'm guessing you won't be staying in town once you're done with schooling."

Sarah's brows slanted. "Why would you say that?"

He stared at her, then shook his head.

"What is it, J-Thomas?"

He sent her a pointed look. "You're too smart to stay here, Sarah."

"I don't think I'm—"

"No, you are." He leaned a little closer. "You've got the highest marks in town. Everybody knows it."

She scoffed. "Sure. But no one wants to admit it."

"You wouldn't be doing it for them though," he replied. "You'd be doing it for you while they'd still be stuck here twiddling their thumbs. You could be the first one, Sarah."

There were light splashes of red in Thomas' cheeks. His green eyes were wide and earnest as the porch light reflected in them. He had gotten himself so worked up.

Sarah was sure her own face was red as a tomato. She glanced at his lips, her heart hammering in her chest. It was only them, the moon, and the stars. They both only had to lean a little closer.

Her curls betrayed her. A few ringlets fell in her face.

Before she could move them away, Thomas had tangled-twisted them in with the others. Sarah stared at him while he worked, but he did not meet her eyes.

When the last curl was tamed, he sighed. "Alright. I should be getting home now."

She blinked.

"Enjoy the pie. Tell your parents I said 'hello,' too." He got to his feet.

"Oh, oh, yes, of course." She stood up and clasped her hands in front of her while he prepared to depart. "Thank you, Thomas. For everything."

He moved down the porch stairs, but stopped for a moment to turn around and look up at her.

"Sarah?"

"Hm?"

"I really preferred when you called me Tom."

Another layer of red coated her face. She fiddled with her fingers, clenching and tugging them as words struggled to form.

Finally, she lay them by her sides and gave him a nod. "Of course. Tom."

"Night, Sarah."

She waved him goodbye, then stayed on the porch until his figure had faded into the night.

When she returned to her bedroom, Sarah could hear her mother crying quietly down the hall. She knew her father was ill and she would have to heal him. She knew people in the town were saying horrible things about her and her family.

None of it seemed that heavy a burden to bear any longer. She crawled into her bed with a light heart.

Because no one, at least on Earth, believed in her the way Thomas had.

CHAPTER 8

"You are happy and sad." Franklin gave her a once over, then a good sniff. "Doesn't smell like anger. Odd scent."

Sarah leaned against Mother Tree and stretched her legs out. He gave her a pointed stare. It was nowhere near as hurtful as the looks her mother had been giving her all last week and during the weekend.

"I don't want to talk about it, Franklin."

He humphed and his jelly stomach shook with the movement. "No morning practice, no conversation?"

The gnome stepped closer and Sarah found herself leaning away from him. But he was determined.

Franklin stood on the tips of his toes, searching her face.

"You're sick," he replied.

"I am?"

He nodded. "I'm certain of it. But not your body, not your mind. Your soul is ill...ill with worry. What happ—"

"Nothing." She turned away from him. Her hands had turned to fists by her side.

There was a light pat on her right fist.

"There, there. All will be well, Sarafina."

Sarah's lips trembled but she forced them into a straight line. She took Franklin's hands in her own.

"I'm sorry, Franklin. And thank you."

He gave her a nod. "It's what friends are for. You were there for me when Margery took off with that berried Bardolf."

The very mention of his adversary's name brought another shade of red to Franklin's already rosey cheeks.

"Now, we've yammered about this already, right Franklin?" Sarah said, patting his cone shaped hat.

He sighed. "We have."

"And what did we decide?"

"If a gnomey does not see my value, then she is not worth my hand in marriage," he replied. "Thank you, Sarafina. Sometimes the old feelings get the best of me."

She smiled. "Like you said, it's what friends are for. I do have a reason for calling you out here though."

At those words, he puffed out his chest and turned up his chin. "How can I be of service to you, Chosen One?"

She hated when he called her that.

"Well, first I was wondering if you, or any of the others, had heard word from Lyrica?"

He quirked a brow. "No, not in years, which isn't odd. You know hardly anyone passes through now."

She nodded. "Fine. Next question. If I wanted to return to Lyrica, without a portal or a large body of water, how could I? Would the body of water have to be bigger than a lake?"

"Hm." Staring at the ground, he tapped his chin, before finally saying, "You can't."

Franklin grinned.

The joy on the gnome's face matched Sarah's deflation. In her time with the gnomes, Sarah had learned their perspective on conversations differed from humans. They were straightforward and honest. Though the gnome hadn't given her the answer she wanted, he had answered her question. That was a victory for him.

"Why do you wish to return?" he asked.

"I...I think Lyrica may be in trouble again. I think there's a war." Sarah slumped her head, before pulling her knees up and resting it along them. "And there's nothing I can do to help them. If I can't get back, what will happen to all the Lyricans?"

The school bell rang in the distance. Sarah wiped her eyes and jumped to her feet.

"I'm sorry. I have to go, Franklin."

"Would you like me to walk you?"

She shook her head. "No, I'll be alright. I can't risk anyone seeing me talking with you either."

He frowned. "Why not? It doesn't bother you usually."

"Things...things have changed. I'll tell you more soon. I promise. How does that sound?"

"Not good. Is it the best I'm going to get?"

"Afraid so. I'll speak with you tomorrow." With those words, Sarah was off.

She knew she'd be late no matter how fast she ran. Still, the mile jog to the white schoolhouse felt nice.In the woods Sarah had almost always felt safe, but the last few nights the trees had been especially comforting. Her mother had ceased communicating with her, aside from cold plates of food left on the table. And she had started to lock their door. Each night.

Sarah pinched her palms to stop the tears.

Today she refused to cry. Today was a new week. She would arrive home and the doctor would tell them her father was on the road to recovery. Once that was done, she'd focus on saving Lyrica. Then, on how to fix things with her mother, though she wondered if what remained of their relationship was even repairable.

And did she want to even try to piece together the shambles?

A tiny bit of guilt gnawed at Sarah. She ignored it.

She opened the back door of the schoolhouse and burst into her classroom. Sarah had an apology on the tip of her tongue, but something was wrong.

"I hope this doesn't become a habit of yours, Sarafina," said Mr. Greensburg. "Take your seat."

She didn't move. A shiver ran over Sarah.

"Must I repeat myself? Take your seat, Sarafina, and stop disrupting the lesson."

Mr. Greensburg slammed his manual on his desk, and Sarah found her way to a chair. She began fumbling with her school items. Her hands were shaking so badly it took all she had to not snap her pencil in half.

Without having to look, Sarah knew her classmates were staring at her. The atmosphere in the room coiled around her like a snake. She had become so used to their negative energies she hardly noticed it anymore. Sensing other's emotions was also not her strong suit. Except this time, her peers were more than angry and disgusted. Even a little hate wasn't unusual for them.

But this time, there was fear.

It permeated the room like winter's wind, touching every crevice and corner.

Sarah kept her head low, looking underneath her lashes. Several of her peers were wearing crosses around their necks.

Most people reserved them for Sundays at church but now…

Her mother had told them. Lucille had told her entire gaggle of hens about her Devil Child and they had spread the lies to everyone.

The feeling of fear pressed down on Sarah. It competed for dominance with the betrayal that dug into her chest.

Her own mother had offered her up.

Sarah's jaw quivered. Her notes became blurry scribbles across her paper. Even her hands could no longer keep up with Mr. Greenberg as he instructed the lesson.

She placed her items on her desk and tucked her hands under arms. They were still shaking right along with her jaw.

Sarah gnashed her teeth together but couldn't keep them steady.

Her classmates' fear still filled the room.

Her mother's betrayal clung to her.

But her own anger raged inside her. And Sarah wasn't sure if she wanted to put it out.

Her mother hadn't packed her any food. It would have been a waste considering Sarah's current state. Her stomach was a tangle of frustration with room for nothing else.

The spring day had become dreary outside. Gray light streamed through the windows. Still, the room remained cast in shadow.

When the instructor announced recess, her peers quickly left the classroom, casting hesitant glances her way. She never joined them or any of the other grades outside and she didn't plan on starting any time soon.

Especially not today.

Alone in the classroom, Sarah sat hunched over, staring at her desk. Red, crescent-shaped lines decorated her palms.

Part of her wanted to cry. The situation definitely called for it. Yet Sarah could not add fuel to the fire. If anyone saw a single tear, it would be more gossip for them to feed on.

Daring a glance outside, Sarah saw nearly all eyes on her. They whispered and pointed.

It hadn't been like this before. She had even learned how to navigate the town and school unseen.

Sarah had always been the local crazy. Yet she had never been truly feared until now. She had never truly been seen as a monster until now.

She closed her eyes and took a deep breath. Sarah got to her feet and left the classroom. Recess had another fifteen minutes based on the clock. That would be fifteen minutes of peace.

The halls were silent as she moved through them, making her way to the school's front. The farther she walked from the classroom, the easier it became to breathe.

She stood by the front entrance, staring at the trees across the road. Her fingers tingled and her feet seemed to head outside of their own choosing. She pressed on the handle, gradually pushing the door open.

She could do it. Sarah could dart into the woods and keep running until her home was completely behind her. She'd go somewhere else, somewhere new where no one knew her name and no one cared where she came from.

She'd start a home there. And if no such place existed, she'd live in the woods with the trees. Because, unlike humans, they never judged her.

"Sarah."

Thomas' hand slipped over hers. He removed her hand from the knob, then closed the door. He faced her.

"Sarah, you don't—"

"Look well?"

She averted her gaze to the floor. The words had come out sharper than intended. Suddenly, her breathing was uneven and she couldn't focus. Her eyes moved everywhere. It felt as if something had a giant's grip around her throat and refused to release.

"I—"

"Let's relax now, Sarah." He placed a hand on her shoulder.

She shook her head.

"Yes, listen to me. Hey, look here. At me."

She couldn't. She couldn't even keep her eyes straight.

He tipped up her chin, forcing her eyes to meet his. Their green color reminded her of the forest trees.

"I believe you, Sarah."

He nodded and she found herself mocking his movements.

"I believe you, Sarah."

She flung herself into him, latching her arms around his back while her eyes stung.

She would not cry. She refused to.

The weight of his arms settled around her.

She bit her bottom lip as a single tear fell down her cheek.

"Tom!"

Sarah stepped from his embrace. She recognized Elaine's voice easily, as well as the expression on her face as she took in the scene.

Elaine stood at the end of the hall, arms rigid across her chest. Her usually perfectly smooth, blonde curls seemed frazzled.

'What's going on here?" she demanded more than asked.

Neither Sarah or Thomas responded.

Elaine looked between the two of them, finally settling on Thomas. She narrowed her eyes at him.

"I would like to speak with you, Tom. Alone." She tossed one sharp glance at Sarah, moving her icy blue gaze over the redhead.

Sarah placed her hands on her hips and glared right back at her old enemy. Her insides burned with hurt and frustration.

"I'm helping Sarah out, Elaine," Thomas said. "We can speak after school."

The blonde's face dropped. Sarah thought she'd misheard her friend.

Had Thomas really asked Elaine to leave?

He stared at Elaine, shoulders pulled back and body sturdy. Yet there was an apology in his eyes.

The tips of Sarah's fingers cooled, along with all of the rage. She couldn't fight back, not if it meant Thomas would be hurt. And by the way he was staring at Elaine, Sarah knew if anything happened to her, he would be greatly hurt.

Sarah sighed. "Thomas, you should go. I'll be fine. Recess is almost over anyway, so we should all be getting back to class. Excuse me."

Before Elaine could spew hateful words or Thomas could convince her to stay, Sarah departed from the hall.

CHAPTER 9

"And you're certain everything's fine, Sarah?" Ms. Carr asked. The two were standing by the school's back door. Dusk was approaching and the sky had started darkening.

Sarah grinned. "Yes, everything's fine, Ms. Carr. See you tomorrow morning."

She was sure Ms. Carr knew she was lying. Teachers usually had a particular knack for sensing deceit and Ms. Carr was no exception.

"I could walk you home. It's late and I'd like the chance to speak with your mother. Tell her what a brilliant daughter she has."

The words were sweet and wrapped in worry. Her teacher was honestly concerned for Sarah and that was enough to end her day on. She had already let her stay after for additional lessons, though they both knew she didn't need any.

Ms. Carr gave a small smile and nod, before wrapping her jacket around herself. The spring evening had an unusual chill and the air smelled of rain.

"Alright then. I did...I did have one more question for you, Sarah."

"Yes?" Sarah was already stepping onto the path that cut through the woods and led to her home.

"Do you remember our lessons on the Salem Witch Trials?"

Sarah hesitated. "Y-yes. I do."

"Good, good. This message was muddled in all the historical fact," Ms. Carr said. "The moral of that event is people...they fear what they do not understand. But what is not understood is not inherently bad."

The two were silent. Sarah stared at the ground, searching for words. Her eyes were stinging again but she fought the tears back.

"Goodnight, Sarah. I look forward to seeing you tomorrow morning." Ms. Carr closed the screen door and stepped toward the front of the school.

Sarah watched her until her figure disappeared into the night. Then, she stared back at her own path and headed home. She had no clue what awaited her there. Would her mother even let her in? Would she try to send Sarah away again?

The thought immediately had Sarah shaking her head. She'd escape before they could catch her.

But what about her father? Sarah wondered if Lucille would allow her to see him. The doctor telling her her father was on the road to recovery was the only thing she'd been looking forward to throughout the day. Even in all the mess at school, Sarah knew there was at least that.

And now she also knew she wasn't alone. Ms. Carr and Thomas were behind her. She only had to make sure if she drowned in the town's scrutiny, they didn't drown with her.

"Run, Sarah."

"Jacob?"

She knew the rock was coming toward her but she didn't know why. It hit perfectly at the rim of her forehead, breaking Sarah's skin. Warm blood trickled along her hairline and down to her jaw.

Sarah wiped at the crimson, smearing it across her pale cheeks and palms.

Another rock sailed through the air, slicing the flesh right under her eye.

"You should have stayed away from him."

Elaine.

Sarah smashed her teeth together. She took in a sharp breath, removed her hand from her bleeding face, and straightened her stance.

Elaine stood on a hill's slant a few yards up from where Sarah was on the path. Beside her were two girls from her gaggle: Beth and Susanna.

Sarah pivoted to face them directly, pushing away at the desire to open the earth beneath the three young women's feet. If there were ever time to test out her magic, her three peers were ideal test subjects.

Still, she had made an agreement with herself. And her town would consider any retaliation on her part an admission of guilt. Though it bruised her pride, Sarah had to play passive.

"Leave me alone, Elaine," Sarah said. "I'm going home and I'll forget this ever happened."

Elaine scoffed. Sarah wasn't surprised. She didn't really expect Elaine to retreat. In her age, the girl had only grown crueler. Her infatuation with Thomas had saved Sarah the last year. Now all that storage seemed to be roaring back to life.

The three descended down the hill.

"First, we'll capture the middle one. Then, her two friends. Understood?"

"Franklin, no!" Sarah peered around the forest, attempting to catch a glimpse of the gnome. She couldn't allow him to interfere.

"She really is crazy." Susanna gave her a once over. She shook her head. "Elaine, we should go. Her mother wasn't lying. Something's got a hold on her."

Beth looked at Susanna. "All the more reason not to run, Susan."

"She already made that Jacob boy disappear," Susan retorted.

Sarah rolled her eyes. *That old rumor is still going around I see.*

"The Father told us not to fear evil, didn't he?" Elaine jutted out her chin and continued her descent.

"Blind them with our dust."

"Ethlen, no," Sarah whispered. "You can't interfere."

"There she goes again." Elaine twirled her cross between her thumb and forefinger. When the three were only a few feet from Sarah, she lay the necklace against her chest.

"You need to keep your evil hands off Tom."

"Thomas is free to socialize with whomever he chooses. And..." Sarah raised her chin. She met Elaine's glare directly. "I'd never hurt him. He's a good friend."

Sarah could have dodged Elaine's slap but she didn't, nor did she return the favor. Instead, she swallowed the small bit of pain and faced her enemies again.

"I'm leaving, Elaine. Goodnight."

Without another word, Sarah spun on her heels and moved

down the path. The sound of urgent footsteps followed.

Nothing I can do. She sighed.

One of the three pushed Sarah to the ground. Her forest friends screamed out to her. She ignored their pleas to help.

Fingernails dragged across her neck as a weight pressed into her back. Someone's thighs pushed into her sides and Sarah knew she was trapped.

"Get her, get her, get her!"

The end of Sarah's long ponytail was yanked up and the plait undone as they pulled at her red strands.

She forced her hands out to remind herself not to attack.

One of them had a grip on her skull and they pushed her face into the earth while another kicked her side. Between the soil filling her mouth and the air being kicked out of her, Sarah's world was becoming blurry. She could feel each kick to her gut vibrate through her. She could hear the three girls panting while she gasped for air.

They were four young women alone in the woods. Everyone had left to town for the day and darkness had begun to settle. There was no one to hear Sarah's agonizing gasps or their panting exertions.

Someone stomped on her open hand.

"Maybe we should stop." That was Susanna.

Her friends didn't listen.

"Elaine. Beth." There were tremors in her voice. "Stop, w-we...her mother's going to have her exorcised, then she'll be fine. We can't kill her!"

Mama wanted me exorcised?

"Sarah!" Thomas' voice was like a clear bell in a sea of white noise. She could hear him stumbling down the hill and running toward them. The attack immediately stopped.

"What are you doing to her?"

A flashlight illuminated Sarah's curled form. She blocked her eyes and turned away from it.

"I'm trying to protect you, Tom."

"By attacking my friend? She's covered in blood. Sarah, can you hear me?" He moved her hair away from her face. The size of his eyes informed her how badly she looked.

The three young women had grown quiet.

"You three need to leave now." He glared at Elaine and her

friends. "Get out of here. Go!"

"Even her own mother calls her a demon, Tom. We were only—
"

"Now!"

If Thomas had been a dwarf, Sarah was certain the volume of his shout would have shaken the forest. Soon Sarah could hear retreating footsteps. When the sound had become distant enough, she flipped onto her knees. Then, embracing the streak of pain that ran along her sides, she forced herself to her feet.

Immediately she began to sway. She knew down the path was her home, the place where her father waited for her. That thought steadied her and she moved forward.

"No, no. Let's take it easy here." Thomas stepped in front of her and placed both hands on her shoulders.

"I'm fine. Just n-need to get...home." The word caught in her throat. She started coughing and before she could protest again, Thomas had lifted her onto his back.

"Just rest now, alright? I'll get you home."

Part of Sarah wanted to push away, yet his back felt solid underneath her. His skin offered a comforting warmth, so she let the last bit of her energy go.

Slowly, the two made their way through the forest back to Sarah's home. As Thomas carried her, Sarah kept her eyes on the moon, wondering if all of Lyrica was staring at the same moon.

The night she had met Alex, the night he had attacked her and she had saved him, the moon had been large and round, as well. Was he staring at the same moon from a balcony in the Alclian domain? And was Serwa by his side?

Thomas sighed. "I had a feeling, I mean I didn't know. I just had a feeling Elaine was up to something. I never once thought she'd be capable of this. I'm sorry I didn't get here sooner."

"Not your fault," she whispered.

"Maybe not directly. I still took too long to listen to my gut. I should have stayed after and waited for you."

She patted his shoulder. "You're here now."

He scoffed and she knew he was smiling. "We'll tell your parents and Ms. Carr what happened. They're not going to get away with this. I'll be your witness. And don't say you don't want to."

He read my mind.

"You don't have to be everyone's punching bag all the time, Sarah."

She placed her chin right between his neck and shoulder. "Thank you, Tom."

"So, you've finally given in and used my short name, huh? Hm, I'm glad to hear it. You want to hear something else?"

"Hm?"

"That story I told you about, way back when I was sick. I started working on it again and I've got a new main character."

"Hm." Sarah was struggling to keep her eyes open.

"She's a quiet but fiesty redhead. And she's smart, too, more than she gives herself credit for."

Sarah laughed outright at that one. Her sides still ached and the action intensified the pain but she couldn't resist. Thomas joined in, his back still solid and steady beneath her.

Soon the familiar light of her porch came into view. Sarah released a long exhale. She tapped his shoulder.

"Here's fine. Let's talk with my parents tomorrow."

"Sarah..." He squatted down some and let her slide off. "It won't take long if that's what's worrying you. Tonight, we only have to tell them. Everything else can happen tomorrow."

She shook her head. "I'm exhausted and everything...well, it hurts. I don't think I'll be in school tomorrow. I'll tell my mama at breakfast."

He glanced toward the house, then met her gaze once more. "Fine. I'm telling Ms. Carr tomorrow though. Then, we'll both come here for her to hear it straight from you. Alright?"

She bobbed her head. "Goodnight, Tom."

"Night, Sarah." He slipped his hands into his pockets and waited. She could feel his eyes on her as she moved into the house. Before closing the door, Sarah gave him one last wave.

The house was quiet. She hadn't seen the pickup outside, which meant her mother had gone into town again. It seemed in her father's absence, her mother had increased her activity with her gaggle of hens.

Looking up the stairs, Sarah took in a deep inhale and prepared herself. Something so simple had never felt so daunting. She leaned against the wall and moved up one stair at a time. On the very top stair the floorboard creaked.

"Lucille, is that you?"

She stared down the hall. Her parents' bedroom light was on.

"Anyone there? Sarah, honey, you getting home?"

So many words rushed through her mind. None of them seemed right. It even hurt to smile, yet Sarah wore the largest grin. Her body shook in delight. The day's events dimmed in her memory and finally she spilled tears of joy. They streamed down her face rapidly, adding a layer of salt to her bruised lips and stinging the wounds along her face.

Finally, gripping the wall's corner, she managed to say, "Y-yes. I'm here, Daddy. I just got in from school."

"Let me get up and—"

"No!" She remembered her appearance. "I'll come to you. I'll wash up and bring you something to eat."

He didn't respond.

"Daddy?"

Under her father's weight the mattress squeaked, followed by a long sigh.

"If you say so," he replied. "Even I'm too tired to argue."

"I'll be right there, Daddy. Just give me a minute."

Sarah ran down the hall and into the bathroom where she filled the tub to its rim. She tossed her clothes to the floor, stepped into the tub, and began scrubbing away the filth. She could hear her father humming away down the hall.

Glancing down at her dress, she pulled it in with her. Better to kill two birds with one stone.

The warm water stung her open wounds. Examining herself, Sarah counted a total of twenty cuts. The two on her face from the rocks, the five on her neck from their nails, three more on her right shoulder, and smaller ones scattered over her thighs. A few of them still bled. They burned from the soap and Sarah found herself biting her lip to counter the pain.

Only this caused more blood to dribble from her busted lip. She had forgotten about that one.

Sarah watched the blood drip into the dirty water. It was an odd color, a shade she realized could only come from a combination of blood, filth, and soap.

Her knees jutted out of the water like two snowpeaks with slashes of red traveling downward. Sarah went to take in some air but her throat had constricted.

She needed to get out of the tub.

Seething tears rolled down her face. She gripped the tub's rim yet her grip would not hold. Her arms and hands had become rattles. Her feet searched for the tub's bottom to stand on but Sarah could not find it. It was as if she were swimming in a bottomless lake, the shore nowhere in sight.

Fresh sobs broke from her. Her father's humming had become a flat noise in the background.

She tried closing her eyes and taking in some air, only to reopen them in the next moment. All she saw were the woods, all she felt were hands grabbing at her, fingernails digging into her skull. Then, everything hurt. Every wound burned and every bone ached.

The tears continued falling. Her father continued humming.

Sarah sniffled and snotted, her body growing heavy. Leaning back in the tub, she gazed at the ugly water. The forest's dirt and her blood.

It made no sense. Once before, Sarah had wished to be like her peers, to make her mother happy. Yet they'd acquired a level of cruelty she couldn't imagine.

Her mother...

She shook her head. Her breathing evened out and, finally, Sarah found rest.

CHAPTER 10

I can't see.

Sarah blinked repeatedly, yet there was no light. She flailed out for something in front of her only to find her hands empty. A vacant bubbling sound mimicked her movements.

Sarah pushed upward and away from the water's bottom. Gradually, the darkness dwindled, a bright moon took shape, and she broke the water's surface.

Gasping for air, Sarah peered around her. A light rain was coming down, hiding everything in the distance. The night and rain blurred the darkness together, an endless canvas of black.

The waves roared to life, illuminated by the slivers of moon as they moved upward, crashing against a figure in the distance. Sarah moved toward the large rock.

There was something caught on her foot. Fear gripping at her, Sarah attempted to swim away from whatever had her yet its hold did not slacken.

She reached below the water and caught hold of her captor, pulling him up from the watery depths. What stared back at her was her knotted dirty dress. She sighed.

There had been no monster after all. Only her ruined dress.

Treading the water, Sarah felt around her body. Though the cold would not allow it to show, a blush had crept across Sarah's cheeks. She was completely naked.

Embarrassment fueling her, she untangled the dress and slipped it over her head. Sarah looked around once more and spotted the protruding rock, the closest piece of land as far as she could tell.

The rain became more forceful, nearly blocking out the moon completely with its speed. Sarah blinked away the droplets clinging to her face. She kept the rock in sight and soon it was within arm's reach.

Both Sarah and the rock were soaked from the rain and water. She struggled to get a firm grasp, finally deciding to wrap her entire body around the stone. She edged up from its base, just nearly reaching the top.

She peered over the water. The rain was heavy and the sea infuriated. The storm showed no signs of letting up.

She pressed her forehead into the stone, before taking several deep breaths. Her body had become nothing more than shivers and spasms.

She allowed what she had just done to sink in, let it settle into her mind while she took thankful breaths of air. Eventually, she calmed.

Sarah rested her head flat on the rock and closed her eyes.

She was alive, she had found temporary sanctuary, and she knew exactly where she was.

Lyrica.

"We need to tell Mother."

"She might have woken up and left by time we do that. Plus, Mother is a slow swimmer."

"She is not! You take that back, Reina."

"And why don't you stop whining, Finley?"

"I'm not whining!"

"You are!"

Sarah cracked her eyes open. Every part of her felt dry and tight, like an old piece of salted leather which had been soaked and left out too long in the sun. Her body was still knotted around the rock.

"You're the worst sister I've ever had."

"I'm the only one you've ever had, you barnacle."

There was a gasp.

"You're not supposed to use that word. I'm telling Mother—"

"Well, you tell her everything anyway, why not that?"

Sarah arched her neck up to look over at who had woken her. A young boy and girl were treading the water on the front side of the stone. They both had light brown skin with wavy dark brown hair cascading down their backs. The girl's hair moved past her shoulders, much longer than her brother's.

The two continued squabbling. It was obvious they were siblings and the boy was the younger of the two. Sarah also quickly realized he was very much a mama's boy.

"If Mother were here, she'd give you a fin spanking," the boy said, sniffling.

The girl rolled her eyes. "I'm too old for a fin spanking. And when Father returns, I'm going to tell him how big a baby you've been."

"I have not!"

"Have so."

"Have not!"

"Have so."

"Uh...excuse me?"

They froze, eyes large and locked on one another.

Sarah waited for them to turn to her.

Neither moved.

"Alright. This is going to be an odd question. Could either of you—"

Plop, plop!

Their beautiful green tails had disappeared almost as soon as they had appeared. Sarah forced her arms free from the rock and pushed herself to its edge.

The sun was beating down on the sea, so she could clearly see them in the water.

She reached out with both aching arms, then turned them inward toward herself. The sea's waves moved with her, pulling the two siblings from their escape.

When they were within reach again, Sarah eased the water back to the base of her little piece of land. She was panting.

The boy hid behind his sister and clung to her waist. She studied Sarah. Her hands were fists by her side.

"You're not human?" the young girl asked.

Sarah shook her head. "Not in the way Lyrica thinks of humans, at least."

"A-are you a witch?" the boy stuttered, still hiding behind his sister. "Are you the ones working with the humans?"

Sarah blinked. "Why would witches work with humans?"

"Please, we've kept our end of the agreement," the older girl said quickly. "This is far enough away from shore."

"No, listen. I'm not a Lyrican human."

"Could she be using one of the witch stones?" the boy asked.

"Hush, Fin," his sister hissed. She returned her attention to Sarah, though her eyes occasionally darted around them.

Using her magic, Sarah examined the space around them. She couldn't sense anyone. They were alone. They were also strangers.

"You're scared," Sarah said.

Neither answered. The girl puffed out her chest.

"There's no need to be. I'm not going to hurt you. I only want to get back on land. I'd get there myself but I'm not sure where I am and...my trip here wasn't smooth."

"You didn't come on the big ships with the humans?" the boy asked.

She shook her head.

"Then, what are you doing this far from the shore?" the girl added.

Sarah glanced between the two of them. She bit her lip then immediately winced when she caught her gash. She wiped away at the thin line of blood before focusing on the two children again.

"Have you two heard of The Chosen One? The Child of Legend from earth?"

They nodded.

"Well, I'm...I'm her. I was in my bathroom, well, you wouldn't know what that is. Anyway—"

The mergirl leapt forward and pushed off the protruding rock, so she was nearly nose to nose with Sarah. Her eyes roamed over Sarah's face. She sniffed, then smiled, finally falling back into the sea.

"That's why you smell funny," the girl said. "Our noses aren't as good as other beings but you do smell odd. It explains everything. You found a portal and returned to stop the humans!"

"She's going to fight the humans with Father!"

The two children squealed. Together they dove under the water, only to shoot straight up into the air, finally landing with a huge splash. The spray caught Sarah and though she was tired, she laughed along with them.

"This is so exciting! Oh, my name is Reina and this is Finley."

"You can call me Fin."

"It's a pleasure to meet you both. Just call me Sarah."

"It's a good thing we found her before one of our cousins did," Fin said, speaking to his sister.

"What's wrong with your cousins?" Sarah asked.

"He means sirens," Reina corrected. "We call them cousins since they are related to us, only not directly. They've been trying to play both sides. They may have drowned you or given you to the humans."

"Sirens never tell the truth," Fin said. "That's why the old king Poseidon cursed them. They tried to take his throne."

Sarah bobbed her head, making note to do more digging into sirens and Poseidon. Ms. Carr likely had a book on Greek mythology.

"But you have nothing to worry about now." Reina beamed up at Sarah, her tail swishing happily in the water. "I'm here and I'll make sure you get back to land."

"I'm here, too!" Fin shouted.

Reina glared at him. "No. You're too small. You need to go back to Mother while I carry the Chosen One to shore."

"I am not too small!"

"You are."

"I'm a much better swimmer than you," he retorted.

The elder sister scowled. She looked at Sarah. "Some people just love to lie to themselves, don't they?"

Fin's eyes narrowed. He sunk just below the water so only the top of his head was showing.

Reina sighed. "That means I've really upset him. It serves him right, though. Younger brothers are a handful. Do you have siblings, Chosen One?"

Sarah glanced between the two.

"Uh...no," she finally sputtered, wondering if she had dodged a bullet as an only child.

She cleared her throat. "And, please, just call me Sarah. Before we leave, could you tell me where in Lyrica we are? I want to know where I'll be landing."

Fin popped his head above the water. "The Eastern Sea. We're right by the plains. Father traveled south near the human's kingdom. That's farther away."

Which means Gan and the wood elves are farther away, too.

"But we're not supposed to tell anyone that." Reina sighed, staring at her brother blankly.

He huffed, then turned away from her.

Reina smoothed a hand over her face and looked at Sarah. She smiled despite her obvious irritation. "Of course, we know we can trust you, Sarah. Just keep it a secret."

"Agreed. The Eastern Sea is by the mountain. Where I returned the stone?"

"It's that way." Fin swerved to his right and pointed off into the distance. "I'll help Reina take you there."

His sister crossed her arms, her eyebrows arched downward. She opened her mouth to respond. Sarah rolled herself into the sea.

"Let's go," she said, praying her distraction had worked.

Reina grinned. "Mother tells us to swim deep. That way the humans can't see us so easily if one of their ships arrive. You'll need to be able to hold your breath."

Sarah bit back a complaint. "How long is the journey?"

The girl tapped her chin. "If we don't have any trouble, it'll be about thirty minutes. We shouldn't run into any humans. Their ships hardly pass here and Father said they're more focused on conquering the land for now."

For now? What's happened to Lyrica? Why are witches working with humans to hurt other Lyricans?

"Are you ready?" Fin asked.

Sarah shook herself. She'd never be able to answer those questions if she didn't get to shore.

"The longest I've held my breath is two minutes. I'll try for longer but if I start smacking your tail—"

"I'll bring you up." Reina nodded. She turned to her brother. "You're going to watch her. Make sure she doesn't drown. Keep up or I'm leaving you."

The smile on Fin's face touched from ear to ear. "I will, Reina. I promise."

"One more thing," Sarah warned.

"Yes?" the siblings replied.

Sarah hardened her eyes and stared down at both them. She broadened her shoulders and pinched her face, putting on her best Serwa glower.

"If the humans come and they see us, you two must leave. Don't worry about me. I don't want you or your family getting hurt on my part. Understand?"

They glanced at one another.

"Reina," Sarah said. "Fin. Do you understand? I do need your help and I'm thankful for it. But you can't risk your lives."

Both children glued their eyes to the water.

"We understand," they mumbled.

"Good. I'm ready whenever you two are."

Without another word, Reina offered her tail to Sarah, who wrapped her arms around her impromptu wagon. Fin positioned himself beside Sarah just before the three dove below the waves.

The temperature dropped as they drove deeper. Reina's tail moved rapidly, knocking Sarah from side to side. She felt like she was on a broken ride at the State Fair.

Fin giggled beside her, releasing a string of bubbles.

Despite her extra weight, Sarah thought they were moving at a good speed. The *swishing* of water was a hollow sound in her ears as they sped through the sea. The trio blasted through schools of small fish darting the little ones in every direction.

As promised, Reina shot to the surface when Sarah tapped her tail, Fin following right after, until land was in sight.

"I can get you closer." Reina gazed at the open sea around them. "There aren't any ships and I don't feel anything large moving through the water. We should be fine. Here."

The young mergirl grabbed Sarah's right arm, while Fin grabbed her left. Together they swam her up to shore, close enough that her feet could touch the pebbly bottom.

Once Sarah could stand to her full height, they released her. She prayed her long dress hid her shaking knees. She could do nothing about the deep gulps of air she was taking in though.

Back slightly arched, hand on abdomen, and breathing heavily, she smiled at the two merchildren.

"Thank you both very much. I wish I could do more to show you my gratitude."

They laughed.

"You're going to do enough," Reina said, smiling.

Fin's tail fluttered in the water. "Once you get rid of the humans, everything will be fine again. And our family won't have to stay away from shore."

Their eyes were like large, round blinding suns shining on Sarah. Only their words felt much more menacing.

She gave them a small grin. "I hope we meet again. Now go. In case one of those ships comes."

"I hope we do," Reina squealed. "Come, Fin."

"Bye, Sarah!"

They waved, before pushing back into the sea and diving under the water. She tried to watch them as they left but they had already disappeared.

Sarah pulled her hair to one side and twisted out the salt water. Then, she fell back onto the shore, choosing to ignore the endless number of rocks under her. There was also a small ledge leading up to what she assumed were the plains. Tan grass peeked over the edge.

The beach was very different than the one in the south where she had healed Alexander.

"Alex!" Sarah sat up. She dug into the front of her dress and pulled out the ruby necklace.

It was still securely tied around her beside Nettle's sword. There was not one knick or dent in either the stone or the silver trim surrounding it.

Sarah gave a hard exhale, letting her head hang between her legs.

"I'm not sure which trip I enjoyed more. This one or the first."

She closed her eyes and forced her head up into her hands, before looking around her. For miles on either side, all Sarah could see were rocks and pebbles. No sand like the beaches in the south. These rocks ranged in color between light grey and night black, casting a unique color pattern down the beach.

She looked out to the sea, then back at the gem around her neck.

"Okay, Sarah, no time to mope. Here's what we know." She held up a finger. "One, we're on the eastern side of Lyrica. Last time we were here it was mostly cracked earth. That seems to have changed. Two, witches and sirens are working with humans to capture or kill other Lyricans. Three, if we stay on this beach, we may be spotted by a ship. That can't happen."

A chill moved across her skin. Sarah chose to take it as a sign. Shaking legs or not, she had to leave soon.

Sarah pressed the necklace to her lips.

I only need to know one more thing.

She pressed her eyes shut and thought of the last time she had seen Alex. She was floating in the sea. He was standing on the shore sending her off. The moon hung above them.

"Alex," she whispered. "Alexander."

A small corner of a room came into focus behind her eyelids. Despite the ruby's red color coating her sight, Sarah could still make out the details. Alexander's arms were pulled back from his body, held stagnant by chains. He was shirtless. Lines of dark green were scattered across his chest with streams of the same color pouring from them.

Lashes.

"Alex?" Her voice was above a whisper. "Alex."

Her friend glanced around. He leaned forward but the chains held him back. Then, a hand appeared above him. The hand patted his head before slamming it down, forcing his arms away from the chains. The slow creaking and cracking of bone followed.

Sarah's vision was blurring.

"Where are you, Alex? Listen to me, listen!" she screamed.

The hand's owner whispered something. Her friend growled in response, which got him a slap to the face.

"No! Tell me where you are. Tell me and I'll save you."

Alex's head was pressed face down again but he jerked it up at the last moment.

Sarah held her breath.

Chin pressed hard against the ground, Alex's eyes focused.

"Run."

The red immediately shrank into a thin line. Sarah could see it cut between the sky and the sea in front of her. And then, it became a small dot touching the sun until it disappeared.

The ruby necklace stumbled from her hands. Sarah stared at her palms, trying to make sense of what she had seen. He had felt so close yet he had never been farther away.

She bit her lip and tossed her head back as the burning began behind her eyes. Her hands fell to her sides and she turned away from the sea. Seething tears rolled down her cheeks as her heart thrummed in her chest.

Someone had Alex and they were hurting him.

It has to be the humans.

Suddenly the tears stopped. The waves pushed the sea water across the shore. Rocks trembled beneath her.

Sarah took in a sharp breath. She dug into the earth as a tension gripped her muscles.

The air whirled around her...

Control, Sarah. It's about control. It's—

Sarah slashed at the air. A piece of ledge jerked to the left, then crumbled, landing a few yards from her. She got to her feet.

"I'm going to find you, Alex." She gripped the necklace. "And I'm going to save you."

Urgency wrapped itself around exhaustion and Sarah began her climb over the ledge. It was short in height, so it only took grasping the right holds before she found flat land.

She looked at the space before her. There were plains as far as the eye could see, covered in the tan grass. The mountain where she had tossed the stone was a shimmering image in the distance. Short trees with thin trunks arched upward and out into flimsy green bushes. They were placed sporadically across the landscape.

And they would offer no shelter.

Sarah ran her hands through her hair, which felt stiff and dry. Tossing it to one shoulder, she quickly worked it into a clumsy braid. Her gaze had not left the distant, shimmering mountain.

"Think, Sarah, think." She tapped her finger against her hip. "I can't remove the stone but maybe I can bring a dragon...or two."

A sinking feeling settled in her. Could she even wake an elemental? And if she could, was she strong enough to control them? Actually, she wasn't certain it was the humans who had Alex.

"Darn it, darn it, darn it!" Sarah started marching toward the mountain. "It's not like I have a choice."

CHAPTER 11

The sun was merciless as it beat down on the plains, causing land in the distance to blur and mesh. Sarah had worked in heat before. She had watched her father work when he said it had become too hot for her. Still, she didn't think the largest straw hat in Montana would do much against the heat.

Maybe it was because she was so tired.

The thought brought no comfort considering she didn't expect rest any time soon. She didn't need it really, at least not as badly as she needed water.

Since starting her march she hadn't seen or sensed any bodies of water nearby. The plains almost felt like a desert, or what she imagined a desert would be like. There was the unrelenting heat, the open space, and the lack of water.

Yet Sarah knew water had to be somewhere. Though she hadn't encountered another person, she had seen many animals scurrying around. Birds, deers, zebras—which she had only seen in encyclopedias, so the sight froze her for a moment—and more. They couldn't thrive without water.

She sighed. *What would Serwa do?*

Several yards ahead, an image formed. Two of the thin trees were exactly adjacent. Their flimsy branches curved around one another to form the perfect canopy.

Sarah sped up her trip and slumped under the canopy's shade. The slight cool relaxed her.

While she nestled in between the two trees, Sarah glanced around her. She was completely exposed but she also knew she had little choice.

Taking one last look, Sarah let her eyes grow heavy. She wrapped her arms around herself, feeling more secure in the position. Then, there was a scream.

"You're not going to get away!" A man's voice followed by heavy breathing.

Sarah shot up. Farther east there were two figures running. One was a man on horseback, the other a child.

An image flashed in her mind of the little boy and the knight with the odd symbol on his back. Sarah remembered them coming to her in the woods. Could this child be the same boy?

"You dirty half-breed!"

There was no time to hesitate. Sarah ran perpendicular to the two, aiming for the man on horseback. She thought of sending a piece of earth jutting upward but wasn't sure if she'd hit the horse, too.

Sarah hiked the ends of her dress above her knee. She pumped her legs, calling to the earth to push her forward and praying she'd make it in time. This child—a girl, she thought as she grew closer—would not end like the boy. She couldn't.

The man wore no armor. Considering the heat, he had made a smart decision. But on his horse's side where a satchel hung, Sarah saw it.

There was the symbol—two cupped hands holding a flame with blue arrows pointing upward. All doubt disappeared. When Sarah was close enough, she grabbed the horse's side and pulled herself onto its back.

The man stared at her, jaw slacked and mouth hanging wide open while the girl continued fleeing.

Sarah smiled. Then, she reeled her arm back and punched him in the face, before tossing him to the ground. He hit the earth with a thump and a thud.

Sarah pulled on the horse's reins, gently rubbing the animal's side and shushing, until it stilled.

The girl who had been running came to halt. She stood some distance away, a satchel wrapped around her. She faced Sarah and her once-pursuer.

Sarah looked her over. The girl couldn't have been more than twelve. She had a dark tan complexion and a crown of tight curls hung to her chin. She took in long, easy breaths while she watched Sarah.

Why wasn't she running?

The man groaned. Sarah forced her attention away from the child.

"I-I will kill you both. How dare you intervene with my hunt, girl?" His hateful glare bore into Sarah.

Staring down at him, she pulled back her shoulders. "You're not killing anyone. I don't know who you are or why you're chasing a child. What I do know is you're going to leave. Now."

The man smirked. He had the palest blue eyes and lightest blond hair she had had ever seen. Maybe once he had been considered handsome. But now scars decorated his face accompanied by unbecoming wrinkles.

A trail of crimson dribbled from under his short strands.

"What I do, I do for humanity," he spat. He eyed her. "If you had not intervened, you would have been spared. Whether you're human or not no longer matters. You will die for your sympathy to the half-breed."

He reached behind him and withdrew a sword.

Sarah tried not to show her panic. She had forgotten to disarm him when she mounted his horse, and aside from Nettle's small sword around her neck, Sarah had no weapon.

She glanced at the girl. The child still stood as she did before, simply watching.

He charged, slashing upward at Sarah. She tugged the horse away, then quickly climbed down, facing her enemy. He was impatient, like a cat waiting for milk, as her mother would say.

He would come to her.

Only a moment passed. Then he charged again, but this time Sarah was ready. It's what all those early morning practices had been for.

He swung downward slightly to Sarah's left. She bent her knees and moved just to the right. Shock decorated his face. She replaced the look with her elbow.

The man stumbled backward, disoriented. Sarah followed after him. When she was close enough, she pulled her leg back, aimed, and kicked him in the groin. He fell knees first. The sword clattered to the ground.

She grabbed the weapon and raised it to his throat.

Hot, angry breaths left his body while he clenched his teeth tight.

"You little—"

"Shush," Sarah warned. She pressed the sword's tip a bit closer to his throat. Reminding him who was in control, as Serwa would have done.

"I want you to tell me why you were chasing this girl," she stated.

The child still hadn't moved.

"You can go ahead and slit my throat. I'll never confess to a sympathizer."

"A what?"

He tsked. "You treat them as if they're humans, as if their lives are somehow equal to ours. They must be maintained!"

"Who is *they*?" Sarah cried, though she was certain she knew the answer.

"All of them. Vampires, werewolves, shifters, angels, trolls, all of them!"

Sarah shook her head. She was trying to fight the tremble in her arm. "You're insane," she replied.

He smirked. "The righteous always are."

Righteous? She gazed into the man's eyes. They didn't falter. He wholeheartedly believed what he was saying. But how could he?

The air moved beside Sarah. Suddenly, the man's head was snatched back. Long nails flashed in front of his pale skin and burgundy eyes stared into Sarah's blue.

Blood spewed from the man's throat.

The girl released her hold and his body crumbled to the ground. She flicked her nails, dashing blood across the grass.

The sword stumbled from Sarah's hands.

"You weren't going to kill him," the child said. "You were stalling."

"I was trying to get information," Sarah retorted. Her entire being was pulsing. She couldn't quiet the drumming sound of her heart.

The girl glanced between the fallen man and Sarah. She moved a few steps in Sarah's direction, then inhaled deeply through her nose.

"Hm." She turned her head sideways and observed Sarah. "You smell funny. But...I think I know you."

Sarah had a similar feeling. But she knew she hadn't met the child the first time in Lyrica and definitely not on Earth. So, where?

"My name is Bolanile," the girl said. "You may call me Bo. What's your name?"

"Sarafina. You can call me Sarah."

Bolanile's eyes grew wide. She closed the gap between them and stared up at Sarah, inspecting her face. A grin broke across her lips.

"Auntie Sarah!" She leapt into her arms, the corpse beside them a forgotten thought. "I knew you'd come. Mother and Father said you would. You look different than the portrait we have of you at home."

"Wait, you're...Serwa and Alex..."

The child pulled back from Sarah and smiled at her. She didn't see it before, maybe because it had been so long. The girl had Alexander's eye color and his sharp nose. Everything else was Serwa from her tight curls to the curve of her face.

Sarah pulled the child close to her and nuzzled her nose in her hair. Her eyes brimmed with tears, which she blinked away. If Bo was anything like Serwa—based on her recent execution, she most definitely was—she would scowl at Sarah's crying.

The thought made Sarah smile.

"This is perfect," said Bo. "Now, let's hide the body and release the horse. I think there are some bushes nearby, or maybe you can put it under the ground. Then I'll take you to the others."

"Others?" Sarah raised a brow while the child leapt from her arms.

Bo nodded. "The other children."

Ten.

Sarah counted once more.

Ten children including Bo and Kwento, her younger twin brother.

"And what happened to everyone else?" Sarah asked.

Bolanile had led Sarah to a small opening among a collection of flat rocks. No one, on horseback or foot, would notice the little nook unless they walked straight for it. Considering Sarah hadn't run into anyone since leaving the shore, she doubted they'd be found.

For now, at least.

The children had gathered in a semicircle within the small space. It was wide but not deep.

Bolanile and Kwento were the only two standing. They leaned against either wall, facing one another. Kwento's eyes were the same color as his sister and father's. He had the same tight curls, though his hair was shorter, cropped with the sides shaved.

Kwento looked at his sister. She gave him a hard nod.

"Mother said after the humans had taken most of the south, they started moving north," he stated. "No one knew because the fairies with Auntie Nettle and the Southern Wood Elves were still fighting. A small group of the human army made their way north."

His sister continued, "Too far north and the land is dangerous to live on. That's what Father said. But the humans had found witches to work with. The Northern Sky Elves alerted us. By then, it was too late. The humans had brought reinforcements. Father stayed behind to fight."

"Mother took as many as she could," said Kwento. "Some people couldn't keep up… We ran all the way to the river but we didn't have a boat, so Mother parted the current. While we were moving across, the humans caught her with black diamond chains. She couldn't fight and keep the water from drowning us. She told us to run."

Sarah was counting her breaths. She was hearing their story yet it didn't ring true.

Serwa had been captured. Alexander was missing. The humans had conquered nearly all of Lyrica aside from the western deserts and most of the east where they hid.

She shook her head. The children stared at her. Alexander's children let their gaze fall away as they told what had happened to them. They didn't sniffle or cry but they would not meet her eyes.

"But, Nettle was still alive and fighting last you heard?"

They bobbed their heads.

The confirmation brought her some solace.

"And Solar? The other dragons? I'm sure they're not—"

"The human queen has most of them," said a small boy among the children. Actually, he was the smallest. He had ash gray skin and bright scarlet eyes. No burgundy at all. And his right leg had a slight twist to it.

He was crippled.

Sarah forced her eyes from his leg.

"Their tears turn to diamonds when left out under the moon, you know," he said. "The queen likes to put them on her dresses."

"But..." She was almost too scared to ask. "How does the queen get their tears?"

A few of the children whimpered. They shook their heads and Sarah could see the young ones rubbing at their eyes.

Bolanile sighed. "Tell her, Ev. You're the one who saw it."

Everyone turned to the smallest child. His eyes were locked on Sarah.

"She has her knights torture them."

No!

Everything inside Sarah refused his words. Dragons were the original beings. They were strong, they breathed fire—how could so many have been taken? Why hadn't they burned the human kingdom to the ground yet?

Sarah wanted to scream. She wanted to call to the earth, make her way to the human kingdom, and destroy it. She wanted to find and hurt the one holding Alexander, the ones holding Serwa. And yet, she couldn't.

She had no idea where they were holding either Alex or Serwa.

She had no idea how or even *if* she could stage an attack large enough to take on an entire kingdom.

Most importantly, she had no army.

Instead, she had pairs of eyes staring up at her. They were round, watery pools looking to her for a solution. But where could they go? How could Sarah travel across Lyrica with ten children to guard?

Her shoulders sank.

"But you're here now," said a little girl. She smiled. "You're the Chosen One and you'll save us. You'll bring back Mama and Papa."

Sarah's jaw tightened. A shiver pulled at her shoulders and her vision grew blurry. She couldn't cry. Not now.

Kwento kneeled in front of the other children, sending them all a great, big grin. "I think it's time for lunch. Bo brought back some food. Are you all hungry?"

There was a quiet, joyous cheer.

Bolanile opened the small satchel she had been carrying. Her brother helped her hand out small amounts of food. There was bread, fresh meat, and jam. Apparently, the humans had brought good supplies if they were eating so well.

"Auntie Sarah?" Bo held up a small cloth with various food items wrapped in it. "Are you hungry?"

As if waiting for its cue, Sarah's stomach growled, which caused her to blush and the children to giggle. Together they all sat, laughing and eating, but something bothered Sarah. During lunch was definitely not the right time to ask.

The children had given her information. She wasn't as lost as when she had climbed from the sea. Still, during their tale no one had mentioned the knights who wore the cupped hands holding the flames.

Were they a special sect of the human army? Maybe like the Templars she had read about in her library books.

Sarah leaned against the cavern wall. Her food was already gone, the sudden hunger abated. She tucked her arms around her. The cavern's shade was a needed relief after hiking under the sun. The children chatted amongst each other, their voices dissolving into the background.

Soon there was silence, soon Sarah closed her eyes, and soon sleep finally found her.

CHAPTER 12

Sarah looked over the map again.

This is not going to be easy.

After several days of rest, Sarah found herself at square one. She and the others were essentially trapped. Most of the south was taken, aside from a small territory still being defended by the fairies and the wood elves. The north would be nearly conquered at this point unless the people had resisted, which wasn't likely. Not according to Bo and Kwe, at least. The humans had grown too strong.

Sarah lay back against the flat stone and let the sun warm her skin. The sky was a light blue above her.

It was easy to become comfortable. They had water and food from hunting the local animals and a pond farther north. Because of the cavern's position, the children could even play outside if it was dark and they were quiet. They had escaped a war and found some peace. Sarah couldn't blame them for growing content.

But the humans were getting closer. The animals had learned to keep their distance, forcing either Bo or Kwe to make the long, dangerous journey to the human camp for supplies.

Their time was running out. Sarah had to come up with a plan.

She dragged her palms across her face.

"Auntie Sarah?"

Kwe peeked at her over the stone's rim, resting his chin on the very edge.

"What are you doing with Mother's map?" he asked.

She sat up and patted the space beside her. He scrambled over, took a seat, and their eyes turned toward the map.

It wasn't the same one Sarah had used during her first time in

Lyrica. The parchment wasn't falling apart and there were new territories, new kingdoms including Alex's and Serwa's.

Smiling, Sarah traced her fingers over the small spot on the map. It was where her two friends had made their home once she left. The Alclian dominion where Queen Isabella and King William once reigned was now the capital of the vampire kingdom. The domains had united. Alex and Serwa had become the king and queen.

"Here's our home," he said, covering her finger with his own. He moved down toward the east. "This is where we are now. And the humans are here and here. Is that what you were thinking?"

Well, he can read me just as well as Alex.

Sarah glanced at him before forcing her eyes away. She tucked and untucked her legs from under her.

"Am I wrong?" he asked.

"Huh? Oh, no, you're not wrong. You're exactly right, actually."

He smiled.

Sometimes it was odd looking at Bo and Kwe. Sarah found herself staring at them often, seeking out Serwa and Alex in their features. Each time, she found them.

He continued, "If we move northeast toward the mountain, there's a small jungle but farther north means closer to the humans. And if we head west, there's the tall grass. Not much cover though."

She nodded. "You hit the nail right on the head."

"I what?"

"Nothing. Let's put the map away now. Kwe, I want to ask you something. I need you to tell me about the human soldiers. The ones who wear the cupped hands on their armor."

His eyes immediately flashed red.

"I don't like to talk about them," he replied, picking at his tattered pants' hem. The children had abandoned their original clothing for something less conspicuous.

Sarah held in a sigh.

Patience. Be patient. The others won't talk. He's your only chance.

She cleared her throat. "That's okay. You don't have to tell me much, just a little bit."

"And how much is a little bit exactly?"

Sarah kept her voice level. "Just three questions. How does that sound?"

He turned his head to the side, looking her up and down. "Will you give me your jam for lunch and dinner?"

She raised a brow. "You want...my share of the jam?"

He nodded. "I'm a growing boy. I have to eat."

"Fine, you have a deal." She held out her hand, which Kwe shook. "Now, the knights with hands and cupped flames, were they the ones who attacked your home?"

The tips of Kwe's fangs peaked from under his top lip. His shoulders had bunched up by his ears. "Yes.They were with other humans, too."

"Good. Do they have special abilities? Something I should know about if I run into another one?"

He shook his head. "No, they don't have any magic. Sometimes they have witch stones, which give them power. It doesn't last long though."

"Good to know. Now, what makes them different from the other human soldiers?"

His eyes fell from hers and his chin hung low. His fangs elongated.

"Kwe?"

Silence.

"You can tell me. What do they do?"

The boy moved his arms across his chest. Rapid breaths left his body and Sarah could hear his teeth gnashing together.

"What—"

"They call us half-breeds and hunt us," he said, finally meeting her stare. "They're the humans who hate people like me and Bo."

"They need to be maintained."

The man's words from several days ago replayed in Sarah's mind. When he said maintained, he meant controlled by humans.

"The humans want to rule all of Lyrica." Kwe released a low growl. His eyes burned that bright red again. "Mother said they think they're better and that they have to lead us. People like me and Bo stop them from getting the control they need. To them we're rule breakers. That's what Father said."

Sarah shook her head. Her gaze paused on Kwe while her mind

raced through what he had told her. What the humans wanted went beyond a war.

Kwe took in a long breath and closed his eyes. When he reopened them, they had returned to their original color.

He touched the ends of his fangs. "Sorry. I didn't mean for my fangs to come out."

Sarah wrapped herself around him. "Don't you dare apologize. It's tough to talk about. Thank you for speaking with me."

"Sure. I'm sorry we didn't tell you before. None of us like to talk about it."

"I told you to stop apologizing. After everything you just said, I understand completely."

"Help!"

Before Sarah could move to her feet, Kwe had already started making his way below. He ran toward the young boy who was waving his hand and panting. Bo had called him Michael.

"Help!"

"What's happened?" Bo stepped out of the nook, followed by several other children.

Tears streamed down Michael's face as he fought to catch his breath. His light brown hair was plastered with sweat.

"T-they took her," he stuttered. "They took Marie."

Gasps followed his announcement. The youngest children clung to each other, except Ev. He stood by Bo's side, specifically by her hip, staring at Michael.

Michael fell forward but Kwe caught him before he fully hit the ground. Whimpers broke from him, his shoulders moving to their rhythm.

"We weren't even close to the shore, only a bit farther than normal. By time I saw the ship, Marie was screaming. And they were dragging her away in a net and I...I..."

Michael pushed away from Kwe, allowing himself to slump to the earth. He slammed his fists.

"I'm supposed to protect her!" he wailed. "Our parents are gone. It's all up to me and I can't even protect my little sister."

They all surrounded him, watching. A growing sense of dread settled in Sarah's stomach. A quick glance around told her she wasn't alone in the feeling.

The ships Michael spoke of had to be the human ships Fin and Reina had warned her about. But they had said they were rare. Marie and Michael had simply been at the wrong place at the wrong time.

Someone started, "What are we—"

"Everyone inside," Bo replied.

"But Ma—"

"Inside." Kwe stood from Michael's side. He directed a bright smile to all the children, then urged them into the little nook. "We will handle this now. Give us some time. Dry your eyes. No crying."

Sarah turned to Michael, who was still lying on the floor. His gaze was to the earth. She placed a gentle hand on his shoulder.

"Let's go inside now, hm?"

He didn't respond.

Sarah pulled his arm around her shoulders and dragged him into their temporary home. Though something gnawed at her about leaving him alone, Sarah knew there were other matters to discuss. The biggest being how they were going to rescue Marie.

She headed outside.

"Bo?"

The child had vanished.

"Bo?"

No response.

She sighed before reaching out with her magic. Following the trail, she found Alex's daughter on the farthest side of the rocks. She stood facing the direction of the ocean.

"Are you alright, Bo?" Sarah asked.

The child did not reply.

"Listen. We'll get Marie back."

She moved away from Sarah, wrapping her arms around herself.

Sarah drummed her fingers against her hip, eyeing her niece, a word that still felt odd. Yet she knew Bo and Kwe were as much her responsibility as they were Alex and Serwa's children. There was a reason Alex and Serwa had spoken of her to Bo and Kwe. There was a reason they knew her on sight.

Because two of Sarah's dearest people in the world believed in her. They knew she could take care of their children. So...

Sarah gulped, then pulled the young girl into a hug.

"Auntie Sarah, what are you doing?" she whispered.

I don't have the faintest clue.

"I don't need a hug. I'm fine."

"Mhm."

"I'm not upset."

"Okay."

"I'm not. I only..." Bo buried her face into Sarah's abdomen, soaking her dress with hot tears. She must have clamped her mouth down because Sarah only heard muffled sniffles. The girl's grip, however, was what her daddy would have called a death grip. If Sarah wanted to get away, she wasn't likely to.

She smiled at the thought of her father. The bear hug was a method she had learned from him. When she had been unable to find words, he had offered her arms and pouch of a belly. That had always been more than enough. She hoped she was enough for Bo.

"Auntie Sarah, what should we do?" Bo whispered. "We need to save Marie but it's not safe here either. The humans have the land and now their ship is here. I don't know what to do."

An idea blossomed in Sarah's mind. The humans had the land and a ship on the eastern sea. Kwe, Bo, and the other children couldn't travel by land—the distance would be too much. But they'd all fit on a ship. And Sarah knew exactly where to get one.

Killing two birds with one stone, as Daddy would say.

"Bo, I have an idea. It's going to take everyone's help."

The girl wiped her eyes before looking up at Sarah. "Everyone will help. I'm certain."

"Good. Because we're going to steal a boat."

"Are you sure they'll be fine?" Michael asked.

Bo glared at him and put a finger over her mouth. Ev, who clung to her back, shook his head at the frightened young man.

Sarah attempted to send him a smile but her focus was narrowed. She and six of the children were treading the water a few yards from the ship. After ensuring the humans didn't plan on moving farther along the coast, they had waited for nightfall to make their move.

Three of the youngest children stayed behind. They couldn't

swim and were all under seven, so the plan was to get them afterwards. Truthfully, they wouldn't be much use in a brawl.

Sarah hoped there wouldn't be much brawling anyway. If they could get all the humans in one room and lock them up, no one would get hurt.

Together, the group made their way to one side of the ship. Sarah called to the water. It lifted her right below rim, so she could peek over. The entire deck was empty.

Quickly, she gestured to her companions before raising them above deck with water, as well. Sarah waited until the last of them was aboard. Then, she climbed on herself.

The boat creaked and groaned with the waves, moving back and forth. Though the night was dark, the moon was bright and Sarah felt completely exposed on the deck. What if another ship came by?

She rattled away the feeling.

Bo turned to her. Without even a nod, they began.

Sarah and three others stayed on deck while the rest moved below to lock the humans away.

Now they waited. A horrible tightening gripped Sarah's chest as she watched Kwe and Bo step into the darkness. She itched to go with them, but someone needed to stay above with the other children. From what Sarah had gathered, they weren't like Kwe and Bo. They hadn't been trained to fight.

A creak. Sarah prepared herself.

They all emerged from the bottom of the ship, Marie included. Sarah smiled until she noticed no one else was.

Michael held his sister to him. As he met Sarah's eyes, he frowned.

She moved toward him and placed a hand on Marie's back. The young girl was breathing steadily. She was alive and well.

Something was wrong but now wasn't the moment to ask. They had more work to do. As long as everyone was alive, there was nothing to worry about.

Sarah moved to the ship's side, looking for the anchor. Since returning to Lyrica, she'd had a troubling revelation: she was very much out of practice. Moving the water to lift the ship's anchor shouldn't have been so difficult. After all, she was older now and supposed to be stronger.

Yet she could feel sweat building on her brow as she tried to quietly place the chunk of metal on the deck.

She'd once used an elemental's own water attack against him. Now she struggled to keep the water moving. Serwa would be disappointed.

The thought made Sarah gnash her teeth.

Come on. Only a little bit more now.

The anchor landed without a sound. Sarah released a long overdue exhale just as a woman with short hair who was dressed in men's clothes appeared from the ship's depths.

Everyone froze.

The woman wiped her sleepy eyes before peering around. Her body reacted first, growing rigid. She took a step back as realization dawned on her face. Finally, she screamed.

Bo moved. Ev got to the woman first.

His small hand turned into a claw, which slashed across the woman's body. She fell to the side.

Ev now squatted by the body with wings protruding from his back. Where hands and feet once were, there were now sharp claws and talons. His eyes glowed.

Sarah was like a statue, staring at him.

A...a gargoyle?

It was too late though. Noise could be heard under the deck.

She cursed.

"Fight!" Bo screamed.

Heeding his sister's command, Kwe stepped to the side of the entrance. He stood just out of sight. When the first man appeared from the ship's bottom, the boy didn't hesitate.

He sliced the sailor's jugular and the body landed beside the young woman's.

Sarah ran across the deck, positioning herself in front of the other children.

"Stay behind me," she shouted as sailors began spilling onto the deck. "Did you hear me?"

She glanced behind her. Apparently, she wasn't as needed as she thought.

While on land, their eyes had nearly watered at the very mention of humans. But now, having the enemy so close within their grasp, that fear had disappeared. It was replaced with a potent hate.

She gulped.

Charging toward their enemies, the children wailed into the night. They had no weapons aside from their fists, feet, and teeth, but they put them to very good use.

The humans' assault came to an abrupt halt. With swords raised, they watched two of their men be overtaken by the children. The men screamed their throats raw as the children clawed at their eyes and pummeled them with their fists.

Marie grabbed at one's hair. Michael squeezed another's throat.

Some bit, others scratched, a few just screamed, but the result was the same.

The men's cries died away with haste. However, the children didn't stop pounding at the bodies.

Sarah tried to move toward them. Her feet didn't seem in compliance.

Just go, just go.

Her hands were tremors. Why was she shaking? This wasn't her first fight! She had killed many during the last battle in Lyrica.

So, why not now?

The night filled with empty thumps and thuds. Bo and Kwe moved on either side of their comrades, facing the human enemy. Their eyes were like crimson stars in the dark sky.

Bo smiled. "For our home!"

On cue, Ev appeared from the side and grabbed the captain—he looked to be at least—with his talons. The man cried out but Ev continued to lift him into the air, only to drop him into the sea.

Using Ev as a distraction, the siblings made their move.

Sarah bit her lip. She winced as the old gash reopened. Yet it was just what she needed.

Moving forward, she called to the wind and blew the men backwards. Their bodies slammed against the deck. Once there, she pinned them down.

"Bloody witch!" one howled.

Sarah searched the space for Bo. When she found the child's eyes, Sarah gave a hard nod. There was no other choice.

"Kill them," Bo ordered.

The impromptu soldiers didn't need to be told again. While Sarah held the sailors to the deck, the children descended on them. The twins made quick use of their targets while the others beat them into unconsciousness. And Sarah watched.

Part of her wanted to close her eyes, to cover her ears. She didn't want to look on while the humans were beaten to death. She didn't want to hear their screams. But she planted her feet to the deck, forced her eyes to remain open, and took in all their painful wails.

Because Serwa was captured. Alex was missing and Solar was likely being tortured for her tears like the other dragons.

Sarah wasn't on Earth anymore. She was on Lyrica.

At some point, the sailors' fight left and they let the children end them. Both Kwe and Bo checked each corpse for insurance.

The remaining children had fallen on their knees. They were panting and staring around wide-eyed. As the moon shone down on them, Sarah could see crimson splattered across their skin and clothing.

Marie snuggled into her brother's arms and held his hand. He squeezed her against his chest in response.

Ev landed on the deck without a talon scratch across the wood. Still in his other form, he squatted directly in the moon's path. His shadow, his skin, a wonderful dark in contrast to the pale, round moon above them.

With a few flutters of his wings, the two appendages folded into his back. Ev stood from his squatted position, coming to his full four feet of height. His claws and talons disappeared, leaving him the same small boy Sarah had met several days ago.

Kwe turned to him. "Ev, can you—"

"I can do it."

The smallest child limped over to Sarah. He patted her hand and pulled her toward the lower deck.

"I don't think we should tell you. Kwe and Bo think we should."

"Tell me what?" Sarah asked.

"About what we found here."

An icy feeling pierced her chest but Sarah forced her feet forward.

Ev moved through a few hallways before stopping at large wooden door. It hung partially ajar.

"It's quiet," she whispered. Her heart hammered in her chest and Alex's warning rung in her ear.

"It is when things are most quiet one has to be most cautious."

"This is why we decided not to lock the humans up. If you listen closely you can hear them breathing," Ev said. Then, he pushed the door open. Sarah followed behind him.

Her eyes widened at what she saw.

Wooden planks in columns of three stacked above one another. Cages between each stack. Lyricans chained to the wooden planks and locked inside the cages. Dying lanterns hung along the walls, casting shadows over the captured.

They didn't speak. But Sarah could hear whimpering. She could hear chains rattling.

"They're mixed like us." Ev stared up at her. He squeezed her hand. "We think...Kwe and me, we think this is where they were going to put us. It's where they had Marie."

Rage replaced all other emotions.

She hadn't wanted to kill the humans. She had been so stupid.

"Release them. Then, check the ship for any remaining humans," she stated. "We don't want any getting away, alright?"

The boy nodded. "I think we got them all. I'll check for food, too. I bet they're hungry."

And in pain.

"I'll send Bo and Kwe to help you. When we're done, we'll make sure everyone's patched up."

He smiled, then walked to the first plank and snapped the chains. Sarah headed above deck.

They had already moved the bodies to the sea. Kwe and Bo stood a single level above at the ship's wheel. Based on the glares they were giving, both twins wanted to steer the ship. But none of them had time to waste, especially if they waited for a breeze. They still needed to pick up the youngest children before starting their journey.

"Both of you?" She turned to them.

"Hm?"

"Just hold it still."

Sarah turned her back on her niece and nephew. She took a long breath, then reached for air and pushed it's current into the sails. Water sloshed along the ship's base as it moved ahead and the wind whistled in Sarah's ears as she moved the children to, what she hoped would be, safety.

CHAPTER 13

Sarah stood at the head of the ship and gazed out at the water. The sea had led them to the river, which was wide enough for the ship to fit through. But when it narrowed at the corner, they'd have to abandon ship. Then she, Kwe, and Bo would take the lead. If they managed to get close enough to the Southern Wood Elves' home, they'd be captured and taken to Gan. Just like before.

Except this time there was a war going on. None of them knew if the elves were still holding the humans off. It was the last word delivered to Serwa before their home was taken, but that was not certainty. Still, it was all they had.

The air shifted behind her.

"Did you see anyone, Ev?"

"No. No sign of the humans," he replied, stepping beside her.

"And you didn't fly too high, did you?" She glanced at him.

"No." He shook his head. "I stayed low, so I don't think anyone would have noticed."

Sarah released a breath. The last thing they needed was a surprise attack. But if that was what awaited them on shore, she'd give herself up. Then it would be up to Bo and Kwe to save everyone.

She chewed on her lip. They had to survive.

"Ev?"

"Yes?"

"Make sure everyone's prepared." She eyed the land around them. "It won't be much longer until we leave."

"Yes!" The little gargoyle tossed his hands into the air. "I can't wait to get off this thing."

"You don't like the boat?" Sarah chuckled, smiling at him.

Ev stuck out his tongue and shook his head. "No, this thing is horrible. It never stops moving. I don't know how anyone slept."

"I think everyone found it peaceful maybe," she replied.

He scoffed. "Yeah, and dragons blow dandelions. I'll tell everyone your orders." With that, the boy spun and walked away.

Sarah found herself grinning and shaking her head. There seemed to be good and bad to having siblings. She felt like it was mostly good after her time with everyone.

The trees had started changing since they took the ship. From thin trunks with arched tops to wide stems of wood with rounded bushes above them. Lyricans may have been at war with the humans, but at least the world was balanced with itself. The elementals remained caged, forests continued to grow, and water flowed.

Sarah straightened her back at the sight before her.

The ship's tread slowed, then came to a jolting halt. It was time to go.

"Alright." Sarah pivoted on her heels just as the children came up on deck. Since releasing the others there were now twenty-one of them. That was more people depending on her to protect them. But there was strength in numbers, too.

"Have we gotten as much as we can carry?" Sarah's eyes fell on Kwe.

He bobbed his head. "All the food and blankets are packed. We found lots of knives and swords, too. All the older ones have a weapon."

"Perfect. Was there one—"

"Here, Auntie Sarah!"

Bo appeared from the lower deck with a short sword raised above her head. She grinned from ear to ear and handed it to Sarah.

"It's not much. I found it under a floorboard in the captain's room. Perfect for our own captain." The young girl beamed up at Sarah and rocked back-and-forth on her toes.

"Thank you, Bo." Sarah squeezed her shoulder. "Are you ready?"

The child elongated her nails. "Now I am," she chimed.

Together they lowered the draw and set foot on land after several days on the sea. As they planned, several of the older children carried the youngest on their backs. Marie clung to her brother's neck while her eyes searched the unfamiliar land around them.

"Bo and Kwe up front. Everyone else link arms and follow," Sarah said. "We won't be stopping until the evening. Let's hurry."

The twins took the lead while Sarah walked to the end.

She didn't know it the first time she stumbled her way into Lyrica, but she must have been close to the river. The sea fed the river, so if she had walked along the shore she would have found it. Instead she had found Alex and heded deeper into the woods.

Her heart hammered in her chest. If they walked perpendicular to the river, they'd be in wood elf land, near Serwa's cottage.

Was it even still standing or had it been lost in the conflict?

Sarah pushed the thought away.

As they traveled deeper into the forest, the woods thickened. Aside from small patches of sunlight, there was only shade. Still, with their heavy packs and some carrying the youngest, their group was soon huffing.

Sarah reached out with her magic, feeling for anything heading in their direction. It only seemed to be them, the trees, and forest animals.

"It's fine, Gharet. Just stay with me."

Sarah stretched her neck out to see who had spoken. It was a short blonde boy, Thobias, she believed his name was. Directly next to him was his much taller other half.

Gharet had at least a foot on Thobias. His eyes were a bright pink and his skin was paler than even Sarah's. His hair was a short curly bush atop his head.

"What if the elves are gone?" Gharet asked Thobias. "Or what if they turn us away? I don't want to go back on the ship." He shuddered.

Thobias patted his shoulder. "We're definitely not returning to the ship. The elves will accept us. Sarah believes in them. We should, too."

He nodded. "You're right."

Sarah averted her gaze. They were all depending on her. They all believed in her.

What if I fail?

Taking in a sharp breath, Sarah clenched her fists and stared ahead. She couldn't let her doubts or fears get to her. She needed to remain focused.

The group continued their journey. As a whole they moved steadily behind Bo and Kwe, keeping a good pace. Despite their efforts, the sun began to dip and the sky changed to a light pink.

Sarah internally groaned. She had hoped the elves would appear before the sun set. She hadn't sensed anything since they left the ship, but Sarah didn't expect that to last long. The humans would come at some point.

She tapped the child in front of her. "We're going to rest for the night. Move it up the line."

He leaned closer to the girl in front of him and passed on the message.

Starting with Kwe and Bo, the line gradually came to a halt. Sarah moved from behind the others and made her way up front.

"It's getting dark and—"

The hair on the back of Sarah's neck stood to attention. Based on the looks Kwe and Bo wore they felt it, too. Their entire group was surrounded.

Sarah placed a hand on her sword while she peered at the trees around them. She couldn't see them, whoever they were. She could feel them though. They had created a large circle around the group and their numbers continued to increase.

She glanced at the twins. They nodded.

Just as Sarah took her first step backward, a branch snapped and a child was snatched away into the trees.

Sarah grinned. The elves had found them.

Bo and Kwe raised their arms up and were quickly lifted into the sky, as well. Sarah went to mimic their movements. The sound of gasps and whimpering stopped her.

"What's happening?"

"Where did they take them?"

"Who are they?"

"Sarah!"

She lowered her arms and turned to the remaining children. "Shush now, alright? Everything's fine." She ushered them together. "This is how we're going to get to the elf village."

"Can't we walk?" Gharet asked, glancing at the treetops.

Sarah shook her head. "That's not how they do things around here."

"Are they using nets?" He quivered. "I don't want them to use nets."

Thobias grabbed his friend's hand. "It's fine. They're not the humans. If they're using nets, I'll stay close by so they'll catch us together. Hm?"

Sarah sent the young man a grateful smile. He had better words to comfort Gharet than she did. Considering what he had been through, his fear made sense. There was no fault in it.

The mass of children huddled together until one-by-one they were lifted away. When they were gone, the only hint they had ever been there was a slight rustling in the trees followed by an unsettling silence.

Something sliced the air and Thobias disappeared. Gharet's hands grabbed nothing. He turned to Sarah.

"I just...I just—"

As Gharet was slung into the air, he reached for Sarah. She tried to find a hold, hoping they'd be caught together and she could keep the young man calm.

No such luck.

He disappeared and his screech was all that Sarah heard before being lifted herself.

Though her heart shot into her throat, she smiled as the air moved past her. She had missed the opportunity to be taken by the elves last time. Now was a time to correct past mistakes.

Suddenly her movement jolted. She bounced upward into the tree branches, then tumbled down. Her feet were what they had caught, she realized, so on the second bounce she prepared herself.

When she penetrated the tree's leaves and the branches scratched her sides, Sarah reached out and grasped the nearest hold. She looked down at where she had stood a moment ago, then at the branch she held.

She sighed. Her timing has been perfect.

The branch she gripped shook. Two eyes stared at her in the shadows.

Like she was an old potato sack, the elf pulled her up by her collar. His nose was less than an inch from her own. No smile decorated his face.

Sarah fought the urge to grab her sword.

"Wait."

He sounds familiar.

He stepped farther out with her still in grasp. Patches of sunlight poured in between the leaves. She narrowed her gaze at the short-haired elf.

"S-Sarah?"

"Skuntz!" She lunged forward, stretching out her arms to wrap around him.

Her green-skinned friend found himself pressed against the tree with her plastered to him. Heavy breaths fell from her. She turned up to meet his gaze, a huge grin tugged at her lips while complete shock covered his face.

"I knew we'd find you."

"You did? I didn't know I'd find you," he replied.

"Ugh. You just don't know what we've been through!" She wiped her hands over her face and shook her head. "I never thought I'd actually get them here safely."

"You mean the children you had with you?"

"Yes! Oh, we need to hurry to catch up with the others. Let's move." She slammed her hands on his chest., still grinning and awaiting a response.

Skuntz glanced between himself and her. Sarah followed his gaze, then stumbled back when she realized her position. Elf or human, her parents would have scolded her for touching a young man the way she had.

"Sorry. I got too excited and ah!"

Skunts had wrapped his hand around her wrist while the rest of her dangled in the air. She tried to meet his stare again but found her cheeks were burning too much to complete the act.

"I've got you."

"Thanks," she whispered and he raised her up once more, positioning her away from the edge.

Skuntz released a breath. "Let's try this again, hm?"

Sarah blushed.

Holding onto Skuntz for dear life, Sarah closed her eyes and jumped. Together they zipped down a tree, the air tangling her mess of curls, until Skuntz brought their descent to a gentle halt.

She peeked one eye open.

"You're alive," he said.

"Thank heavens." She slumped to the ground. The blades of grass tickled her nose.

Skuntz chuckled. "You didn't scream when I caught you. Why so scared now?"

She placed her forehead against the cold soil. "There is a difference between going up and going down. And you didn't say anything about jumping without a rope."

"There was a vine a few feet down. The rope wasn't long enough."

She scoffed. "I don't exactly sail through the sky every day, ya know?" She lifted her head and glared at him.

Skuntz puckered his lips and stared upward. "Hm. You should try it more often. Gets you places quicker."

Her jaw dropped. He smirked.

"Auntie Sarah!"

Her niece and nephew rushed toward her. Concern decorated their faces. Sarah ran for them without thinking.

"What's wrong?"

"It's Gharet. He won't stop shaking and screaming. We can't find Thobias."

She looked at Skuntz, who said, "We never drop at the same location. He's here but I don't know where exactly."

She took a hard breath. "Take me to him."

The three made their way to the camp's center. As the distance closed, the young man's shouts became more audible. Sarah ran faster.

Soon she could see his figure. He was rolling around on the ground, covering his head with his arms. The elves surrounding him offered their hands only for him to push them away.

"Stay back, stay back!"

"Gharet."

His pink eyes found Sarah. She moved toward him and encircled him in her arms. He was taking in jagged breaths.

"We were only trying to help," said a woman.

Sarah nodded and gave her a smile.

"Is he well?" Skuntz asked, standing behind her.

Gharet shuddered.

"We're going to need some space. He only needs a moment." She didn't believe the words even as she spoke them.

Still, Skuntz began to disperse the crowd that had formed.

"What's wrong with him?"

"The boy seems like he needs help."

"Some sort of madness?"

Sarah clamped her mouth shut.

They mean well. They mean well.

"The boy apparently is to weak for a good tree run." Several men laughed and Gharet covered his ears.

The scolding words were poised on Sarah's tongue.

"They locked him in a jar!" Bo screamed. "It's from when they captured him. He turned into air and they locked him in a jar, so stop all your gossiping right now!" She stomped her foot and met the eyes of anyone who dared look.

Kwe stood by her side, matching her scowl.

The dispersing crowd fell silent. Even Skuntz looked back at them with eyes full of surprise.

Sarah pulled Gharet closer to her. "You're alright," she said. "You'll be alright now."

Thobias squeezed Gharet's left hand while Sarah held his right. Shadows decorated the hut walls as the sun began its final descent.

Gharet took a long breath. His eyes fluttered closed and Thobias' eyes watered. The medicine had finally drifted Gharet off to sleep.

Sarah licked her thumb, then pressed it against his cheek to remove a dirt smudge. *Probably from rolling on the ground.* She shook her head.

"I should have held on tighter," Thobias whispered. His eyes were cast down and he still held onto his friend's hands. His lips trembled. "If I had gotten to him sooner, I…" Thobias took a sharp inhale, then pinched his eyes closed. When he finally cleared his throat, he didn't meet Sarah's gaze.

He said, "Kwe and Bo, they tell me Queen Serwa was—she is— friends with the elves?"

Sarah nodded. "And she trusted their medicine. It'll help him sleep, Thobias. I promise."

He turned his neck and peered around them. Sarah followed his gaze around the hut and toward the opening.

She gave a small smile. "We're alone. Everyone else is at dinner."

When Thobias finally turned back to her, he released a large sniffle. His face contorted, wrinkling upon itself as slow tears raced down his cheeks.

"I am so sorry, Thobias," she whispered.

Though Sarah wished Gharet was better, seeing the healer's hut empty eased some tension around her heart. The first time she traveled to Lyrica, the elves had fallen ill to some plague. Now she was returning in the middle of a war, yet she had only seen a single man with a crutch.

Despite the war, they were prosperous.

She gripped Gharet's hand at the very thought, causing the young boy to groan.

"Oops!" She let his hand go and placed it on his rising abdomen. "Sorry, Gharet. Got too excited."

"Thank you, Sarah," Thobias said in between sniffles.

"Don't thank me."

"I have to." His thumb traced circles along Gharet's palm. "You could have left us. You already had ten others with you."

"Thobias—"

"No, please listen." He ran a hand through his blond hair. His eyes found his friend. "I only knew Gharet a short time before we were taken. Our parents were part of a group that thought they could remain neutral if they moved north. Closer to the part where not much grows and no one lives."

Pioneers. Sarah's mind raced back to Lewis and Clark—two men from her history books who ventured across the western United States. She imagined their trepidation and excitement at the prospect of their journey. Except, Lewis and Clark weren't running from a war like Thobias and Gharet.

Thobias' thumb came to a halt, stopping the circular motions. He patted his friend's hand, then placed it at his side.

Turning his full attention on Sarah, he said, "My mother was an angel. She left after I was born, returning to wherever angels call home. My father is human. He's who raised me. Most people...most people treated me like I shouldn't have been born. That was another reason my father decided we should move north. Once they found out the wandering woman who visited him gave birth to a half-breed, no one spoke to him anymore."

"Don't call yourself that!" Sarah hissed.

"What?"

"Half-breed. Don't call yourself that."

"But it's what—"

"No!" Air spiraled inside the hut and blew at its walls. Sarah had clenched her teeth and was breathing sharply through her nose. Her blue eyes were deadlocked on Thobias.

His own were like saucers staring back at her.

"Where'd you learn that word?"

"Um, it's what...everyone, I...besides my father. Everyone calls me half-breed."

"And who are they?" Sarah snapped. "Who are they to tell you what you are?"

He stumbled. "I...I don't know."

Sarah knew her face was as red as a tomato but she didn't care. In that moment, nothing else mattered except erasing that dirty word.

She crossed her arms. "You're only what people make you out to be," she said. "Back home, everyone calls me crazy. I'm only different though. No better, no worst. And you are, too, Thobias. All of you."

He watched her, his eyes still round and wide, as if they were nets capturing her words. A small smile pulled at his lips.

"Thank you, Sarah." He seemed to lighten. "You're definitely our captain."

Sarah's face was even redder, this time for a different reason. She looked away, knowing the blush had crept all along her face. Thobias couldn't have been much younger than Sarah. But she was speaking to him like he was nine.

She cleared her throat. "It's fine. I'm sorry. I interrupted you, didn't I? Uh, you were talking about your father."

He bobbed his head. "I want to tell you this, so you'll understand the things humans have done. And why you need to stop them."

An image of Alexander flashed in her mind.

"I met Gharet with the others on our journey. We found land and we settled. There were a lot of half...people like me," he corrected. "Both Gharet's parents were there. His mom was a werewolf and his father an air nymph. We all became fast friends. But then..."

Thobias chewed on his thumbnail. He gazed off past Sarah while she fought the urge to swat his hand from his mouth.

"We were so isolated. We didn't know the humans were coming. They took my father. I think only because he was human. Gharet..."

His eyes drifted to his sleeping friend.

Sarah held her breath, waiting for his next words.

"Sometimes, when I think of that day, it's like I can only see the memories in red and white. Red against the snow and...they killed Gharet's mother. She was trying to save us. The humans filled his father with arrows before he could turn into air. There was nothing we could do except run. Only, we didn't run fast enough."

He trembled.

Sarah reached for him. "You're safe now." Her magic pulsed inside her. "And no one is ever going to harm you or Gharet again. I promise."

He gave a small nod.

Rising to her feet, Saran turned to leave.

"Wait, Sarah, where are you going?"

A fluorescent fire orange shown beneath her palms. She looked back at him.

"I'm going to end this war."

CHAPTER 14

Sarah stood in the shadows, away from the village center where everyone had gathered. Like her first time with the elves, there was a raging fire, food, and lively dancing. Kwe and Bo led their shipmates around introducing them to their temporary neighbors.

Though there had been plenty of tears upon arrival to the village and the children were still a ways from home, at least they were smiling. And laughing. Since Maria's capture, it was Sarah's first time seeing her beside her brother instead of wrapped around his neck.

Of course, they all stayed huddled together. They moved as one, just as they had practiced on the ship, just as they had done once they reached land. Still, some tension had eased from their shoulders. Sarah wished that could be her case, as well.

She turned up to the star-filled sky. The stars in Lyrica seemed brighter than those on Earth. She wondered if the two worlds shared the same sky or if they were completely separate, in their own little pockets of the universe.

Sarah closed her eyes and took in a long inhale. She gave herself a moment, then focused back on the children. She had no time for silly questions. There was a war to end.

She peered over the crowd around the fire. "Nineteen, twenty, twenty-one," she counted. "They're all still here. Aren't they? Maybe I miscounted."

"Self-doubt has brought down even the greatest warriors, my friend."

Sarah jumped where she stood, reaching for her weapon, then immediately cursed herself. She had left it in the hut with Thobias and Gharet.

"Calm yourself, child. Have you forgotten me so easily?" The woman smiled and her layer of wrinkles became more pronounced.

"Gan!" Sarah nearly cried out in excitement, running forward to hug the small elf. A shiver ran through her. "Your heart still beats with the forest." She pulled back from her old friend, tears brimming in both their eyes. "I could feel it as soon as I touched you."

Gan placed her cane in one hand and took Sarah's hand with her other. "Of course you could. You are still as much a part of Lyrica as Lyrica is of you. My child, there were days I doubted I'd see you again. Yet here you stand!"

The woman raised her arms up and out, gesturing toward Sarah. "And how you've grown. Tell me, what happened to the short, red-headed child who stumbled over every word, hm?"

Sarah chuckled. "I grew up some."

"More than some," Gan corrected. "I have to look up to you. How old are you now, child? How much time has passed on Earth?"

"Only two years, going on three. It's been much longer here, hasn't it?"

"Twelve years since you brought balance. Sadly, it feels much longer with the war." She grasped her cane with both hands and glanced up at Sarah. "You received my message?"

"Yes! I tried to reach back out," Sarah said. "When I did, I spoke with Skuntz instead. I need you to tell me everything about the war. Where's Nettle? I need to join the battle as soon as possible."

The elf's grin shrank some. She patted Sarah's back. "Walk with me, my friend. I will tell you all you need to know."

The woman started off, and Sarah began to follow until her sights fell on the children.

"They will be fine," Gan said, following her stare. "I promise it is safe here."

Sarah sighed. She wrench herself away and followed after Gan. They walked along the edge of the camp, then farther into the village. The noise dwindled. The campfire's light dimmed, leaving only the moon's light to guide them.

"When I sent you my message, the human queen Leonna had advanced east and was pushing us farther into our village," Gan said. "We and many others were fighting beside the fairies. Their size and ability to move between Lyrica and their realm was our main advantage."

"Nettle's leading the fairies, isn't she?" Sarah asked.

"Yes. Before moving north, she ordered a few of her kin to remain and help us. There will be history books written about her, I'm certain. Along with Nettle we managed to keep the humans at bay. Several had moved past us, crossing east over the river. We set up archers. A few traps, too. That came to a quick end. No one crosses the river unless we want them to."

Gan's shoulder straightened with the words. She held her chin just a bit higher.

Sarah beamed at her. "I like the sound of traps."

"It's how we managed to contain the humans until they moved north. By the time we heard word, it was too late. They had taken the vampire kingdom. And Alexander and Serwa, as well."

She shook her head. A light breeze brushed across their faces.

"Nettle and I both feared the children had been killed in the attack. You have no idea how happy I am to see Bo and Kwe here. All of them!" Gan said. "I've already sent word to Nettle. When the northern attacks started, most of our force moved there to see what, if anything, we could do. It's mostly been scouting. Still, our traps and the humans' ignorance of our numbers have left us in peace for the last few months."

"They haven't attacked?" Sarah raised her brows. "Not even a threat?"

"Oh, there have been small skirmishes. But I believe their numbers are as divided as ours. We didn't exactly take their war lying down. Serwa and Alexander dispatched soldiers to help us. They've returned north with Nettle for the time being."

"And..." Sarah held her hands behind her back. "Alexander and Serwa. Have you heard anything?"

"I have no clue where either of them are. I am sorry, my friend."

Sarah nodded. She placed her fists by her side and kept her eyes forward. "It doesn't matter. I'm going to find them."

"We will find them," Gan agreed with a nod of her head.

The two walked in the thick of the forest. The village was left behind, placing them in an open clearing with a large tree. A tree Sarah knew had roots that were old and deep.

"The Great Spirit."

Gan chuckled. "You remembered? I'm glad to hear you did not forget your other home."

"I couldn't even if I wanted to." Sarah placed a hand on the old tree, tracing its carved face which still resembled an elderly woman.

"Sit with me, child."

Together Gan and Sarah sat in the small nooks of the tree's roots. The moon cast strings of light against the trunk. Sarah stared up through the leaves. She sighed.

In all this peace, how could there be a war?

"I have thought of using the Great Spirit to search for Serwa and Alexander," Gan said. "But the risk has been too great. A few witches are working with the humans. I'm not certain how skilled they are, but I'm afraid one might sense me while I look. If they were good enough, I could lead them right to the Great Spirit. They'd alert the humans I was looking and...I don't want to think about what actions would follow that."

The old elf shook her head grimly. Like Sarah, she leaned back against the tree, placing her cane over her soft middle. She closed her eyes.

Sarah could feel her own magic shifting inside her, pushing against her skin in hopes to move along the tree. Her lids grew heavy.

"I must move north." Sarah yawned. "Once I join Nettle, we'll figure out how to end this war. I can't take the children with me though. I wanted to ask—"

"Of course, they can remain here. We will find host families for them. Did you really think I would turn them away?" The elf's eyes were still closed, though a smirk played on her lips.

Sarah smiled. "No, but I thought I'd still ask. It's always good to put manners to use."

"That is true. I wish Skuntz had those manners."

"What?"

Leaves rustled above them. Sarah stood up, looking into the branches when Skuntz suddenly slid down the tree's trunk. He stopped right beside Gan and frowned with disappointment.

"How long did you know I was following?"

Sarah gawked. She hadn't sensed him at all. Was she that tired or was she that out of practice?

Gan opened her eyes and sat up. "Since we left the center. You're getting better each time, grandson. Be happy."

"I won't be happy until you can't sense me at all."

Gan barked out a laugh. "You have a few decades until then."

"Another five years I think," he retorted.

Sarah still stared. His eyes finally found her and he gave a once-over.

"Are you well? You look like you've seen a three-headed dragon."

Sarah narrowed her gaze. "Why couldn't I sense you?"

"Don't feel bad, Sarah. Skuntz blends in with the forest better than any in the village," Gan replied, turning to her. "Like you, he is no longer the child from all those years ago. Would you like to sit with us, Skuntz?"

He answered by plopping between the two of them.

Sarah rolled her eyes and returned to her spot.

"We were talking about you following Nettle to the north, Sarah?" Gan asked.

She nodded.

"That's a horrible idea," Skuntz chimed in.

"And why is it?" Sarah retorted. "The children including Bo and Kwe are safe with you all. I should be on the battlefield. Unless you need me here. Are you worried about an attack? Gan, if you need me to defend the village against humans, I'll stay."

"No, my friend," the old elf said. "Everything here is fine."

Sarah watched her carefully.

"And no, I am not lying."

"If you need me to stay, I will. I will save—"

"We haven't exactly been twiddling our thumbs, you know?" Skuntz laughed. "We've taken care of ourselves quite well since you left. You don't see any human hordes, do you?"

Deep breath, deep breath.

"Skuntz." Gan's tone held a warning.

Sarah exhaled. "I didn't mean it that way. If everything's fine here, why can't I join Nettle?"

"Many reasons. The most important being there is another mission." Gan grabbed her cane and rose slowly to her feet. The old elf looked down at Sarah and Skuntz.

"In both the north and south the humans are at bay. But if Serwa and Alexander's thrones remain empty, their people will remain dispersed. We'll need them to retake their thrones."

Skuntz nodded. He turned to Sarah. "To gather more troops and, if I'm being honest, to boost morale, we need Alexander and Serwa. We must find them and take back their home together. The other battles can wait."

Sarah glanced between them. "You're saying my mission is to find Serwa and Alex first?"

"Exactly."

"Fine. I want to find them, too, except I don't even know how to start. And we can't search with the Great Spirit."

"No, but there is another way," Skuntz said. "Ellen and Emma are the only other witches for certain we can trust. They'd never betray Serwa, and she trained them herself so they should be able to track her. There's a bond, too. It's less risky than using the Great Spirit."

"Where are Ellen and Emma, then?"

"Kwe and Bo haven't mentioned them?" Gan asked.

"No, not at all."

Skuntz got up and stood beside Gan, leaning on her shoulder. "Well, now you have somewhere to start, don't you, *Chosen One?*" He winked.

Sarah was certain her mouth had mashed into a thin line. She looked away from him.

Gan chuckled. "You two are going to work so well together."

Sarah snapped to attention, her eyes darting from Gan to Skuntz.

A sneaky grin decorated Skuntz's face. "Ready to leave when you are."

"No. Gan, I—"

"There is strength in numbers, Sarah." The old elf gave her a pointed look. Sarah chewed on her bottom lip.

Gan was right. She just didn't want her to be.

Not only was Skuntz a talented warrior but he was experienced. He was more familiar with battling the humans than she and—though she hated admitting it—he could naviagte Lyrica better than her, as well.

Skuntz's grin widened.

Sarah swallowed her pride. "Fine, but I have two tasks before we leave."

He held up a single finger, waving it in the air. "First, speak with the twins. We've already established that. What else?"

Sarah spun on her heels, then shot a glare over her shoulders. "That is none of your business. Good night, Gan. Skuntz."

She marched away from the two elves, trying her hardest not to stomp as she did so.

His hearty chuckles followed her departure, along with a final statement from Gan.

"You two are going to work so well together."

The next morning, Thobias held Gharet's hand while they stood underneath the Great Spirit with Sarah. The late afternoon sun poured down through the trees. Yet their rays seemed nonexistent to Gharet.

He shivered and looked between his two companions.

"Are you sure?" he asked. "You think it'll be okay?"

Sarah sent him a wide smile. "Definitely."

Thobias patted his hand. "And Sarah's here. If you get lost, she'll will be able to bring you back."

Sarah stretched her grin. She wasn't so sure about that part...

"Fine." Gharet took in a quivering breath, his shoulders rising to his ears. He snatched his hand from Thobias'. "I'm going to do it. I can do this."

He turned to them both for a final affirmation.

Sarah and Thobias each gave him a hard nod.

Gharet took a step back. He shook out his arms before holding them out to his sides. After taking several deep breaths, he closed his eyes.

Sarah's heart raced in her chest. She fiddled with her fingers and bounced on her toes as she watched her friend. An unsettled energy was zipping through her.

Gharet had to do this...he would.

A slight chill fell over the three. Gharet's clothes began to flutter; the air above him turned and twisted, spiraling downward until he was consumed. The gusts weren't too strong but Sarah could feel their force, the magic in the air.

And then he was elevated, just slightly lifted from the ground before his pale skin became translucent. His clothes faded, as well, and soon there was only air.

Gharet had transformed. He whirled in between the trees surrounding them, then twirled around Thobias and Sarah.

"Yes! Great job, Gharet."

"That's perfect." Sarah clapped her hands and beamed.

Gharet moved away from them and spun around, picking up stray leaves and twigs as he formed a small twister. Gradually, the wind faded. Gharet reappeared and stepped back onto the forest floor.

His pink eyes were large circles and his mouth a gaping hole. He stared at himself, then met his friends' gazes.

"I did it," he breathed. "I did it!"

Sarah surrounded him in her arms. She felt Thobias' soft strands tickle her cheek as he joined them.

"Thank you both," Gharet whispered. "Thank you both so much.

Sarah fell back on the hut floor, sprawling her limbs out and shaking her head.

Kwe and Bo appeared above her. They exchanged glances.

"We're sorry, Auntie Sarah," Kwe said. "Cousins Ellen and Emma didn't even tell Mother which direction they were going."

"Ethereal Quests never have a destination, Auntie Sarah," Bo added. "Not until you've spoken with your ancestors and nature."

Sarah looked beyond them, focusing on the slanted ceiling. Her one clue had been dashed to the wind. Ellen and Emma were their only hope of locating Alex and Serwa. Except they were missing, as well.

"Ethereal Quests are an old practice," Gan said. "Serwa doesn't support many of the old ways. I'm surprised she'd encourage it."

Sarah sat up, tossing her curls to one side before saying, "If Serwa didn't support it, then Ellen and Emma must have decided themselves." She turned to the twins for confirmation.

They both bobbed their heads.

Skuntz stepped inside from the hut entrance. He continued staring out at the village, before spinning on his heels and facing the group. "There has to be another way to locate them so they can locate Serwa and Alex. Did they leave any hints? We at least know they're together."

Raising his hand, Kwe said, "I think I might have an idea. Dwarves are connected to the earth. Father said they could speak with it. Maybe if the dwarves speak with the earth, they can tell us where Ellen and Emma are?"

"You're a genius, Kwe!" Sarah surrounded the young boy with her arms, and squeezed him.

"Well, I try." He smiled at his own humor and Skuntz sent him a wink.

Sarah glared at the elf. *Less time together for those two I think.*

"Oh wait, I have something too, Auntie Sarah!" Bouncing on her knees, Bo raised her hand. "The grumpy, old dwarf who visited Mother and Father. What was his name, Kwe?"

The boy shook his head but Sarah knew exactly who she meant.

"Abelard. You mean Abelard."

"Yes!" she squealed. "Abelard can help find our cousins, then they'll find our parents."

"Thankfully, we know exactly how to find dwarves." Gan smiled.

Sarah raised a brow. "Don't they live underground?"

The old elf wigged her finger at Sarah. "There is one thing dwarves always come above ground for. Sunflowers . And plenty grow in the woods."

"Go where the sunflowers are and we're bound to find a dwarf." Skuntz nodded. "Easy enough. We should leave as soon as possible."

"The sooner the better," Bo replied.

Slanting her brows, Sarah stared at the child. "Bo, you...you and Kwe can't come."

"What?" they both shouted. Kwe wrenched free of Sarah's hold and moved beside his sister.

"Why can't we?" he asked.

"We can fight," Bo retorted. "We've shown we can take care of ourselves."

"Both of you are more than capable, but Serwa and Alex trusted me for a reason." Sarah shook her head firmly. "You have to remain here with the others. I have to keep you safe."

"But we will be safe," Bo pleaded. "Safe with you."

"No, it's too risky. I can't put your lives in danger."

"You'll protect us."

"Bo, I—"

"No!" The young girl shot to her feet. Her eyes had become that bright crimson, and her fangs protruded from her mouth. "They're our parents and we're going. You've been gone since before we were born. Why should we listen to you?"

Sarah's mouth felt dry. She lifted her chin. "B-because I know best. What if you get hurt? Your parents would never forgive me."

"We're not anyone's children. We're know how to fight," Kwe added. "We can help you, Auntie Sarah. Let us go."

"You're not going and that's final." Sarah gave them a flat stare.

Bo's shoulders bunched up by her ears and trembled. She stomped her foot, screeched, then stormed outside the hut. Kwe followed behind her.

He looked back at Sarah, his fists their own balls of tremors.

"You didn't even ask us, Auntie Sarah," he said. "You didn't even give us a choice. They're our parents."

With those words, he disappeared behind Bo.

Sarah blinked. Her eyes remained locked on where her niece and nephew had stood only a moment ago. Words raced through her mind but only one seemed appropriate.

"Ugh!" She slammed her fists on the dirt floor and pulled at her hair. "I cannot believe she's so upset. I'm trying to protect them. Don't they understand? I'm trying!"

A gust of wind shot through the space.

"Calm yourself, Sarah." Gan rubbed her back. The corners of her mouth were tugged up into a smile. "Children often cannot see beyond what is right in front of them. Their needs and wants are immediate."

"But I need for them to be safe, Gan." Sarah rubbed her eyes. "Why can't they see that?"

"Because they need their parents," she replied. "If it helps you, I believe you are making the right decision."

Skuntz plopped down across from Sarah and his grandmother. His eyes were trained on her.

She matched his stare, straightening her back and narrowing her eyes. There was no time for weakness. Not in front of anyone.

Skuntz cleared his throat. "The plan is to return Alexander and Serwa. However, we need a backup, as well. Kwe and Bo are the backups. If we cannot save Alexander and Serwa at least their heirs are safe. You're doing the right thing, Sarah."

Refusing to make eye contact, Sarah gave him a small nod. "Thank you, Skuntz."

"Of course. Now, I say we rest for today, pack with the sunrise tomorrow, and leave before noon. How does that sound to you?"

"That all sounds fine except Kwe and Bo are not going to give up easily."

"You think they'll follow us?"

She nodded. "I'm certain. We should prepare tonight and leave as the sun rises."

Skuntz crossed his arms and stared at the floor. He released a hard exhale. "Fine, but they are Serwa's children. I'll make sure they don't follow us despite when we leave."

Gan chuckled. "Do not feel guilty, Skuntz. It is for their own good. I'm sure they'll forgive you."

He huffed. "I'd hate to trick them. I don't think I really have a choice though..."

Sarah raised a brow. Glancing between Gan and Skuntz, she narrowed her eyes. "What exactly are you planning to do to them?"

Dusting his pants off, Skuntz stood up. "Trap them."

CHAPTER 15

The sun had begun to peak over the forest, casting the sky in a beautiful hue. Sarah and Skuntz made their way north toward where the dwarves tended to venture. It was the part of the forest with the most sunflowers.

The two had said farewell to Gan, and left the village when the sky was still dark. Kwe and Bo had followed them.

Sarah had to admit she was impressed. The twins did a good job of keeping themselves hidden. Still, with a good ear and a little magic, they were easy to spot.

She chanced a peek at Skuntz, hoping he'd initiate whatever trap he had planned. He didn't even give her a glance.

She held in a sigh. They couldn't let the twins follow much longer or—

"Here's good, I think. Try to keep up."

"What?"

Skuntz was already several yards in front of Sarah and gaining distance by the second. Temporarily amazed at his speed, she stumbled after him, before finally running at full speed herself. Still, Skuntz was taller than Sarah, and his legs longer. And he was more familiar with the forest.

She panted behind him. Why were they running?

Sarah tried to pick up the pace and, to her surprise, the distance between her and Skuntz lessened. Soon, they were at each other's sides again.

"Now, at least I know how fast you are."

"Excuse me?" she huffed.

"Not bad. I'm going to need you to be a little faster by the time we end this war though."

Sarah's fingers tingled. She had never wanted to punch someone so badly.

"You're more intolerable than a spud muncher," she hissed.

He raised a brow. "A what?"

"Nothing. What are we even doing?"

"This."

Skuntz pulled Sarah to the right. She could feel herself falling past him but he held tight onto her arm, keeping her steady.

"No!"

Sarah looked behind them. Where there once had been earth, there were now two large holes.

"Let us out!"

She turned back to Skuntz, tilting her brow. "Is that Bo?"

He nodded, before releasing her arms and approaching the holes. He leaned over one and waved.

"Hello, Kwe."

There was silence.

Skuntz groaned. "I know you're mad at me now. I promise you'll forgive me later."

No response.

Sarah followed Skuntz and peered down at her nephew. He didn't have the same seething glare his sister or mother could conjure. Instead, he had mastered what Sarah's mother called "puppy dog eyes."

She had to turn away.

"Auntie Sarah, I want you to let me and Kwe out right now."

"I'm not going to do that, Bo," she said, walking over to the other hole. "This is for your own safety."

"If you don't help us, we'll just climb out and track you. We're going. No matter what."

"Not likely," Skuntz said.

He reached into his satchel and pulled out a glittering net. It looked like regular rope with bits of shimmer all over it.

"Fairy dust?" Sarah offered.

"Exactly. The strengthening effect has faded some. It's been a while since their last coating. I still think it'll do the trick. Can you grab the other end?"

Together Sarah and Skuntz nailed the rope nets over the traps. Despite Bo's yammering and an attempt to climb over the edge, they managed to finish the job.

Placing her hands on her hips, Sarah examined their work. She nodded. Even if Bo and Kwe climbed to the top, they wouldn't be able to cut through the nets. Skuntz had already told Gan to pick them up for lunch. They'd be fine.

"Alright, Bo and Kwe, we're leaving."

"I'm never speaking to you again, Auntie Sarah!"

She sighed and turned to leave. "Let's go, Skuntz."

The tall elf was still leaning over the trap that had captured Kwe. He ran a hand through his hair.

"Can you at least say goodbye, Kwe?"

The boy remained silent.

Skuntz huffed. "This isn't easy for me either. Listen, just wait for my grandmother. We'll see you when we return."

With those words, Skuntz turned on his heels and marched past Sarah, deeper into the forest. She gave the traps a final glance before following after him. The elf's brows were creased.

"I thought you agreed leaving them behind was the best option?" Sarah asked.

He nodded. "I do. I also said I hated that I had to trick them. Kwe's going to be upset for a while."

"Hm. I thought you'd be more concerned with Bo," Sarah offered. "My niece doesn't seem the forgiving type."

Skuntz mouth turned up at the corners. He tucked his chin and chuckled.

"What's so funny?" Sarah asked, eyeing him.

He shook his head. "Unforgiving isn't the word. Once, when Serwa brought the twins by for a visit, a few of the village children were teasing Bo. One boy made a very un-elf life comment about witches."

A chill ran through Sarah. "Um...what happened...is he okay?"

"What? Oh yes, of course. We managed to break them up while he still had some hair left."

The shock must have shown on Sarah's face because Skuntz tossed his head back and laughed. His brown hair caught in the sun, lightening it to a glossy caramel complexion. His shoulders tensed and loosened with each chortle.

Sarah's gaze moved over him. Her heartbeat quickened.

No.

She faced forward, gripping her satchel and keeping her eyes ahead of her. Did he notice?

Skuntz smacked a hand on her shoulder. Sarah knew the blush was spreading across her face.

He said, "Well, if you think that's shocking, wait until you hear Serwa's stories about Bo and Kwe. Those two tend to leave quite the impression."

"Mhm." Sarah moved her hair over her left shoulder, covering her face. "Let's find these sunflowers, hm?"

With those words, she walked ahead of her companion, her entire body as rigid as a plate of syrup in winter.

Skuntz followed silently behind her.

Sunflowers on Lyrica were smaller than those she had seen on Earth. While the tallest ones she had seen were from pictures in library books, the sunflowers on Lyrica were closer to the size of tulips.

Gradually, these small flowers began to appear all around the forest, hidden in the little crevices of tree roots, or among the blades of grass. But they were there and as Gan said, where there are sunflowers, there will be dwarves.

"Want to wait here?" Skuntz gestured around them. "There are enough flowers here, I think. We don't need to walk into an entire field."

"I wouldn't mind that at all," she whispered and placed herself beside a tree.

Skuntz plopped down on the tree's other side. He leaned back against the trunk and kicked his feet up.

The forest was a light chorus surrounding them. The quiet sounds of rustling leaves, birds chirping, and claws scratching against the earth filled the background. The bushed tops of the trees provided a wonderful shade with only small splotches of sunlight breaking through the thicket.

Sarah leaned back and listened. She closed her eyes, her heart calmed as she took in slow breaths. Even the air on Lyrica smelled fresher somehow.

She'd barely had time to process it, barely had time to fully understand that she had returned to her second home. An easiness settled over Sarah. Her skin was a comforting cool, much more enjoyable than the blistering heat of the eastern plains.

She shook the thought away.

The children were safe, they had a plan to rescue her friends, and she wasn't going into battle blind. This time, Sarah would be ready.

An energy moved nearby. Sarah opened her eyes. She looked at Skuntz.

"I heard them," he said. "Dwarves aren't known for their stealth."

There was someone else. Sarah shook her head. "Skuntz, they're—"

A short man jumped from the tree where they rested and landed bottom first on the elf. Skuntz flailed to the ground, sprawled out like a blanket.

The dwarf stroked his beard and laughed. "Want to say that again?"

"I think his mouth might be too full of dirt," said another dwarf, emerging at Sarah's side. The short man bowed. "Good noon, miss."

Sarah returned the favor. "Hello. Good afternoon to you, too."

The dwarf in front of Sarah had a long black beard along with a perfectly bald head. He twitched his pinched nose while giving her a hard top-to-bottom stare.

"You were waiting for us?" he asked.

She nodded. "Yes, we—" she gestured to Skuntz who still had the other dwarf on his back, "both were. My name is Sarah. This is Skuntz. We're not here to fight."

The dwarf scoffed. "I know that much. Your friend there hasn't moved an inch since Calvin landed on him. If that's fighting, I've got fairy dust pouring from my ears."

The two men laughed and, finally, Calvin stood up from Skuntz's back. He offered the elf a hand, which Skuntz took.

"Alright," Calvin said. "You know me. This is my brother, Basin. Now, what can we do for you? If it's asking about joining the war again, you've already convinced a few of our young folk. The rest of us have made up our minds."

Sarah narrowed her eyes. *Does Abelard know Serwa and Alex have been taken? He'd never miss an opportunity for a good fight.*

Skuntz placed his hands on his back and pushed forward, cracking it. He sighed. "Not this time, but we do need your help."

Calvin—who had a full head of blond hair with two plaits on either side—crossed his arms. He sucked his teeth, then tapped his foot.

"If it's not about the war, what are you in need of?" he asked.

"And make it fast," Basin added. "We're here to pick our sunflowers and go about our business."

Sarah moved beside Skuntz, so she was standing directly in front of Calvin. She put on her best smile.

"We're looking for two friends," she replied. "But we're not sure where on Lyrica they could be."

The dwarves nodded.

"And we hoped to ask the dwarves for some help. Actually, I want to ask Abelard. Not sure if you know him."

At the mention of her old friend's name, the dwarves hung their heads. Short, dry sobs escaped them and a fear gripped Sara's heart. She wanted to ask the question yet her mouth had dried.

Basin wiped a hand over his face before meeting her gaze. A redness had filled his cheeks, just under his watery eyes.

He cleared his throat. "Abelard is dying."

People died. Sarah knew that. Humans, elves, vampires, dwarves, everyone at some point died. What Sarah didn't understand was why Abelard had to be the one dying. And why right in front of her eyes.

The old dwarf hadn't stirred since she and Skuntz arrived hours ago, after traveling through Lyrica's underground caverns. While they walked, Sarah felt like an eternity had gone by. Now that she was sitting with her old friend while he faded beside her, she wished she could go back to that walk.

Then none of it would have been real. Not yet.

"Would you like some more water?" Klara, Abelard's daughter, asked.

Sarah smiled at her but shook her head. Skuntz declined, as well. He pinched his chin and stood quietly in the corner.

"I'm sure he'll wake soon," Klara said. "He'll be happy to see you."

Klara had an angled face, encircled by lovely shoulder-length orange hair. Her eyes were the greenest Sarah had ever seen and her cheeks held a few freckles. If Sarah had to guess, she wouldn't have pointed Klara out as Abelard's daughter at first glance. But the wide build of her shoulders, the way she carried herself, head held high, and how easily she moved with an ax strapped to her...well, that seemed more Abelard-like.

Sarah had cried when she first laid eyes on Abelard. Her eyes still stung, and she sniffled at his bedside. Klara, on the other-hand, seemed perfectly content. She even hummed beside Sarah.

"The roast should be done shortly." She gave Sarah and Skuntz a large smile. "It's Da's favorite."

Sarah gave Klara a slow nod, before returning her attention to her old friend. She tried glancing at Skuntz but his eyes were downcast.

"Um..." Sarah began. "How long has he been ill?"

Klara stared at the ceiling for a moment. "It's been a few months now. We're all waiting for his final day now."

"What?" Sarah gaped.

Klara narrowed her brows. "His final day. It means the day he dies. We know it's coming."

A tension shot through Sarah, forcing her neck up, so she looked down at Abelard's daughter. The young woman seemed none the wiser, continuing to sway and hum.

Sarah ground her teeth. "How do you know he'll die? He might get better. He could!"

Klara shook her head. "He won't."

"You're wrong!" Sarah jolted from her chair and marched away from the unfeeling woman. She turned to Skuntz. "I know. We can find a cure. Skuntz and I will go looking for one. Klara, you just need to keep him alive for a few more days."

The dwarf stared at her. "This isn't an illness from a wound or plague. My father's old."

"That doesn't mean he has to die," Sarah replied.

The young woman shook her head. "Yes, it does. We're all going to die at some point."

The air twisted in Sarah's chest, shaking her from the inside. Suddenly, she wanted nothing more than to move her sword across Klara's face.

She had done everything she could to save her own father, including incurring her mother's betrayal. Why wouldn't Klara do the same for Abelard?

"This is what my father wanted," Klara stated. She rose to her feet, moving along the bedroom walls decorated in weapons. She smiled. "Healers came to see him. They all gave him medicine, which he whined about taking, by the way." She moved her hand along a sword, then placed her palm over its handle. "The remedies worked for a while. He'd always become sick again in the end. That's when he knew it was time."

Skuntz sat up from the corner and turned to Klara. Gripping his chin, he could barely keep his eyes off the floor.

"You have our sincerest condolences, Klara. I'm sorry Abelard could not perish on the battlefield." He gave a quick turn of his lips. "From what I'm told of him, he would have preferred it that way."

The young woman laughed. "Now, that is one thing we can agree on. But when the battlefield is not an option, when old age is what takes a dwarf, we have our graveyards, too."

Klara looked at Skuntz. He nodded.

"From earth we are born and from earth we return," Klara whispered. Taking in a long breath, she closed her eyes.

Finally, she met Sarah's gaze once more. "Because I am his only child, I will finish my father's business. Fill his role as a warrior in our army and fulfill his unfinished tasks including helping you both. My father did consider you a friend, Sarah."

Sarah had crossed her arms and was staring Klara down. Reason or no reason. Abelard was dying. The least his own daughter could do was show some emotion. Yet Klara had none.

"I can help you find the two witches you seek," she said, placing the ax by her side. "And then I will escort you on your travels. I'm certain my father will agree. He'd want to make sure you both were safe."

Skuntz nodded. "It wouldn't hurt. And we'd be grateful for your assistance."

Sarah gawked at him.

Who made him her leader? And when did he suddenly become so kind?

She directed her eyes downward and shook her head. When she looked up once more, she met both Klara and Skuntz eyes.

"I want nothing to do with this."
She slammed the bedroom door behind her.

CHAPTER 16

A small patch of night sky was visible through a hole in the caverns' ceiling. Even if someone peered straight through, down into the caverns, they'd only see darkness. That was exactly what Sarah needed at the moment.

Torn between anger and embarrassment, Sarah had stormed away from Abelard's home, until she realized she had no clue where she was going. So, she found the nearest collection of rocks in the tunnel and sat behind them.

After escorting her and Skuntz, Calvin and Basin had warned them to stay within the main tunnel. Leaving it would lead to many other tunnels, which were connected to several other tunnels and so on.

Though Sarah was furious, she still had enough sense to stay near the house. And now that she had had several moments to herself, that burning anger had simmered into a reddening embarrassment.

The interaction between her and Klara raced through her mind repeatedly. A nightmare that wouldn't end.

She sighed. "I'm an idiot."

From what Sarah could tell, the caverns were nothing more than large, empty chambers connected by large, empty tunnels. Empty aside from the dwarves who occupied them, of course. Still, there was a loneliness in the mass of rock and shadow—a loneliness Sarah sought for comfort.

"I want nothing to do with this."

She grabbed at the roots of her hair. Who was she to tell someone how to deal with loss?

Stretching her legs out, Sarah leaned back against the rock, and stared up into the patch of night. Her chest constricted as she fought back a sob.

The sky blurred.

"He just...for a moment, I was thinking of my daddy and...I need to be home!" She slammed her fists against her thighs. Her red curls fell around her like a curtain as she hunched over. She clenched her fists against her abdomen, while salty trails ran down her cheeks.

A furious tension twisted inside Sarah. She kept her fists clenched, squeezing her nails into her palms as her entire body palpitated.

Sarah could hear her breath bursting from her in short gasps. Yet she almost felt like she was hearing it from someone else. Like she was watching another person decompress their sadness, hurt, confusion, and frustration...only for all those things to restrict once more.

"I need to be here, too."

Her fists relaxed in her lap. The palpitations stopped, and Sarah stretched out again. Slowly, she breathed in through her nose, then out through her mouth, easing her muscles after their strain. She wiped at her cheeks, and looked up into the night.

The sky wasn't blurry anymore.

She sighed.

"Now, I need to go apologize." Sarah rose to her feet and began marching in, what she hoped, was the direction of Abelard's house.

Deep breath, deep breath. You were the wrong one here, Sarah.

She gave a hard nod before throwing the house door open and moving into the back bedroom. The door was ajar.

There was a familiar groan.

"You're not the only one. I've knocked a human or two on their backside in my day."

Abelard's laugh filled both the room and Sarah's ears.

She stared.

Skuntz and Klara sat around the old dwarf's bed laughing, steaming mugs in their hands.

The old dwarf caught her eyes, and a large grin—with a few teeth missing—spread across his face. "I'm glad I've lived to see the day."

"Abelard," Sarah whispered, feeling her mouth curve up. She stood by slightly opened door, fingers grazing the door frame. "You—you're awake. " The words left her mouth like a secret.

Klara said, "Come in, Sarah. I'll get you a bowl of roast. Here, take my seat."

"Oh no, I can stand."

She shook her head. "What sort of host would I be? Here, please." She gestured toward the chair, and Skuntz patted the seat.

Sarah sent a smile her way, hoping Klara would see the apology in it. When she took her seat, Abelard grabbed her hand and gave it a hard squeeze. She looked at him but refused to meet his eyes.

They blazed with an earnest welcome she couldn't match knowing they'd have to say farewell soon.

Taking a deep breath, Sarah briefly closed her eyes. He gave her hand a gentle pat.

"Klara told you, didn't she?"

Sarah nodded.

"Though I won't be able to fight at your side this time, as my only heir she will fill the role," he replied. "I've taught her everything she knows. The rest she learned on her own."

Holding a cup and bowl, Klara made her way to Sarah's side and placed her food on the nearest table. She wiped her brow and sent the entire group a grin.

"A hearty meal and hearty conversation? Tonight's looking to be a good one."

With his free hand, Abelard reached out to Klara, his blue eyes gazing into her green. "Since the night you arrived at my doorstep, each night has been a hearty one. You're a very memorable surprise."

Klara's face crumbled for a moment. She turned away from her father but Sarah could see the dwarf wiping her eyes.

How could Sarah have ever thought this was easy for her?

"Hm. I think I'd like to hear about that. You were a surprise, Klara?"

The young woman laughed. "To him, yes. To my mother, not so much. She didn't know she was with child, until Da had already gone on to another battle. She didn't have many other options except to raise me."

Sarah mashed her lips together, feeling the question brewing on her tongue.

Klara sat on the edge of her father's bed. She looked over Sarah and Skuntz. "I'm certain you're wondering where my mother is now."

Sarah and Skuntz glanced at one another, before shaking their heads and shrugging.

"No, of course not," Sarah replied.

"Never crossed my mind," Skuntz added.

Klara raised a brow, a smirk pulling at her lips. "Uh-huh. Well, in case you *were,* when I was twelve, she decided it was time I grow up. She had been the same age when she began supporting herself. So, my mother abandoned me with a few belongings. I knew she had written about my father in her diary. That's how I got here."

Abelard huffed. "It was her loss, dear Klara. Don't forget that."

"Yes, I know, I know, Da."

"Oh, and Sarah?" Abelard asked, moving his attention to the redhead.

"Yes?"

He sighed, casting his eyes away from her. "I can only hope," he whispered, "that you won't think less of me."

"Why would I ever do that?"

He sighed. "Because Karla's mother and I were never married." The old dwarf sniffled which caused his wrinkles to move across his face like waves.

Sarah bit back a laugh. "What?"

"I know!" He covered his face, and shook his head. "It was not the decent thing to do. I was young. When her mother came to —"

"No, no, no!"

Klara, Skuntz, and Sarah glanced at each other. Apparently, none of them was interested in hearing the details of Abelard's unsanctified love affair.

The old dwarf slanted his brow. His bottom lip dropped into a pout. "You don't think different of me, then?"

"Not at all," Sarah assured him. "You'll always be noble in my eyes, Abelard."

He smiled. "That's—" Sarah's old friend gripped his chest.

"Da!"

Shaking his head, he held up a hand to Klara. Ragged coughs

wracked Abelard's body and chips of earth shot from his mouth.

They were covered in blood.

Klara grabbed his head while Sarah placed a hand on his back. With her other hand, she placed her mug to his lips.

Abelard drank gratefully but when the cup was empty, he met Klara's eyes.

"Fetch Calvin and Basin."

Sarah had never been to a funeral. She had definitely never been to a warrior's funeral and definitely not when the mentioned warrior was still alive. Yet it seemed like her second trip to Lyrica was going to be full of nothing but new and painful experiences.

Leaning on Klara, Abelard walked in front of Sarah. His lips were turned to his daughter's ear and she bobbed her head while he spoke. Without having to hear, Sarah was certain he was providing Klara his last instructions. The dwarf equivalent of a will and testament.

Sarah's eyes burned.

Why isn't there something I can do?

She sniffled and set her trembling jaw. Abelard's last memory of her would not be ruined with tears and snot.

The brothers Basin and Calvin marched behind them. Dwarves lined their small group on either side, each carrying a lantern. The sound of their footsteps against gravel filled the caverns. Their shadows moved along the walls, sometimes crossing over one another due to the number of attendees.

Apparently, Abelard had been more renowned than Sarah had known.

A low groan filled the space, gradually increasing in volume until the very noise shook the earth beneath them.

Sarah peered around her. Each dwarf had placed a hand on their abdomen and was humming in sync. To her surprise, even Skuntz had found the rhythm.

Standing tall and straight beside her, the elf stuck out even more than she did. Height aside, his leaf-green skin and light brown hair would draw anyone's attention. However, he hadn't seemed uncomfortable once since traveling beneath Lyrica with dwarves.

Sarah, on the other hand, had cried twice and thrown a

tantrum.

She sighed. Everyone around her appeared more familiar with loss than she was. Was that good or bad in Lyrica? Sarah couldn't decide.

The march continued.

Soon two large statues came into view. Both depicted a dwarven warrior, axe raised in the air, pure battle rage decorating their faces. Right below where the axes clashed, there were tall metal gates leading to an illuminated room.

The dwarves leading Abelard's march pushed the gates aside for everyone.

Sarah's eyes widened when she entered the room. Her march came to a gradual halt as she took in the dwarven cemetery.

There was a hand on her back. Skuntz gently ushered her forward.

Sarah had expected tombstones or even names carved into the walls. Instead, the space was full of sculptures of dwarf men and women. But something poked at Sarah.

There was no organization. The sculptures were placed randomly around the cemetery. No columns or rows. And they all were so different. Not only in features but in poses, as well. Some had looks of peace, others sadness, or some combination of joy and melancholy. However, no matter which sculpture Sarah looked at, she had a sense they were all saying goodbye.

She knew this was where Abelard would say goodbye.

The dwarves that marched beside them spread out around the edge of the room. Sarah and Skuntz continued following behind Abelard and Klara.

The humming stopped. The room filled with an unsettling silence, aside from Abelards's grunts as he made his way. The old dwarf was breathing hard. Blood covered pebbles trailed behind him.

"Here is fine, Klara," he said. "Here is fine."

Klara nodded before stepping away from her father. They grasped hands once more, staring into each other's eyes. Despite his age or illness, Abelard's hands were still larger than Klara's. They enclosed her own, wrapping around the hold she had on him.

He grinned that toothless grin.

"Your hands will be much more capable than mine ever were,"

he said.

Klara shook her head, tears pouring down her face. Abelard grabbed her chin to still her and she closed her eyes.

"You knew this day was coming," he stated.

Klara nodded.

"And you know you are my daughter."

Again, she recognized his words.

"Then you know what blood runs through your veins. You're strong, Klara. And you're not alone."

Abelard looked left where Sarah and Skuntz stood. Sarah had started crying long before he had turned to them. She had promised she wouldn't. Then her lips began to tremble, her jaw began to quiver, and her heart felt raw.

She was going to have to say goodbye. Again.

"Sarah," Abelard said, offering her his hand. She gladly took it, giving up on his last memory of her involving anything more than snot and tears.

He set his eyes on her. "Whatever may come, you're more than capable, Sarah. Find Serwa and Alexander. Restore their kingdom. And, please," he briefly turned to Klara, "look out for my daughter."

Sarah nodded, her breaths coming out in short bursts. She wiped at her eyes.

"Thank you, Abelard," she said. "Thank you for fighting beside me, believing in me. You helped make me strong, helped turn me into a warrior. I'll always be grateful."

He bobbed his head, then smiled and stepped away.

Klara immediately grabbed onto Sarah.

Abelard looked at Skuntz. "Complete your mission and keep them safe, elf."

At the words, the elf straightened. He crossed his arms and gave a short bow.

Abelard looked around him before waving his hand in the air. His comrades roared and applauded. They stomped their feet and beat their chests.

While the farewell symphony played, Abelard shot one last smile in Klara's direction.

"Goodbye, Da."

The old dwarf didn't respond. Starting from his feet, a light coating of earth formed, hardening around him. Slowly, the earth moved farther and farther up his body, until he had become another statue.

"From earth we are born," Klara whispered, "and from earth we return."

There was a moment of silence. Everyone bowed their heads.

Finally, those surrounding the cemetery's perimeter began their exit.

Sniffling and wiping at her eyes, Klara peered around her. Sarah mimicked her movements, narrowing her brows when she saw a line of young men standing aways.

Why weren't they leaving with the others?

"One moment," Klara said. She untangled herself from Sarah and approached the men.

Stepping beside Sarah, Skuntz said, "He was brave enough to know death was coming and still face it. It wasn't on the battlefield but it was courageous."

Sarah gave a heavy sigh, still watching Klara speak with the waiting dwarves.

"That's one thing we can agree on. Thank you, Skuntz, by the way. I know this wasn't part of our rescue mission an—"

"Missions don't always go to plan." He shook his head. "We had to be here. And he was important to you and Serwa."

She smiled. "Very. More reason to get Serwa and Alexander back. I won't lose anyone else." She placed all her determination into those words. An oath.

"I said 'no,' David!" Klara stormed away from the men. Fuming, she marched past Skuntz and Sarah. Her hands were fists at her side.

"Stupid men," she hissed. Her orange hair was on edge.

"What did they want?" Skuntz asked.

She rolled her eyes. "To marry me. I told them no. I am not promised to anyone and Da made it very clear what I had to do. Tonight we rest. Tomorrow we head to the Whispering Wall."

She met both their eyes before wiping her own and storming from the cemetery.

"It's not what I expected," Sarah said to Klara the next morning.

The dwarf smirked. "What did you think? I was going to fall the ground and start chatting with all of Lyrica?"

"That's exactly what she was expecting," Skuntz laughed. "Look. It's written all over her face."

Sarah glared at him, before focusing on Klara once more.

"Ignore the idiot. I wasn't sure what to expect, just not...this." Sarah held both her hands out, gesturing to the space around them. The Whispering Wall was actually three walls, each with a collection of holes precisely burrowed in even columns and rows. The holes in the bottom row were all labeled. The higher rows—the dwarves had ladders to reach these spots—did not have the same bronze plaques.

At least from what Sarah could see. The rows continued up beyond her eyesight.

"Sure, sure. Of course you weren't." He sent Sarah a wink.

She could feel the blood rushing to her cheeks. Skuntz was such a pain.

"Well, whatever you may have thought doesn't matter now," Klara said, adjusting the shiny axe on her back. She had made sure to polish it before they departed that morning.

Looking at Sarah and Skuntz, she placed both hands on her hips.

"There is a Cavern Hole that we have to use. Any messages sent there will be delivered to all dwarves. But," she held up a finger, "we don't want to disturb anyone else, meaning we must stay quiet."

An elderly couple walking by made it a point to frown at Sarah and Skuntz. Shaking their heads, they continued walking and Sarah realized the problem.

"If we're not quiet, messages can overlap?"

Klara bobbed her head.

"Skuntz should stop laughing like a cackling hen, then?" Sarah said. "That's fine by me."

"I do not—"

"Shhhh." Both women held a finger to their lips.

He scowled.

Following behind Klara, they made their way to a hole in the right wall. It was slightly larger than the other and its plaque was in gold instead of bronze. Sarah couldn't read the actual words on the label.

"Old dwarven," Klara said when she caught her staring. "It's not used often for writing anymore, but we do like to preserve some of the old ways. Give me a little space, please."

Tucking her orange strands behind her ear, Klara placed her mouth beside the hole and raised her right hand over her chest. She began humming.

The noise started low and deep, gradually rising to a more throaty sound. Both Skuntz and Sarah had stepped back when Klara warned them. Yet, at the start of her humming, Sarah found herself leaning toward the dwarf, her ears perking at the odd vocals.

How could any of what Sarah had told Klara about Ellen and Emma be translated into that?

Several moments passed. Klara finally straightened and stepped back. She dusted off her hands.

"I did the best I could with the little information we had. Now, we must wait."

Skuntz asked, "How long do replies usually take?"

She shrugged. "It depends. Sometimes—"

Wisps of grunts and groans poured from the Whispering Wall all at once. Almost like whispers that were too low to fully hear but loud enough to catch one's attention—and there were many.

The group covered their ears, waiting for the onslaught to stop. Instead, the responses became more rapid, growing louder and more frazzled.

Others around them stared as the wall shook. Then, finally, the noise slowed, the shaking came to a halt, and there was quiet.

Sarah looked at Klara, eyes wide and bewildered. Klara was giving her the same look.

"What was that?" Sarah asked gesturing toward the hole.

Klara raised her brows. "I think the better question to be asking is who are these women you have me searching for?"

"They're witches. They were tutored under Serwa," Skuntz replied.

Klara scoffed. "Well, they've left quite an impression on a few of us. And, Sarah, why do they always finish each other's sentences? It's apparently very irritating." She stared at Sarah, waiting for a reply.

Sarah had none.

"At least we know we have the right people," she replied.

"Ellen and Emma are quite unforgettable," Skuntz said. "Serwa didn't usually bring them when she would visit us. I think there was a reason for that."

Klara sighed. "Well, the good news is I did get a last location."

"Where?" Skuntz asked.

She tsked. "I don't think you're going to like my answer."

"Wherever they are we have to go. They're our only clue in finding Serwa and Alexander."

Klara gave him a sad smile. "We'll have to travel north into human occupied land. From there, we'll need to head to the coast...and across the sea to Esmer's Island."

Skuntz's face dropped.

"What is Esmer's Island?" Sarah asked.

The elf leaned forward and took in a deep breath. He thrust himself straight, huffing out a groan while he crossed his arms and began pacing. Skuntz wouldn't stop shaking his head.

Sarah felt a prickling of fear. She pushed it away, then turned to Klara.

"It's an island north of here," the dwarf said. "It was only discovered about five years ago, after King Alexander improved relations with the merpeople. They had known about Esmer and the other islands for centuries." She shrugged. "But even the merpeople avoid Esmer. Rumor has it that the water around the island is freezing. It's always winter and nothing grows."

Sarah blinked. "An island where it's always winter? But how...no, that's not important." She ran a hand through her hair. There was only one how that mattered.

"Klara, if no one has ever traveled to Esmer, how can we get there?" asked Sarah.

Skuntz stopped pacing, planting his feet perfectly between his two companions. He met Sarah's blue eyes.

"People *have* gone," he said. His gaze faltered, and he looked away. He swallowed down whatever was impeding his words.

Barely a whisper and through gnashed teeth, he said, "But no one has ever returned."

That prickling of fear came back and spread all over Sarah, tightening her skin.

"What Skuntz says is true," Klara added. "If Ellen and Emma traveled to Esmer, they may be—"

"No!" Sarah slashed her hand through the air, narrowing her eyes at Klara. Passerbyers threw their own glares at Sarah, but this time she ignored them.

Finding Ellen and Emma, stopping the humans, ending the war! That was all more important than any silly message being sent. The dwarves around them were just ignorant of the fact.

Klara gave Sarah a sad smile. "I'm not saying they are...passed on. I'm saying it's a possibility."

"And I'm saying I don't believe it," Sarah spat. Her skin continued to tighten, the fear sending multiple what-ifs through her mind.

Ellen and Emma couldn't be dead.

Abelard was already gone.

Alexander and Serwa could be on their way to death as they stood there speaking.

If everyone was going to die, why did Lyrica bring Sarah back?

"A possibility is still a strong enough reason to go." Skuntz looked between the two of them. "We don't have any other options."

The young women nodded.

"I made a promise to my father," said Klara. "If both of you think Esmer should be our next destination, I'll follow you. We must work *together*." She gave Sarah an even look.

Sarah's body tensed, prepared to go on the defensive. But she caught her fists at her side and released them before nodding. Klara was right.

Turning to Klara, Skuntz said, "We'll need to get some proper clothing for Esmer."

"I know a shop," she replied. "They'll have some winter clothing placed away and we'll get a good discount because they're friends of my da."

"All agreed then?" Skuntz raised a brow.

They bobbed their heads.

"To Esmer."

CHAPTER 17

Sarah felt like she was walking on eggshells.

When she, Klara, and Skuntz had returned above ground, they had immediately started north. The trees there felt familiar. Though they had long left Gan and the elves behind, remnants of the Great Spirit could still be sensed. If Sarah focused, she could trace the tree's energy, feel it wrapping around her like a parent's arm.

Then they crossed the river. Sarah sensed less and less of the Great Spirit, less and less of Gan. Their loss acted as a reminder: they were in enemy territory.

Perhaps in the village with Gan she could feign blissful ignorance. But not while traveling north in lands occupied by humans. Especially not with a tall green-skinned elf and orange-haired dwarf carrying a battle axe almost twice her size.

If they were spotted, they would have to fight.

Klara had suggested their path lean slightly west to decrease the likelihood of running into enemies. Sarah and Skuntz had agreed. Farther east would mean crossing into Serwa and Alex's kingdom, which was overrun.

The plush forests had started thinning, and flat, rocky land with mountain peaks in the distance had appeared.

Sarah gritted her teeth. *At some point, they're going to come.*

"I'm surprised."

The sound of Skuntz's voice took a moment to register. Sarah already had her hand raised, her palm coated in a thin layer of ice.

Klara chuckled. "Easy now, Sarah." She grabbed her hand and lowered it. "We might need him."

"Might?" Skuntz peered down at her. "*Definitely* is the word you're searching for."

She scoffed. "Keep telling yourself that."

They laughed. Sarah attempted to join in but the effort felt half-hearted. She was completely on edge. Did Skuntz and Klara know when the Great Spirit's energy left? Could they feel its absence the way she could?

Or was she completely lost in her own world?

"Do you travel back home, Sarah?" Skuntz said.

He was on Sarah's left side, while Klara was on her right. They both smiled at her.

It must be only me.

"Uh...no. Only to and from school. Sometimes into town to shop."

Skuntz eyed her rucksack. They each carried one to store all their supplies, especially with the additional winter clothing.

"Honestly, I thought everything would be too heavy for you. But you haven't asked for a break once."

Sarah glanced back at everything she carried. The very top of the rucksack peeked over her head. Attached to it was anything they could carry ranging from food to weapons to small skillets for cooking. The straps dug into her shoulders but they didn't hurt. She had carried heavier loads on the farm.

She looked up at Skuntz. "My parents and I have a farm. I'm used to the exercise."

He gave her a once-over. "I'm impressed, Sarah."

Her brows slanted. Why would she care if he were impressed?

Before Sarah could start her retort, Skuntz laughed—probably noting the shock she wore—and strolled ahead of her and Klara.

She shook her head. He was such a pain.

Beside her, Klara jabbed out her elbow. She sent Sarah the happiest smile, then walked ahead, as well.

Sarah glanced between the two of them. They had become fast friends apparently.

"I'm coming, Sarah!"

"Jacob?"

"Who?" Klara and Skuntz asked.

"No, I—" Something zipped through her. Sarah could discern their energy. She had been tamping down her magic but now they were so close, there was no hiding.

Skuntz's face darkened. "They're quiet. Not quiet enough though."

Klara dropped her bag to the floor and pulled out Abelard's axe. No questions necessary.

Their location was not ideal. Not only were they exposed but the enemy had the advantage. Whereas Sarah, Klara, and Skuntz had walked along a flat path with a few trees, the area surrounding them were spread out with trees and rocks to hide behind.

"The path continues farther up. We could try to outrun them. They wouldn't have any cover there." Skuntz waited. "What's the decision?"

"I'm staying." Sarah dropped her portion of their supplies and unsheathed her sword.

Klara raised her axe. "A dwarf never runs from a fight. It's time to chop these humans down."

Skuntz smiled. "Glad we're all decided."

A flaming arrow followed his words. Skuntz easily dodged, and the arrow—unable to puncture the rock—fell uselessly behind them.

The enemy still hid.

Bow raised, Skuntz peered at their surroundings. He steadily moved with the weapon, ready to release an arrow at the enemy's first appearance.

Sarah dispersed her magic. She allowed her energy to spread around them, hoping to determine their enemy's location. But something stopped her. Her magic was trapped within a short radius of where she stood.

She could only register Klara and Skuntz's energies. And the absence of another's like the missing piece of a puzzle.

Sarah glanced at the fallen arrow. She touched it with her magic, yet its presence didn't register. She could see it there behind her, but all her magic sensed was an empty space where something should have been.

The flame was still burning at the arrow's tips.

Sarah squinted her eyes; a nagging feeling pulled at her.

Then, she saw the carving on the arrow's shaft. Serwa would have identified the symbol. She would have been able to read entire texts of its language. But Sarah was not Serwa. All she had was her gut.

"It's a trap!" she screamed.

Her comrades' bewildered faces were quickly replaced with fear when a ring of fire spread around them. They each stumbled backward from the heat, cursing under their breaths.

"Back to back," Skuntz ordered.

They followed his orders with weapons still ready. Sarah's heart was pounding. The pressure of Skuntz and Klara's shoulders calmed her. What she couldn't see, they could.

She wasn't alone.

Klara huffed. "They wanted us to wait here. Damn it!"

"You're right," replied Skuntz. "But we're here now, so we need a plan. They're going to reveal themselves soon."

Sarah peered at the fire. Considering she could create her own flames, being surrounded didn't really scare her. Yet these flames were different. The odd carving on the arrow's shaft had told her that.

"They have a witch with them," Sarah whispered as figures began marching into view. "These flames aren't from oil and fire."

Skuntz's shoulders tensed beside her. He hesitated.

"If we can avoid killing the witch, we will. Otherwise, we have no choice," he growled. "Th-the mission comes first. Sarah, can you do anything about this fire?"

She had once seen Serwa absorb another witch's magic. Could Sarah do the same?

"I'll try. And, if I can't, I can at least use it and my own magic against them," she replied.

The humans stood just outside the spiraling flames.

"We're not going to die."

Klara scoffed. "Agreed."

Where the fire had once roared around them, the spirals of orange had now settled some. Smug faces welcomed them.

The first belonged to a woman. She was the same height as Sarah but that was where their differences ended. She was older with choppy black hair and a stocky build. The cupped hand holding fire decorated the woman's armor.

An immediate fury ignited in Sarah.

"They call us half-breeds and hunt us." Kwe's words echoed in her mind. These were the people trying to hurt her family.

On either side of the woman, there were several other soldiers, all wearing the same armor. Most were men, a few women. Two held a pair of dark chains that led behind a rock.

They may have been dirty and smudged but Sarah knew what those chains were made of. She had seen Serwa forced to wear black diamond before and knew the effect.

Sarah eyed each one of them, taking note of their large builds. She wouldn't be able to beat them with her physical strength alone.

Thankfully, she had other tricks up her sleeve.

The woman placed both hands on her hips. She smirked. "And I thought today was going to be uneventful. Glad I came out."

Her eyes danced around, finally landing on Klara. She stepped back and walked over to her. Then she squatted down before speaking.

Sarah could see Klara's axe twitch.

"We have a dwarf, I see. Hmm. Lucky," she mused, stroking her chin. "Your people have been very wise, limiting your time above ground since we've conquered Lyrica."

The woman wiggled a finger at her.

"But we've got you now, don't we?" She locked her sights on Sarah, briefly glancing at Skuntz.

"I'm happy to have an elf, too. Not a sky elf though, are you?"

Skuntz didn't respond.

"No, you're from the woods. Your ugly, green skin tells me all I need to know." She rose to her full height again. "Your lot has been giving us trouble. Revenge is in order. Now, what are you?"

This woman was good at getting under people's skin. She and Elaine would have been fast friends, Sarah was certain.

"No dwarf, no elf. Not an angel. Haven't been able to get our hands on one of those. Hmmm." She tapped her chin, then narrowed her eyes as a sly grin spread across her face. "A sympathizer?"

Like Skuntz, Sarah remained quiet. The woman was just another version of Elaine. Sarah knew how to play her game.

Suddenly, she laughed—an open mouth, head tossed back laugh.

Waving her hand while cackles still poured from her, the woman said, "Well, that's fine. You don't have to actually answer my questions. We have other ways of making you talk, including ways in which you don't need your tongues."

Her comrades chuckled.

Sarah bit back her own retort.

When they had finished mocking them, the woman stepped back and met Sarah's eyes. "You and your friends will call me Captain. And you're coming with us."

The captain leaned forward, above where the flames still burned.

"Now, what do you think about that, sympathizer? Hm?"

Sarah shot the flames up and outward. The captain shrieked as the fire poured over her face.

Skuntz took the opportunity. "A little less on my side, Sarah."

She thrust her arms out and pulled the flames in so they made a semi-circle around her and Klara. Skuntz was now exposed but the humans didn't have a chance. The arrows were already leaving his hands.

"You bastard! Put out her flames. Why didn't you tell us she was a witch?"

Chains rattled. Sarah looked to her left. The human soldiers had pulled the witch into sight. He was a scrawny thing and shivering. Something was wrapped over his mouth.

Sarah peered around. Initially on the offensive, Skuntz was now putting his agility to use and dodging the humans' arrows. Klara was slicing down a soldier who dared to move past their ring of fire. And the captain was shriveled up on the floor.

Seeing their leader crumble must have shook the soldiers because the others hesitated. But Sarah knew that wouldn't last long, especially if they had a witch.

The trembling witch raised his hands. Sarah moved.

Without pause, the humans holding the witch were engulfed in flames, their solid wails of agony assuring Sarah she had done well. Their remaining comrades started toward them. She called to the earth and nearby rocks shot out at their enemies.

In terms of numbers, the humans had the advantage. In terms of intelligence, Sarah was confident she was ahead.

"Skuntz!" she called.

"I'm already here!"

She glanced right. The elf was on the attack. There was barely a moment before each arrow zipped through the air.

Headshots were their best option if they wanted the human numbers down.

The clink of metal against stone drew Sarah's attention. Klara had dropped her ax. She raised her fists, then slammed them into the ground, creating small craters. A roar erupted from her throat and two stone hands burst from below them.

Sarah suddenly remembered her first encounter with Abelard. She smiled.

The hands grabbed the nearest humans, pulling them beneath the stone. Their screams were short-lived.

Sarah prepared to start another burst of fire. She would use it to incinerate the remaining humans. Then she would rescue the witch and they would continue north.

The sensation of punctured flesh made Sarah grab her shoulder. The feathery end of an arrow tickled her fingers.

There's no time to feel it.

She turned, ready to complete her plan, but a man was running toward her. The rocks had long stopped flying. The distraction was over; Skuntz and Klara had ended several of the humans but a handful still remained.

Sarah hadn't been quick enough.

Shoulder first, the man tackled her. Sarah went flying, her back slamming against the stone beneath them. His remaining friends approached Klara and Skuntz.

"Pay attention, girl!"

His fist slammed into her face and Sarah's head was jolted. She saw everything that was happening, could describe it detail for detail if asked by the sheriff. The stormy, grey sky above them. The tips of green leaves tickling the edge of her vision. The hate in the man's eyes.

Sarah had never been hit like that before.

But she couldn't react.

Even when he raised the knife. Even when he pushed it into her free shoulder.

"You're coming back with me, you little witch," he sneered, wrapping his hand around her throat. "And you're going to work for Queen Leonna."

He pressed his full weight against her. His stale breath

permeated her nostrils.

"And you're going to be a good little worker." A smirk.

The man was older.

The man was bigger.

The man was stronger.

Except Sarah was not done fighting.

It laced her with pain but Sarah raised her hand and gripped the man's face. Before he could rip her hand free, she turned her thumb and pushed it into his eyes. There was a moist, slimey pop as her thumb slipped under his eyeball. She pulled forward and his eye hung from his socket.

Of course, he screamed. Sarah needed the time.

She slashed her nails across his face, leaving long streaks. While he whined, Sarah pulled his knife from her shoulder. She slammed the sharpened metal into him repeatedly. She didn't aim anywhere specifically. She only wanted flesh.

At some point, the man stilled. Sarah's stabbing was the only thing making him move. She stopped, and before she could escape, the monster had slumped on top of her.

"No!" she screamed. Sarah tried pushing the corpse off her but he was too heavy.

His weight compressed against her chest, forcing her to take longer breaths. An ache zipped across her ribs from where Elaine had attacked her. But those wounds were healed. She was only imagining the pain, wasn't she?

An apprehension wrapped around her panic and she had to blink repeatedly to remove Elaine's face from her mind. It hovered above her, mocking.

No.

The man was someone else. He was another enemy.

The unwanted heat from his body made Sarah sweat. His chin hair brushed against the skin of her collarbone.

He was touching her. Even in death, he was touching her, suppressing her beneath him just as Elaine had pinned her in the woods.

It was happening again.

Sarah beat at his body. Anywhere she could, Sarah slammed her fists and dragged her nails. He was dead but he was still there.

She didn't have to be done with him. Not yet. Not until she had ripped away enough flesh to lighten him.

A breeze rushed through, making Sarah's eyes water. She closed them and turned away. The man's weight was lifted.

Her chest swelled with the relief. Sarah took in a deep breath. She turned to thank Klara or Skuntz.

"Sarah."

She stared at Jacob.

"Don't move. I'll help you up." He reached for her, and then was slammed onto the ground. Sarah's stare searched for him even as her mind clouded with a conundrum of joy and betrayal.

Something shifted above and deep green eyes stared down at her with worry.

"Sarah. Here. Grab my shoulder if you want to sit up," Klara said.

Sarah did as instructed and found herself leaning on Klara's side.

Skuntz had Jacob pinned. The elf had gripped Jacob's wrist and forced his arms straight. He moved his face, so their noses were only inches apart.

Skuntz looked him over. "What do you think you're doing exactly?"

Jacob tensed under him. "I was trying to help her."

His voice sounded familiar but the way he spoke was not. Instead of sounding like her Montana neighbor, Jacob was speaking like a Yankee.

"Hm. Sarah, was this angel trying to help you or can I kill him?"

Sarah glanced between the two. Skuntz's entire body was taut as he glared down at their latest intruder. The words had left his mouth through gnashed teeth, the low tone accentuating the fact that the elf meant his threat.

Her eyes roamed over Jacob. Some emotion spiraled in her chest, a feeling she couldn't pinpoint.

She took a breath. Jacob may have been a liar. But she wasn't.

Sarah opened her mouth to respond. Her voice cracked on the first attempt. She cleared her throat. "He was trying to help me, Skuntz."

"Are you certain?"

She nodded. "Yes. I'm sure."

"Fine."

Skuntz released Jacob and stepped back, so that he stood with Sarah and Klara. Without asking, he wrapped an arm around Sarah's back and helped her to her full height. Even with both their support, Sarah felt dizzy.

She placed a hand on her forehead, breathing in through her nostrils in an attempt to steady the world. When she had found herself, Sarah uncovered her eyes and turned to speak with Skuntz.

But he wasn't looking at her. His gaze was locked on Jacob.

It had been nearly three years on Earth since she last spoke with him. It had been twelve on Lyrica and Jacob showed the age.

The dark, shaggy hair was gone, replaced with a trimmed, short cut. His short bangs fell just above the brow.

Before, Jacob had a couple feet on Sarah. Now, only a few inches. His shoulders had broadened but not by much. His jaw had carved out, making his features more discernible. Wearing brown trousers, black boots, and a white cotton top, he looked more like the romantic lead in the town play. Not at all the boy she remembered.

Aside from his hazel eyes.

"Why are you helping us, *angel*?" The way the words shot from Klara's mouth made even Sarah wince.

Jacob raised his hands. He looked between each of them though Sarah noted he made the longest eye contact with Skuntz.

"I've been watching and—"

"Your people excel there." Skuntz scoffed and shook his head. "Watching is all you can do, isn't it?"

Jacob barely batted an eyelash. He started again.

"I've been watching Sarah since before she returned to Lyrica. I traveled with her the first time," he said. "When I saw the human was one step away from turning her into that," he pointed to the chained witch who sat awestruck several yards away, "I knew I had to intervene."

Sarah pulled her attention away from the captive. Despite the pain rolling through her, Sarah lifted her chin and scowled at Jacob.

She shook her head. "I heard you before he attacked me. You were coming before he had me."

Three sets of accusatory eyes fell on the angel.

His shoulders slumped. "I was delayed."

"By what?" Sarah asked. "Or are you telling another lie?"

He took in a sharp breath, then met her eyes. "I'm telling the truth, Sarah. As I'm sure you know, I've been reaching out to you since before you arrived on Lyrica."

"Is this true?" Skuntz glanced at her.

She nodded.

A bit of tension left Jacob's body. He continued.

"My family was the reason I didn't arrive sooner. I'm here now though and I want to help."

Klara crossed her arms. She looked him up and down. "And why do you think we need your help?"

"Um. The more the merrier?"

The dwarf shook her head. She turned to Sarah. "You know him better than we do."

Sarah's head throbbed. Her face was swollen and her legs' wobbling had worsened. She wasn't in the mood to make any decision.

"We need to help the witch," she replied before leaning away from Skuntz.

Sadly, she kept leaning. Skuntz grabbed her to stop her from falling over.

"Easy," he whispered.

He examined the arrow in her shoulder. "It wasn't poisoned. I'll take care of your wounds, and then we'll free the witch."

"No time. Do both at once?"

He nodded.

Sarah took the lead, approaching the prisoner first. At the sight of their group approaching, the witch's shoulders rose to his ears. His breathing deepened and his eyes grew as wide as saucers.

Sarah kneeled in front of him.

"It's going to be fine," she cooed. "You're not in danger anymore. Here, let me take this off you."

He shook his head while Sarah reached for the colored paper hanging over his mouth. Blue lightning zapped her palms. She pulled her hand back, pain racing across her palm and her fingers twitching.

Klara examined her burned hand. "Today is not your day,

Sarah."

She sighed. "Apparently not. The paper's enchanted."

"Is there any way we can remove it?"

"I have an idea," Jacob offered.

Skuntz glared at him.

"The paper may be enchanted. That doesn't mean the paper itself is protected. If we can destroy the paper without touching it, the spell might falter."

His logic was sound.

Sarah was also exhausted. As the heat of battle gradually dissipated, aches and pain took its place. Her eyes felt so heavy.

"If I pass out, please wake me up." She raised her hand and narrowed her eyes until all she could see was the colored paper. She noticed it had an odd symbol on it, as well.

The tips of her fingers tingled. She slowed the sensation down until her fingers were nearly numb. Then, slowly, she released the tiny spirals of flame from her fingers until the paper was incinerated.

The ashes fell to the floor and the witch took in a gulp of air. It must have had been a long time since he had breathed freely.

Two green arms surrounded Sarah. Her shoulder screamed in protest as Skuntz snapped the arrow in half and pulled it from her. She groaned through a clamped mouth, glaring at him while he worked.

He sent her a quick smile. "It's best to do when one's distracted. I'll get some medicine."

"Th-th-thank you," the witch stuttered.

Sarah tried to look friendly. Her shoulder was still screaming.

"You're welcome." She cleared her throat. "My name is Sarah."

"Havel." His shoulders were still bunched around his ears. The tremble remained in his voice. "My name is Havel."

Skuntz returned with the medicine. He tore Sarah's sleeve from the shoulder down. If she hadn't been in so much pain, she probably would have blushed. But it was only her arm.

Yes, only her arm.

"Havel, I'm Klara. Would you like some water or food?"

"No, I...I need to return to the human kingdom."

"Wait. Why do you want to return to the humans?"

"They have my brothers." The deep breaths turned into short, gaspy ones. He attempted to stand only to easily fall. His gaze became scattered. "If I don't return, they'll kill them. I know it. Queen Leonna takes life each day."

The human queen.

"Is that why you're helping them?" Sarak asked.

He stopped. His wide eyes took her in. "Leverage is the only reason any true witch would help them."

"I knew it," Sarah said, a smile pulling at her lips. "I knew the witches would never betray Serwa."

A few tears slipped from Havel's eyes. "Betrayal is not necessary. They find other ways. Like my brothers. I have to go to them."

Havel tried to stand once more. His legs crumbled under him.

"You need to rest," Klara warned.

He shook his head. "I'll crawl then. But I can't abandon them. Thank you for your help."

"Wait!" Sarah met Klara's eyes.

The dwarf nodded. "I'll get some of our rations. One moment, Havel."

Sarah peered over the witch. His clothes reminded her of an old potato sack. Or maybe it was only because he was so thin.

Klara gave him a small pouch of food. He thanked them again before heading back the way the they had travelled.

Sarah stared down at her right hand. Thin black streaks from the lightning decorated her palm. There was a gentle pressure on her injured shoulder.

"We're going to have to look at your face. And your other shoulder."

Skuntz stared down at her.

She nodded.

"Sarah?"

"Hm?"

"You did well."

CHAPTER 18

Odd wasn't the right word. Uncomfortable?

Sarah shook her head. No, that wasn't it either. The mixture of silent ignorance and thick tension that permeated their group, plus Jacob, was a unique one.

She glanced behind her. Jacob sent her a friendly smile, which she did not return.

"I don't trust the angel." Skuntz looked between Jacob and Sarah. "His appearance is too convenient."

She hated to admit it but Skuntz was right. The angels had remained extremely neutral since the war began. They had offered no aid to the other Lyricans, simply allowing the war to play out while they watched.

"I've been watching Sarah for a long time."

She huffed, tightening the straps on her shoulders.

"We won't know until we ask," stated Klara. "Even if he's lying to us, he may leave a slither of the truth."

"So?" Skuntz raised his brow.

"So, we ask." Klara reached behind her, before slamming her axe into the earth.

The loud thunk caught Jacob's attention. His walk became a stroll as Sarah and Skuntz took their posts at Klara's side.

Sarah crossed her arms. She wanted to be angry. His betrayal from their last trip to Lyrica was not forgotten. Yet she couldn't summon the emotion like before in the heat of battle. Like his betrayal, after seeing him, the good memories sprung fresh in her mind.

Them walking to school together, him holding her hand, talking about the holidays...and how he wished he had a *real* family.

He had said his family delayed him but could anything Jacob said be true?

The angel had stopped his stroll and now stood several feet apart from them. Like he was about to lecture a class, Jacob crossed his hands behind his back. He lifted his head, awaiting judgment.

"You must tell us why you want to help." Klara had spoken first.

"Sarah was in trouble, so I—"

"No." Klara waved at his words. "Since returning to Lyrica, Sarah's been in trouble on several occasions. Why now? Angels have remained very quiet throughout the humans' conquest."

"I never agreed with that decision," Jacob countered, his gaze sweeping over them. "I always believed we should offer aid. There was a vote and the decision was made."

"I didn't know angels weren't able to make their own decisions. The dwarves have stayed out of the war as well, but look who we have traveling with us." Skuntz nodded toward Klara. "What's your excuse?"

A noticeable line formed between Jacob's brows. He worked his jaw, then cleared his throat.

"There isn't any. I'm trying to correct my mistake now," he replied. "And I owe Sarah a debt."

She shook her head. "Do not use me, Jacob."

"I'm not. I swear it. I was forced to lie to you before. I was going to steal the stone if you failed." He closed his eyes briefly, then took in a hard breath. "This is to make up for that past mistake. I should have been honest with you."

Sarah reached within herself, trying to find any spark of hate or rage. Still, there was none. It was like grasping at air.

"You got your wings, didn't you?" Sarah replied. "What good is your helping me now?"

Jacob moved to respond, then stopped and hung his head. He moved a hand over his face.

"Just watch."

Staring straight at Sarah, Jacob flexed his shoulders and released two large wings from his back. They arched in the space above him, casting shadows over his face. But that was only one thing Sarah noticed.

Her shoulders sagged and Sarah found herself moving toward her old friend.

"You're still fallen."

He lowered both the black and white wing.

There was a bitter tone to his words. "The council...they don't think I've done enough. I haven't paid for what I did. Even though I wasn't the one who commited the crime."

Sarah shook her head. "But, if you didn't—"

"Enough." Skuntz stepped to her side. He held a carved blade in his right hand.

Jacob's eyes followed its length.

"Here's what I've gotten from your sad story. You're a fallen angel. Your council won't give you your wings, unless you help us complete our mission. I'm sure you already know what it is."

"You're wrong," Jacob retorted. "I'm here of my own choosing. I don't want to be with them, my people, any longer. You don't know what it's like to never be forgiven for something I didn't do."

Skuntz held the knife out. Jacob didn't flinch. Whatever fear he had felt for the elf appeared to have vanished.

"Sarah seems to trust you, which makes me want to," he said. "But I don't. I know the games your people play. You're in favor of whichever side wins. So, know this. If you in any way interfere with our mission, hurt Klara or Sarah, I'll cut both your wings from your back."

"I second that," Klara replied, leaning on her axe. "Skuntz, you won't have to use your knife. Two swipes of my axe will have them off."

The words were filling Sarah but she swallowed them down. She couldn't protect Jacob. She *shouldn't*.

Skuntz and Klara's suspensions were justified. Still, she could feel the heat boiling on her cheeks, her hands turning to fists.

Jacob's gaze didn't falter. "It's a risk I'm willing to take. I'm here to help, to leave the angels behind, and to start over. Fresh."

Skuntz held the blade steady, while Sarah leaned on her toes, her eyes darting from the knife to Jacob.

"Fine." The elf sighed. "Let's see how useful you can be." He cast a sideways glance at Sarah, then turned and marched forward. Klara trailed after him, while Sarah was left at Jacob's side.

He turned to her. "Thank you."

"For what?"

"Defending me."

"I didn't."

Jacob smiled. "You did...in a way."

Sarah started after Klara and Skuntz, with Jacob behind her.

"Think what you want," she said over her shoulder, "but our threat still stands."

Yet, her voice held none of the conviction that Skuntz's had.

The northern cold quickly set in. It wasn't a winter cold where snow was certainly on its way. Instead, it was the type of chill created from lack of sun, casting everything in a dull grey. The low temperature was both tolerable and noticeable.

Klara pulled on her cloak. They had all added a few extra layers as they traveled, agreeing Jacob was allowed a hood at least. Considering he was now carrying Sarah's share of supplies, she thought it was deserved.

As they traveled, leafy-green trees became more of a rarity. Instead, they were replaced with thinner, leafless versions of themselves.

Sarah stared at the jagged mountain peaks to the east. She had never forgotten her time in Lyrica, but the jagged tips of those mountains were always crisp in her mind. They were where she had met the former Queen Isabella and King William. The mountains were also where she'd helped kill them.

Her first purposeful kill.

Sarah gripped her sword. Isabella and William thought they would break her in that prison cell. They had been very wrong.

A breeze moved across Sarah's face. She winced and pulled her hood up.

"You need more salve on your bruises or the swelling won't stop," Skuntz said, keeping his eyes forward and twirling a knife in his hands. "We can stop if you need to, Sarah."

The hold on her sword tightened. They weren't even halfway through their journey. Their breaks needed to be few and far between.

"I'll be fine," she whispered while touching a hand to her throat. The human's handprints decorated her neck.

"Your skin is sensitive after the battle," he replied. "It's because it's healing. The salve and rest can help. How are your shoulders?"

Sarah's natural response was to glare at Skuntz. Now it felt odd. How could she meet someone's eyes when her face was blue and swollen?

In the end, she had defeated the human. However, he had not left her without scars. And...he had frightened her.

In a way he had bested Sarah, though admitting the fact caused a flurry of anger in her chest. She took in a long breath through her nose, hoping to quench the fire.

Sarah didn't have time for anger. She needed to remain focused.

"Oh!" Klara's shoulders sagged and she bent over, placing a hand on each knee.

"What's wrong?" Jacob asked.

She ignored him.

Skuntz placed a hand on her back. "Not feeling well, Klara?"

"Hm. I think I'm just a little tired. Do you think we could rest for a while?" She gave him a quick glance.

He patted her shoulder. "Agreed."

Turning away from Sarah, the two marched toward a large rock where Klara plopped down.

Sarah bit her tongue.

I don't have a choice anymore, do I?

She placed herself opposite Klara and crossed her legs. Her eyes looked over the rock, watching as the dwarf sighed and rested against it. She looked comfortable.

Straightening her back, Sarah tore her gaze away. She didn't need to rest.

Jacob took a seat right beside her. Sarah sighed again.

"Well, do you think they're going to let me sit with them?"

"No, but there's plenty of open space, Jacob." She waved her hands at their surroundings. "You see? Hm?"

Not even a blink.

"Have your shoulder wounds opened up again?" he asked.

"What does that have to do with our conversation?"

He shrugged. "Nothing. I'm simply asking as a friend."

Sarah's eyes rounded. She shook her head at him. "Do you

really think it's that easy?"

"Wait. I didn't—"

She leaned close to him, having to tilt her chin just a bit to meet his eyes. She clenched her teeth, letting the rage burn in her chest, and praying he could see it in her stare. A line of tension moved across his shoulders. Sarah's skin was hot.

"I haven't forgotten what happened between us Jacob," she hissed. "I do not trust you. We are not friends. The only reason you're even alive at this moment is because you *helped* me. That doesn't mean I still don't believe you have your own interests. I am not the same naive child you fooled. Understand?"

His eyes roamed her face.

"I understand, Sarah."

"Good." She moved away, creating the distance between them once more.

He moved his hands along his knee. "What if I tell you how I became fallen?"

She stilled. The mountains' shading would have hidden her reaction if they weren't so close. But Sarah was certain he had seen it—the flash of curiosity.

"I'll tell you, Sarah. You can ask anything you like."

She drummed her fingers by her side, looking at one of the few trees surrounding them.

"I promise," he said. "I'll tell you anything."

She could know. Sarah could finally know what was so terrible to make her best friend lie to her.

She sighed. "No. I don't want to know and I don't care."

Talons scraped against stone.

"Skuntz!" Sarah leapt up and ran to his right side. Klara had him covered on the left.

"It's in the air," he said, withdrawing an arrow. "What do you think it its?"

"Harpee?" Klara suggested.

Sarah shook her head. "They don't usually travel alone, do they?"

Removing Sarah's items from his back, Jacob walked past them.

She stared at him. "What are you doing?"

"Figuring out what it is." Without another word, he shook out his arms. His wings quickly followed and he shot into the air.

Clouds coated the sky as well, creating the perfect curtain for Jacob to disappear. They all had their necks bent back, hoping to catch a glimpse of whatever was flying above them. Misshapen shadows appeared here and there, but Sarah couldn't tell which belonged to Jacob or their surprise guest.

There was a hissing sound from the air.

Jacob spiraled downward with his wings encasing him. When he was only a few feet from the ground, he flared his wings and moved into a horizontal position, darting past Sarah.

"Where's he going?" Skuntz asked.

The air sounded above them once more, drawing their attention.

Sarah's eyes bulged.

"Yahooooo!"

A young woman perched on a large bird's back barreled toward the earth. Like Jacob, at the last minute, she pulled on the bird's reins and redirected. Jacob had already shot back into the sky but the woman was in hot pursuit.

Staring skyward, Sarah narrowed her eyes. The pursued and pursuer moved up and down through the clouds. The young woman's chuckles persisted.

Sarah raised her brow.

Skuntz groaned.

"Is...is this a game?" Klara asked, speaking Sarah's thoughts for her.

He shook his head, a scowl pulling at his features. "Yes. She's a sky elf."

"A sky elf?" A grin broke across Klara's face. She gazed into the sky. "I've never seen one. Da had during the Great War with Sarah."

Sarah remembered fighting alongside a few sky elves at the mountain. But the memories were vague. Another bout of laughter drew her focus to the acrobatics once more.

"They're isolated on their mountain peaks and few ever travel down," he said. "Only a handful have ever visited us in the forest."

"Enough!" Jacob bellowed, his voice permeating the atmosphere.

Just as he had done previously, Jacob spiraled to the ground. He pulled earlier than before and stumbled onto his feet.

The sky elf followed him. The giant bird who resembled a sparrow landed gracefully.

"She's insane," Jacob shouted, pointing at the young woman.

He had spun around to face his pursuer. They began a toe-to-toe as he sought his escape.

"Uh-uh, not there. Oh, almost! Not that way." The sky elf roared with chuckles while Jacob's eyes grew wild.

Sarah's red hair flailed around her because she was giggling so much.

Then, she heard Skuntz and Klara join in. Their giggles mingled together, bringing happy tears to Sarah's eyes though her sides had begun to ache from it all.

"This is not funny," Jacob said.

"Hm. I think your friends would disagree," the sky elf retorted. "Easy, Beaker. We'll leave him for now."

The giant bird stilled and the elf jumped down. Her skin wasn't exactly pale. No, it was more like an opaque white as if a storm was just brewing under the surface. Her build was much more lanky compared to the forest elves and her hair was a tangled starch white. The only color on her was her light, blue eyes and layered, grey clothing.

She grinned. "Hello! I'm Ree."

Sarah took her all in, from her head to her toes. She knew she was staring but Ree didn't seem to mind.

Ree's gaze found Skuntz. She blinked. "You're a...you're a—"

Before she could finish her sentence, Ree had grabbed Skuntz by the shoulders and moved their faces within inches of one another.

"Forest elf." The word came out like a breath. Her eyes examined his face and a tightness built in her shoulders. Her grin widened.

"Amazing! I've never seen one before," she said, turning to Sarah. "A forest elf." She looked at Skuntz again, assessing him. "You're so colorful."

Klara dropped her ax when the laughter became too much. Both she and Sarah covered their mouths in an attempt to hide it, but their shaking shoulders were a dead giveaway.

Skuntz ignored them. "Nice to meet you as well, cousin."

Ree beamed. "You even use our formal greeting. Oh, I knew there was a reason I felt like flying low today. If I hadn't, look what I would have missed out on?"

She tossed her arms wide like she was prepared to engulf them in a giant hug.

"A dwarf!"

She pointed at Klara.

"A forest elf. And a human. A good one, too!"

Sarah slanted her brows. "A good one?"

"Why are you so certain she's a good human?" Klara asked.

Ree shrugged. "Would she be traveling freely with you all if she wasn't?"

Point taken.

"Though it's nice to see you, cousin, we have to go." Skuntz kneeled down, then slipped on his rucksack. "Tell your elders Skuntz from the Southern Wood Elves greets them."

"Wait. I don't think you should go."

"Why?" Klara had already slipped on her supplies, too.

"Because—" Ree pointed at Sarah. "The human is bleeding."

Sarah looked down at herself. On both her shoulder blades, small spots of blood had begun to appear on her clothing.

"Sarah—"

"Skuntz—"

He sighed. "You were laughing too hard. You opened your wounds."

"You can just use the salve again."

"It won't work if they keep opening."

Jacob gave a low cough, staring off here and there. "You know, I'm not a healer but I can—"

"No, Jacob." Klara finished his thought.

Ree shot a hand into the air. "You can fly with me and Beaker. There are plenty of healers in my village. They'd be happy to meet Sarah."

"Fine. It's our best option," Skuntz said.

Sarah crossed her arms. "Don't you think it's stupid for me to walk off with a stranger, Skuntz? And I do have a say, though you didn't bother asking."

"I'm not a stranger," Ree replied, shaking her head. "Skuntz is my cousin. I'll treat you as the same."

Trickles of blood ran down Sarah's shoulders. She took in a sharp breath as a shudder settled on her spine.

"Foolish, stubborn child," was what Serwa would have told her.

Sarah gritted her teeth. She needed to be smart.

Pinching her eyes closed, Sarah ran a hand through her hair. She turned her face skyward before opening her eyes.

"I don't have much of a choice." She sighed and turned back to look at everyone. "I'll go with Ree."

Skuntz shoulders eased. "Good. The rest of us will walk. Ree, can you describe how to get to your village?"

"Of course! It'll take you a week walking though."

He balked. "A week?"

She nodded. "But by then, Sarah will have seen the healers and be recovering."

"I can fly up with Sarah and Ree," Jacob offered. "If Sarah wouldn't mind, I mean."

Skuntz opened his mouth but quickly closed it. His nostrils flared as he took in Jacob.

Sarah stared between them. He couldn't be left alone with Klara and Skuntz, after all, and at least she'd have familiar company. Very unwanted company but familiar nonetheless.

She rolled her eyes. "I don't care, Jacob. Do as you wish."

He flexed his wings. "Perfect. Lead the way, Ree."

She scoffed. "Are you going to be able to keep up? You weren't too fast when I was chasing you."

Klara snickered.

"I'm more than capable," he replied. "Just lead and I'll follow."

A sly smirked pulled at Ree's lips. "We'll see," she said before mounting Beaker in one leap.

Sarah was tall, but nowhere near as tall as Ree. She moved back a few steps before trying to get a running start. Klara held out her axe, blocking Sarah's path.

She stared at the dwarf. "What are you doing?"

"Stopping you from opening your wounds even more."

"I'm fine, Klara," she retorted.

Klara huffed. "The blood on your shirt says otherwise."

"Hm. Very true." Ree gave Sarah a hard look, then Klara a sharp nod.

Skuntz stepped in front of her. She looked at him but his eyes were focused just above her head.

"I can lift you onto the bird, but only if you want me to."

Sarah tried to find his gaze but he diverted. A small line was noticeable between his brows and his arms were taut at his side.

"Only if you want my help, Sarah."

Foolish, stubborn child.

She bit her lip.

"Yes. Please." The words were barely audible.

Skuntz kneeled down, scooping Sarah into his arms. His hands were under her knees and placed flat against her back. Still, Sarah could feel the heat rising in her cheeks. Her heart started hammering in her chest.

What am I doing?

Having to stretch up just a bit, Skuntz placed Sarah on Beaker's back. From there, she lifted her leg to the other side and scooted behind Ree.

The sky elf leaned down by Skuntz's ear. She cupped her hand around her mouth and began whispering. When she was done, Ree sat up again and sent her cousin a large grin.

"Understand? I don't want you to get lost now."

"We'll be fine. See you in a few days."

She turned to Sarah. "Hold on to my waist. We don't want you falling off."

Sarah sent up a brief prayer.

"Keep up if you can, angel! Let's move."

Beaker bounced on his talons before spreading his wings and soaring into the air. They curved upward like moving along the underside of a bowl. Sarah gripped her arms around Ree, as the whipping air caused her eyes to water.

Through her tears, she saw a hazy image of Jacob beside her. Wings fully extended, arms outstretched as he broke through the clouds. And he was smiling.

CHAPTER 19

Once, when Sarah was a child, she had hiked up the mountains outside her home alone. Her father had been working and her mother distracted with housework. It was too easy for her to sneak out.

She spent the better part of her day alone in the mountains, traveling farther than she ever had. At a certain point, her tiny frame ached with exhaustion. A thin layer of sweat built over her skin, despite it being a cool day. Her steps became weighted, her brisk walk slowed into a tread, and the higher she climbed the harder it became to breathe.

But the air on the Montana mountains was nowhere near as thin as what Sarah was experiencing now.

Once Ree had stopped teasing Jacob and ceased her onslaught of questions, the three had lulled into a comfortable silence.

Jacob flew beside her and Ree, an easy smile still on his face.

Apparently, he was not having the same problem as Sarah. Each time she breathed through her nose, a groggy whistling sound followed. If she breathed through her mouth, there was a horrible wheezing sound.

She put a hand to her swollen cheek. Despite the salve, the swelling had only worsened. Even just using the tips of her fingers made her bite her lip because of the pain. The air whipping around them didn't help.

Ree patted Sarah's folded hands, which were wrapped around her middle.

"We're almost to my village. We'll take care of you there." She sent Sarah a wide, gummy smile.

Pulling her hood over head, Sarah gave her a small grin.

Ree pulled on the reins, sending Beaker into an upward curve.

The bird pumped its wings, sending them higher and higher into the sky. Clouds flew by them in a rapid flurry. Sarah's hair hung away from her with how fast they were flying. Even her cheeks were jiggling from the force.

Her grip tightened around Ree.

Finally, hanging vertically in the air, they broke through the last of the clouds.

A flash of light touched Sarah's face. She could see the sun in the distance—a warm, radiating yellow far off and away. Her skin warmed as the sun's light fell over her. Sarah took in a sharp breath, letting the heat refuel her.

Then it was gone. They moved past where the sunlight reached as Ree straightened Beaker out. Leaning to the left and to the right, she peered below them, then pointed off somewhere Sarah couldn't see.

"What is it?" Sarah asked. "Your village?"

Ree nodded. "We're going to start the descent. You ready, angel?"

"I have a name," Jacob retorted.

"Me too!" Ree shouted.

Before Jacob could respond, she sent Beaker zooming downward. Sarah looked over Ree's shoulder. Gradually, a shape began to take form in the distance. There was a flat slab of rock atop the mountain. On it were small specks, which Sarah assumed were houses.

Beaker stalled. His claws were noiseless as they landed, leaving thin scratch marks in their path.

The bird shivered, flashed its wings once more, then hunkered down.

Jacob landed beside them.

Sarah slid off Beaker's back before Jacob or Ree could offer to help. She used the bird as her support when her legs touched the ground and nearly fell from under her. Perhaps the flight plus her exhaustion were finally catching up to Sarah.

But she didn't have time to rest.

"What have you brought up here this time, Ree?"

Ree flinched. Turning around, both she and Sarah came face-to-face with an elderly man. He wore robes of long clothing all a pale blue. A stone necklace decorated his neck and he walked with a cane.

Like Ree, he was also that opaque white, and had at least a head over Sarah. His face skin sagged, and there was an evasive feeling of annoyance and lassitude. The old man tilted left to where Jacob stood.

The angel bowed but the old man didn't acknowledge him. Instead, he turned back to Ree and glowered.

"You've brought an angel this time. That's unexpected even for you," he said. His fingers clenched and unclenched around his cane. He examined Sarah.

"And a human? Hm. I'm assuming she's a traitor to her kind, then?"

"They are not my kind!" Sarah pushed away from Beaker to stand on her own. Her legs still trembled.

The old man sniffed, then wobbled over to Sarah. She fought the urge to move back.

"Do you know what the humans have done here?"

"Of course. They've—"

"Then you would know being a traitor to the humans is a high compliment. Do you understand now?"

He hunched over to meet her eyes. Sarah suddenly felt like a child being scolded by a teacher.

"Good." The old man turned his back was to them. "The dwarf and forest elf on the bend are with them, as well?"

Ree narrowed her eyes, a smirk pulling at her lips. "Panu, how'd you know?"

He tossed her a look. "I see everything, Ree, you know that. Now, let's get your friends settled. Especially the human, she's bleeding."

Sarah had tightened the bandage, so the bleeding had actually slowed. Still, the trickles had found their way to the bottom of her shirt. She looked like an artist had sprinkled her in red paint.

Sarah pulled at her hood and followed behind the sky elves.

Ree and Panu chatted in their native language, which sounded nothing like the forest elves. Instead of long drawn out vowels, the words were short and clipped with most of the noise coming from the throat.

"You understand any of that?" Jacob whispered.

"Not a word."

"I've studied different Lyrican languages. Never came across a scroll on Sky Elves. Hmmm." He stroked his chin.

Sarah rolled her eyes.

Following Ree and Panu, more homes became visible. Unlike the forest elves who primarily lived in huts built around trees, the sky elves had no trees to build around. Their homes were stacks of polished rock and stone built into short towers. Wooden doors with carved birds were at the front of each home.

The elves were busying themselves around the village. Everyone's arms were filled with tools, stones, or a crying baby. They carried baskets on their heads, people traded goods outside of their homes, and a few large birds like Beaker were being led around by the reins.

The village was alive and buzzing until the villagers caught sight of Sarah and Jacob. Their brisk walks slowed. They stared long and hard at the foreign visitors, turning their necks as far as they would go.

Sarah gulped. Some of her red hair had spilled from under the hood. She tucked the strands behind her ears and pulled at her hood for the umpteenth time.

Could they still see her? Could they see the bruises?

She stared down at her shirt. If anyone were to get close enough, they would see the blood trails.

Moving her eyes to the ground, Sarah hugged herself. She watched her feet as she walked, hoping to drown out all the stares and whispers. It was almost like she was back in the schoolhouse, surrounded by her gossiping classmates.

"I think we're almost there."

Jacob.

"And trust me, no one can see your face. You're fine." He patted her shoulder, careful of her wounds.

She moved to look up at him but thought better of it. After all, it was embarrassing for him to see her beaten up, as well. Even if he had been there when the attack occurred.

"Thank you," was all she said.

"Of course, Sarah."

His hand lingered for longer than a moment. Sarah closed her eyes and pictured Montana. She thought of her hometown, walking in the woods, traveling to school before the first bell.

The Earth Lyricans like Franklin were always there with her. Yet, each time she reached her destination, they disappeared. Or, sometimes, she would have to pretend they weren't there, and she would again find herself alone.

What would it have been like if Jacob had stayed?

The world she was supposed to belong to didn't want her.

But Jacob lived in both worlds, too.

What would it be like to have a friend who understood what it meant to live in two worlds?

"Oh, I see Ree brought some more friends."

The voice drew Sarah's attention. There was a young man standing outside a towered house. He wore an easy smile and waved at the approaching party.

"Better than the mermaid she tried to catch," replied Panu. He turned, making sure to meet all their eyes. "This is the young man who will heal you. Kerem, this is a human and an angel Ree found. Sarah and Jacob."

He held out his hands, which both Sarah and Jacob shook.

"Very nice to meet you. Please, come inside."

The inside of Kerem's house was decorated with rugs and cushions. There was a wall with nothing but shelves, viles, and books.

Sarah peered over the different items, wondering if she would recognize the names from her time with Serwa. None of them stuck out.

Everyone found a cushion; Kerem placed himself next to Sarah. Not meaning to, she flinched away and drew her hood in. She knew red had flared to her cheeks underneath all the bruising.

"May I look? It's fine if you'd like to wait. I'm sure I've seen worse though."

Glancing down at her hands, Sarah saw they were quivering. She folded them together and squeezed until the shaking stopped.

She undid the clip, then pushed her hood away from her face.

Kerem didn't even blink. He simply took her face in his hands and moved the pads of his fingers over her skin. When she flinched, he softened his touch.

"You used some medicine on these wounds?"

She nodded.

"Hm. It helped. It's not the right mixture though. There are also a few light cuts."

His hands traveled down to her throat.

"I have just the right ointment for this. What else? I see the blood on your shirt."

"I...I was hit in one shoulder with an arrow. The other was a knife," Sarah muttered. "The knife didn't go all the way through." She gestured toward her left shoulder.

"I will need to examine the actual wounds. Would that be fine?"

Sarah's eyes had rounded and she was shaking her head. It was hard enough when Skuntz patched her up. She wouldn't undress in front of a man she didn't even know.

Kerem's smile didn't falter. "Would you prefer if a woman healer helped you?"

Sarah paused, then nodded.

Why did she feel so silly?

"I'll see who we can bring in. She'll knock on the door before she enters."

"Thank you." Sarah met his eyes briefly. "This is very kind."

"Of course. Just wait here."

Kerem got to his feet, Panu wobbled, and Ree jumped up without effort. She turned her large smile on Jacob.

He gulped.

"No boys!" She pointed at him. "Including you. I'll show you around while Sarah is treated."

"Um...I can wait outside if—"

"Young man," Panu said, clasping both hands behind his back. "Pick and choose your battles wisely. Now, let's leave Sarah for the healer."

Jacob's face dropped. Once he had recovered, the angel heaved a sigh and rose to his feet behind the others. He was the last one to leave the house, and sent Sarah a small wave before leaving.

Soon, she was alone.

Sarah slumped over and nestled up on the cushions. She held the hood against her chest, taking in several long breaths. She felt leaden. The cuts in her shoulders were burning.

She rolled from her side to her back. Her eyes closed but she kept forcing them open. She couldn't sleep, at least not until the other healer came.

No, she would stay awake.

She had to.

She would definitely stay awake...

Sarah jolted up. There was a fire burning in the room's center; the smell of spices and fish wafted through the air.

Her stained, dirty cloak fell off her, revealing tightly wrapped bandages. Her shirt was gone and replaced with a short-sleeved white tunic. The fire crackled beside her.

Sarah sighed and fell back onto the cushions.

She had fallen asleep. The healer must have bandaged her while she was out, which didn't make Sarah feel great. Still, at least it was a woman, rather than some man. And, she had to admit she felt better.

The burning had stopped. She could actually touch her face without wincing.

Progress. She grinned.

There were shallow sounds from outside Kerem's house. Even the smell of fish and spices was coming from whatever was happening beyond the door. But Sarah didn't move.

She stretched out as far as she could go before pulling the cloak up to her chin. She released a hard exhale and snuggled up.

There was a peace in the darkness.

Sarah was rested but was not ready to move. She let her body slouch against the soft cushions.

Where was Jacob?

She reached out with her magic to ensure she was alone.

"Maybe Ree took him out for another race." She imagined them zipping through the clouds again, specifically with Beaker chasing Jacob.

She laughed. In moments like that, it was almost easy to forget that he had once lied to her.

But he saved me, too...

She clutched her cloak.

What if Jacob had had to take the stone from her? Would he

have actually done it?

Sarah didn't know the answer. But Jacob did seem different. Just as she wasn't the same naive thirteen year-old, he wasn't the same carefree fifteen year-old. His accent was gone, for one thing.

He was older, actually Jacob was twelve years older than Sarah considering the Lyrican-Earth time difference. That made him twenty-seven.

She shuffled under her cloak.

"When did he grow up so much?"

Jacob had once been her closest—really, only—friend. Then, they were separated by a lie, and now there was time and age too.

Sarah thought of Mr. Greensburg and her stomach roiled.

Jacob was old enough to be her teacher.

Her cheeks grew warm. Sarah covered her face, and shook her head.

"No, no, no, no," she whispered. "Not appropriate, Sarafina!"

In school, Sarah had heard a few of her peers giggle and whisper about the younger teachers. A few even dreamed of marrying a teacher once they graduated.

Sarah always thought it was odd. But now, with Jacob, could she have those same feelings again?

She hadn't felt anything like she had with him before, had she?

Sarah groaned and pulled at her hair. There were too many questions and no answers.

She scrubbed at her face. "Resting gives me too much time to think."

With those words, Sarah re-clipped her cloak, stretched, and headed outside. Most of the houses around Kerem's were dark. The only light was from a bonfire several houses down. She could hear a few voices.

As Sarah approached, one voice in particular stood out.

"Oh, Panu, it was so fun! I had never seen one of our forest cousins before," Ree said with a squeal.

Jacob was sitting across from her shaking his head.

"Well, at least you're making better choices on what you bring back to the village," said Panu.

"What has she brought before?" Jacob asked.

The three were the only ones around the raging fire.

The old man crossed his arms and stared at Ree. "Yes, tell our guest all the creatures and items you've brought here, hm?"

She gave him a sheepish look. "Um, let's see. There was the mermaid..."

"And I had to travel to the shore and explain that one," Panu added. He gave her a pointed look.

Ree averted her gaze. "And the baby giant spider which was not poisonous, Panu. He could have stayed."

Scoffing, the old man waved away her words.

"Once I brought home a baby werewolf but, in my defense, he was lost. Oh, I found a plant with four leaves and red trim. Everyone was allergic though. The drunk human's horn, a soldier's helmet. What else was there?" Pouting her lips, she turned to Panu.

"Is there anything you didn't bring?" asked Sarah, stepping into the firelight.

"Sarah, how are you feeling?" Jacob shot her a smile.

Her thoughts from earlier surged forward. "Um...much better. I...I'm rested."

"Good. Would you like to have a seat?"

She plopped down beside Ree and squeezed in as much as she could.

"Kerem's a miracle worker, isn't he?" Ree said. "There was an injured child at the other part of my village, so he had to leave before we celebrated our new guests."

Sarah's brows furrowed. "The other part?"

"There are many mountain plateaus in this area." Panu lifted his cane and slowly waved it in a circle. "Where we are is the main village. Our smaller villages are hidden by the mist and lack of sun on days like this."

"That's amazing! So, the birds are your only way to get around?"

Both Ree and Panu bobbed their heads.

"Do the forest elves have anything like?" Jacob peered at each of them.

Ree looked at Panu.

The old man started, "I have been told centuries ago the forest elves had a special breed of horses. They've gone extinct since then."

"Due to what exactly?" Jacob moved his seat, so he was sitting right beside the elder elf.

Panu gave him a side look to which Jacob returned a grin. He moved one seat down.

Satisfied, the old elf continued, "Stories like this will repeat throughout time. When other Lyricans heard of our cousin's horses, they began to hunt the beasts down. They thought to breed them. But they didn't know the horses were wild and died in captivity."

Shaking his head, the old man sighed. "We've managed to keep our birds alive, thankfully. Skuntz may know more about the horses than me."

Sarah's ears perked up. "How much longer until they arrive? Have any of the scouts checked their distance?"

Panu chuckled. "I'm glad to see Ree can still keep a few secrets."

Jacob glanced at Sarah, then crossed his arms. "What do you mean?"

Ree grinned. "No one arrives at our village. Everyone is taken here. We'll pick them up in a week's time."

Sarah sighed.

Now, doesn't this sound familiar.

CHAPTER 20

The morning air was cool against Sarah's skin. Unlike yesterday, the sun was not tolerating the clouds' disobedience. The sky had cleared and Sarah could see it beaming in the distance.

She was sitting with her chin perched on her knees, resting on the outskirts of the plateau. Though the sky elves had gotten used to her appearance the last few days, they still often twisted their necks into knots to catch a look at her.

She hated it. Even though she understood their curiosity, being the center of attention made her clam up.

"Maybe too many years of bullying," she said.

Sarah examined the freckles on her skin. The small, red marks had always been an easy target for her peers. When Jacob had appeared in town was the only time the bullying had stalled. Whether everyone was too busy talking about him or if he had shielded her from their sneers, Sarah wasn't certain. All she did know was that when Jacob walked beside her, she had felt better.

And no one had an ill word to say to her.

Then, he disappeared without explanation. Of course, Sarah knew what happened. That didn't stop the rumors claiming she had done horrible things to him. When in truth, he was the one who had betrayed her. Yet she was the one who had to suffer the dirty looks and sharp tongues, the attacks...

Elaine's vengeful face appeared in her mind. Her beautiful sky blue eyes had darkened as she straddled Sarah's back, pressing her to the ground.

Where was Jacob then?

Sarah dug her nails into her palm.

"How's that fair?" She huffed, scooting away from the sun and shaking her head.

She closed her eyes tight. They were burning.

"No time for crying, Sarah. We've done enough of that."

Sarah fanned her face before rubbing her palms against her knees. She stretched in front of the morning sun, then stood to start making her way back to the guest house.

Steadily, the village was coming alive but the strolls she saw were nothing compared to the afternoon rush.

Sarah's walk slowed some as she approached their temporary home. The door stood ajar.

Had she forgotten to close it?

Glancing up, she checked to see if any of the windows were open.

Each one was shut.

The hair stood up on the back of her neck. Letting inklings of her energy move ahead of her, Sarah knew two living creatures were in the house. One of the two was Jacob. The other...

She stilled and drew her magic tightly inside. If she could sense them, they might be able to sense her, as well.

Sarah easily moved between the frame and door before stepping into the shadows. The first floor of the house was like a living room. Rising up, there were small ledges all around meant for sleeping.

She had slept on the first level. Jacob was three above her.

Peering upward, Sarah searched for a physical sign of the unwanted house guest. If she climbed the ladders, she'd be noticed.

Sarah kneeled down in the dark corner and waited.

It didn't take long.

"You must return, Jacob."

"I refuse."

Sarah's ears perked up. Was it another angel?

"And I am telling you, you must," the intruder warned. "Your family sent me here to bring you back."

He scoffed. "Then they're going to be disappointed."

"You're acting like a child. What good will staying here do you? Who do you think you're fooling, trouncing around with these unelected?"

Sarah caught a breath in her throat. The house, the atmosphere...it felt heavy, like it was bearing down on her shoulders.

"At least they're not punishing me for a crime I did not commit," Jacob shouted. "At least they're not cowering in a corner of Lyrica waiting for the war to end!"

The intruder groaned. "If you hadn't lied..."

"And if they hadn't ordered me to kill a child. All the blame isn't on me, Michael."

"That was only a test, you fool. One you failed."

The wooden panels above creaked as one of the two shifted.

"How can you be so certain?" Jacob asked. "Our people have done worse things."

"Because I have faith!"

"I'm done speaking with you," Jacob spat. "Test or not, I would have done the same. You can tell them that."

There was a moment of silence. The tension scratched at Sarah's skin.

"Goodbye, Jacob. Until you come to your senses."

The atmosphere lightened. Sarah took in a long breath, releasing it steadily to remain hidden. Her palms had become clammy while she toed the edge of anger and sympathy.

Was he really being punished for *not* killing a baby?

Jacob was exhaling deep breaths above her. She imagined the compressed frustration building in his chest for twelve years, steadily transforming into a ball of wire that prodded him.

A daily reminder of the horrible crime he had failed to commit.

Sarah turned her hands into fists. She had not been the only one suffering, after all.

She jolted to her feet and began making her way up the ladders.

Jacob head appeared over the ledge. "Sarah?" His eyes grew wide. "How long have you been there?"

"Long enough, Jake." She reached the fourth level and started toward him.

"Sarah, I-I can explain," he stuttered. "I didn't call Michael here. He—"

His words were muffled by her grip. Sarah had wrapped her arms around his neck.

"I'm so sorry, Jake."

His body loosened. The arms which had been at his sides wrapped around her, too. He relaxed his head between her shoulder blades.

Feelings of security spread over Sarah and she hoped she was radiating the same.

"I didn't want you to hear that."

She shook her head. "No, I'm glad I did. Now...everything makes more sense." Sarah stepped away from him, taking hold of his forearm. "I-I'm sorry I doubted you before."

"I can't blame you," he replied, moving away and taking a seat. "I lied to you in the past. Your suspicions were justified. I don't believe I could have taken the stone from you but the thought was still there."

Sarah moved beside him. "And you didn't. Even when things started looking bad."

Jacob gave her a small smile. He still had morning hair and his dark strands were askew. As soon as Sarah caught his gaze, Jacob turned away. He stared at the wall, elbows on knees while his thumb picked against his index finger.

"Do you want to know why they asked me?"

Her stomach turned into knots, and she took in a silent inhale. "Yes" was on the tip of her tongue, yet fear tightened her stomach. The desire to know why he had lied to her battled with her apprehension. What horrible story was behind his reasoning?

The knots grew tighter. She nodded.

Jacob stopped fidgeting with his fingers. He stretched his legs out and ran his hands over his trousers. Finally, he sat straight again, eyes facing the wall.

"In my family, I'm the eldest son. I have a sister who is several years my senior but my father believes in the old ways. I'm supposed to be her...*superior*."

He cast a quick glance at Sarah.

Though no one in her town abided this courtesy, Sarah knew what it was like on the receiving end of another's judgment. So, she stretched out her lips, giving Jacob all the encouragement she could muster.

Internally, she was bristling. Men always seemed to want to control things.

Jacob leaned back and folded his hands over his stomach.

"My sister Hannah, she didn't agree with our parents' teachings." Shaking his head, he chuckled. "That's not describing it well. My sister completely rejected their teachings. She wouldn't listen to me. She left our realm without permission and...and then she met a human...man."

Sarah's spine became rigid. The knots in her stomach were replaced with butterflies.

He continued, "They, um, she became pregnant. When our parents discovered it, they were livid. When she told them it was a half-breed—"

"Don't use that word," Sarah snapped.

"What?"

"Half-breed." Kwe's young face flashed across her memory. "It's rude. They don't need to be labeled something different than we are."

"I'm sorry. I didn't know," he replied with a slight shrug. "Honestly, that's the term we're taught. Good to know it's not acceptable here."

She gave a hard nod. That was one less person who'd hurt Bo or Kwe.

"When they discovered the child was...part human, they were no longer livid. They were dangerous. Interacting with other Lyricans in that way was not permissible. All angel-born must be only of angel blood. That's the rule. Even now it sound ridiculous, doesn't it?"

Sarah squeezed his shoulder. "You took the words right out of my mouth."

Jacob sighed, his chest deflating with the act.

"My family was embarrassed but not enough to break the law. They reported her. By then, my sister had already fled. She never returned home."

For a moment, Jacob's face pinched together. The veins protruded in his neck and the skin over his jaw stretched. He closed his eyes, then cleared his throat.

"Anyway, she never returned home. We still had the baby to worry about. Because my sister was gone and she was my responsibility, I was tasked with finding the child. And disposing of it. Except, except, when I did, I couldn't." He turned his gaze downward. "I saw him. He looked so much like Hannah. He even had my nose, I think. Then I saw how his father admired him. How could I take that away from someone?"

"You can't, Jacob. Because you're not a monster. If that's why you fell, better to be fallen than with them!"

He smiled, his gaze narrowing. "You're so good, Sarah."

"And you are, too. Thank you for telling me what happened."

"I did promise," he replied. "Besides, through all of it I got the chance to meet you. I still need to get rid of something though."

Moving under his shirt, Jacob revealed a long, golden necklace with a small circular ball at the end. He ripped it from his neck, then crushed it under his boot.

"Every angel has one," he replied to Sarah's confused look."We use it to communicate and stay close. It's how Michael found me but—"

He stood up. "I'm ready to move on. Completely."

Sarah wrapped him in another hug.

Wild laughter could be heard outside, followed by birds cawing.

Both Sarah and Jacob slanted their brows. They climbed down to the lowest floor of the house and headed outside. The elves were staring into the sky, pointing as two of their birds flew toward the village.

But that wasn't why they were laughing.

When Sarah caught sight of Skuntz and Klara hanging from the birds' talons, she nearly doubled over. Battle axe pressed to her chest, Klara looked as if she were praying while Skuntz clung to the bird's leg.

The sky elves roared with joy. And Sarah couldn't blame them

A forest elf and a dwarf hanging from two giants birds wasn't something one saw everyday.

Skuntz was angry. It had been nearly a week yet the grimace had not left his face.

Sarah mashed her mouth shut and held in her giggles.

The sight of Skuntz hanging from a bird's talons, zooming toward the earth, still made her chuckle. He and Klara didn't find their *surprise capture* as comical. The dwarf couldn't walk in a straight line the entire day after they arrived.

Jacob nudged Sarah as they sat in the guesthouse and ate

breakfast. Ree and Kerem had joined them.

"Who do you think's going to get sick first when we leave this afternoon? Klara or Skuntz?"

Sarah smirked. "Skuntz. Klara's a bit tougher."

"Hm. It's no fun if we agree."

"Fine. Klara, then."

"And what does the winner get?" He raised his brows, staring at her.

Sarah tilted her head to the side. "A slice of the other's sweet bread?"

"Deal."

They shook each other's hands, falling into a bout of chuckles. Sarah tossed her head back, catching sight of Skuntz.

He was watching them.

She gulped and pulled her hand away. Narrowing her eyes, she said, "May the loser have the sweetest bread."

"Why can't there be a land bridge to Esmer?" Klara asked. She tapped her foot and swirled her spoon around the bowl's edge. "I hate traveling by water...or air, now that I've experienced it."

"Flying is the quickest way," said Jacob, biting into an apple—a rare treat for so far north, according to Ree.

She pointed her spoon at him. "Perhaps, but I still don't like the idea of dangling from a bird. Again."

Ree tore into her slice of bread, glancing between Klara and Skuntz. She sighed, settling into her cushion. "I wish we didn't have to fly, either," she said. "The birds hate Esmer. Their wings always get coated in ice."

Klara raised her brows. "How cold does it get there?"

"Cold enough that we haven't explored the island," Kerem replied. "We've only landed. The birds always start acting strangely, then their wings chill, and we never get very far."

"But now we've got the chance," Ree said with a grin. "They can tell us about the island, once they've returned."

"Esmer is small but it's not that small, Ree." Kerem shook his head. "They'd need more than one day to explore it all."

She frowned. "I'll get my feet on that island one day."

He patted her head. "Not while Panu is the village head. Maybe not even after. I'm certain once he passes on, he won't stop giving you his advice."

"Nagging." She scoffed.

Jacob propped his chin up in his hand. "He and Sarah have a lot in common."

Chewing on her bread, Sarah glared at him, narrowing her eyes. Everyone chuckled, their sides shaking from the effect. Except Skuntz.

Sighing, he placed both hands on his knees and rose to his feet. He looked around the room, making sure to meet everyone's eyes.

"We need to make up for lost time. By bird is our best option. Jacob?"

He turned to the angel, who had became as still as a statue.

Skuntz's gaze traveled up his wings. "You should put those away before we reach Esmer. I'm sure you don't want them falling off."

Barely giving anyone a chance to grab their next breath, Skuntz had already walked to the door and closed it behind him. Because he didn't slam it, there was no echoing or resounding tremor. Yet the humor in the room had dissipated.

The monstrous rock edged upward, then curved down at its tip. Shorter pieces of shaped stone surrounding it eventually spread out into trees. From the trees there were pebbles and from the pebbles a sandy beach.

Along the edge of the monstrous rock was a split in the stone. Almost like a jagged smile.

Sarah held her fear in her stomach and sat up right as they came in for the landing. Without a pause, Ree placed Beaker gently on the ground while the others followed behind.

Klara still had her eyes closed when she landed. She had gripped the elf in front of her so tightly a strain had started in his neck. He looked to Sarah. She gave him a small smile before stepping from Beaker and tapping the dwarf's shoulder.

Klara parted her eyes ever so slightly.

"We're here. You can, uh, release him now."

"Huh?" She glanced up, then immediately unlocked her arms from around her rider. The veins in his neck relaxed.

Klara sent him an apologetic grin. "Sorry. I forget my own

strength sometimes."

Jacob and Skuntz's birds arrived next. Soon, the four of them stood on the beach with their rucksacks piled high and wearing their winter clothes.

Sarah flexed her shoulders. Because the pain was still there, Jacob still carried some of her load. But she felt much better than she had when they first moved north. Kerem was definitely a miracle worker.

Beaker and the other birds shivered. Their chests puffed in and out as they tapped their talons in the sand.

Ree sighed. "I think it's time to say farewell. They're getting restless. We'll return in one day."

"Thank you, Ree," Sarah replied. "You all have been very kind to us."

"Of course! It's not every day a sky elf comes across a forest elf, a dwarf, an angel, and a human traveling together, now is it?"

"Not at all," Jacob replied. "Thank you for not feeding me to Beaker."

"You're welcome," she said before turning to Skuntz. "Take care, cousin. Panu will be very upset if you die."

"I'll try not to. Let's head out."

They said their final farewells, the elves took to the sky, and the group turned toward Esmer. Sarah could feel the shared moment as they all took a collective breath, then followed Skuntz deeper into the island.

With no map or hint of how the island was laid out, it was up to Skuntz and Klara to do the tracking. Jacob had wanted to take to the sky for a better view but the island's chill kept his wings tucked away.

Standing on the sand, Sarah hadn't felt too much of the cold. Yet, as they made their way around, the temperature dropped quickly. Her breath began to form mist and her exposed fingers would have gone numb if she hadn't placed them beneath her cloak.

The others around her panted, leaving their own ringlets of breath in the air. Aside from the large rocks at the island's center and a few hills, most of Esmer was flat. Leafless trees with grey bark surrounded them along with stiff patches of grass. There were no flowers, fruits, or vegetables. The sun's light waned as they traveled.

"I don't think there are any signs of Ellen or Emma," Jacob

whispered, walking beside Sarah.

She turned to respond but realized he wasn't speaking to her. Jacob's gaze lay ahead on Skuntz.

The elf looked upward and to the left, not meeting Jacob's stare. "None that I've seen," Skuntz replied. "Klara?"

She shook her head. "If they are here, they haven't arrived recently. Any tracks they may have left are likely gone."

"Could you try reaching out with your magic, Sarah?"

She shrugged. "I doubt I can cover the entire island but I'll see."

Sarah came to a halt before placing her rucksack on the ground. She wiggled her arms and legs while her friends waited. Taking a deep breath, Sarah cleared her mind. She allowed that clarity to move through her muscles and relax them. As the stress eased, her magic pooled out from her.

Sarah urged it forward, dispatching her energy in every direction.

Where are you two?

She could feel the island, feel the trees and rocks pulsing with their unique vibrations. But there was nothing else.

Opening her eyes, she groaned.

"Anything?" Skuntz asked. His stare was hopeful.

"I'm sorry," she replied. "It seems to be only us on this island."

There was a collective droop in everyone's shoulders.

Without looking, Sarah grabbed her rucksack and placed it on her back. Immediately, her supplies tumbled to the ground. She had picked the sack up by the wrong end.

Gnashing her teeth together, she fought back another groan.

"Here, let me help you."

"No, it's fine. I just wasn't thinking…"

Skuntz had already kneeled down and was scooping items into his arms. He slanted his brows as Sarah stopped mid-sentence.

"What is it?"

She shot to her feet and met their bewildered stares. "We're not thinking."

Their only response was to blink.

"We're not thinking," she repeated. "Not how Ellen and Emma would. Even if they arrived yesterday, they would never be foolish enough to leave a trail for someone to follow them."

"And if they did leave a trail, it would lead to a trap." Skuntz pinched his eyes. "How could I have been so stupid?"

Klara hmphed. "Don't be too hard on yourself. If these twins are anything like what the other dwarves told me, they're not exactly predictable."

Thrusting her palms outward, eyes wide and round, Sarah shouted, "Yes! If we're going to find Ellen and Emma, we have to think like them. We can't be logical."

Jacob tapped his chin. He moved his gaze to the mountain.

"So, if I were a traveler here looking for shelter, where would I go?" He pointed to the curved rock. "There's likely to be caves there where I could rest."

"Meaning they aren't at the island's center," Skuntz replied. "That still leaves an entire island for us to search."

Sarah shook her head. "Not if we think about the worst option. Where would a traveler never go to seek shelter here?"

The elf shrugged. "The shore? There's nothing except rocks, sand, and saltwater. And when the tide comes in any shelter would be destroyed."

"Bo and Kwe said witches are supposed to be challenged during these quests," said Sarah. "They'd stay on the rockiest part of the shore where there's nothing to help them."

"When we were flying in, it looked like the eastern shore was covered in pebbles." Skuntz turned to the others.

They all nodded.

"East we go then." Klara grinned.

CHAPTER 21

"**W**ell, if they're here, they're doing a great job at hiding."

Klara kicked at a small rock. It was one among many that rested across the shore.

Skuntz stood opposite her, staring at the land in front of him. He kneeled down, picked up a pebble, then tossed it into the woods. "Ellen and Emma aren't always logical. That doesn't mean they're foolish." Sighing, he placed his palm where the pebble had been. "They would find a way to survive."

"But where?" Jacob asked.

Sarah stood beside the elf. "I agree with Skuntz. I think here is our best option. If they're not here, maybe they've left a hint of where they've gone."

Klara scratched her head. "I have an idea but I'm not sure it will work."

"Anything is worth a shot at this point," Skuntz said, rising to his full height. "What are you thinking?"

"Hm. I've never done it with pieces of stone this small. I could try humming and see how the sound echoes."

"How will that help?"

"If the sound comes back flat, that means the stones are weighed down," Klara replied. "Maybe these two are lying somewhere along the shore we can't see. Or there's a marker we're missing."

Skuntz looked at Sarah.

She nodded. "Like he said, it's a worth a try. How can we help?"

"You can't," said Klara. "Give me some space, please. And time."

Klara bent down. She placed one hand on the stone and the

other on her chest. Unlike before, the humming did not start low with a gradual build. No, instead Klara began from a higher pitch, expanding the volume as the song continued.

The pebbles around them trembled. Sarah held her breath, and Skuntz leaned toward her. She looked up at him.

"She can do it," he whispered.

Sarah nodded and tried to force those words into her heart. She doubted anything else would calm it.

Skuntz grabbed her hand and squeezed. His own hand dwarfed hers, and as quickly as he had taken hold of hers, he released it. Trails of warmth along Sarah's palm followed his departure.

The idea of calm became foreign. Her heart thumped in her chest so hard, for a moment she worried it would disturb Klara.

Her eyes were locked on Skuntz though she knew he was purposefully looking away.

Why did he grab her hand? And, more importantly, why did Sarah enjoy it?

The humming stopped. Klara rubbed her throat and cleared it a few times before speaking.

"Follow me." Her voice was raspy. She reached into her sack for some water, then made her way west along the shore.

They had only walked for a few yards when Klara dropped to her knees and began rummaging through the small stones.

"The sound reflected from here was odd. I'm not sure what it is."

Jacob turned all around them. "Where's *here* exactly?"

She sighed, and tossed her orange hair back. "This portion of the beach. Start from where I am and keep moving outward. Any questions?"

Obeying her instructions, they began grabbing at any rock they could. Sarah had only gone a few feet when the sound of sliding stone pulled her attention. She looked behind her and gawked as she took in the scene.

Jacob was on his knees, arms spread wide open. The surprise on his face was the equivalent of Sarah's. A perfectly square hole and its top lay in front of him.

Klara rushed over. "This was the odd sound. This is why these rocks didn't echo like the others."

The dwarf continued examining the tunnel while Sarah broke

from her spell and found her footing. Three stones were in the shape of a triangle and had been attached to a slab on the land. This slab opened up into the tunnel that Sarah found herself staring down.

Jacob sat back on his knees. "Well, I think we've found them."

A breeze blew in from the tunnel and chilled Sarah's face. She balled her fists.

"We don't have time to waste." Sarah turned her palm upward and a small flame appeared. She lowered the flame into the darkness until the space was illuminated. There was no ladder or rope but small holds had been carved out. Sarah only needed to make the trip a little easier.

She slammed her free hand and called to the earth.

Nothing happened.

Sarah tried again, hoping to form steps for them to walk down. The earth remained stagnant and the flame vanished from her hands.

"What's happening?" she asked, staring at her palms. Her hands shook and her heart raced while she tried to comprehend the element's response.

I can't use my magic. I can't...no, no, no!

Spinning on her knees, Sarah shot her hand out and called to the stones surrounding them. Instantaneously, they began zooming through the air.

She shook her head. "What?"

"Sarah."

She looked behind her at Skuntz, who was staring at her straight in the face. His own face held no emotion aside from his brows being slightly raised.

"You still have magic. Ellen and Emma must have cast a spell to prevent magic usage," he replied. His gaze fell on her still raised arm. "You can lower that now, you know."

Humiliation slapped her on the cheek and Sarah knew a rosy red was showing. She took in a sharp breath, then got to her feet.

"Where are you going?" Jacob called after her.

She didn't respond. Instead, she snapped several branches from the nearest tree and started making a fire. Her father had shown her how to do it once and she prayed she remembered his instructions. The only other option was to stumble around the tunnel blind. That didn't seem smart on a mysterious island.

Sarah intently focused on her task. Once the first spark caught and the flame was large enough, she used her cloak to grab the largest branch. Still averting her gaze and after dousing the flame in water, Sarah marched toward the tunnel again and began making her way down.

The others rose from where they had been sitting while waiting for her to finish. They climbed behind her with Klara bringing up the rear. Skuntz was just behind Sarah.

She tightened her hold on the branch. The thought of not having her magic, even for a moment, frightened her. She had panicked.

Skuntz walked next to her. "I wasn't trying to embarass you, Sarah," he whispered.

She released a slow breath. "I know. That doesn't make my reaction any less embarrassing."

"If I woke up one day and forgot how to shoot an arrow, I would react the same way."

"But it's different...with me." She sighed. "Please, pretend it didn't happen, that we even had this conversation."

He was quiet. Sarah was certain he was rolling his eyes.

Finally, lowering his voice, Skuntz said, " We're all here with you. You're not alone is all I wanted to tell you."

Slowing down, the elf found his way behind Sarah once more.

"You're not alone."

No, she wasn't, which was both a problem and a solution.

Shadows crossed over one another in the space ahead. The tunnel ended and instead they were all standing in a circular room. In its center was what looked to be a well. Beyond that, there were two large rectangular tombs made of stone. Torches lined the wall.

Sarah gulped.

Skuntz moved first, making his way to the right container and pushing the top off. He gasped.

"Ellen?"

Sarah's heart skipped a beat. She raced to where he stood and came face-to-face with one half of her old friend. She didn't have the braids from years before. Her hair was shorter and had grown outward, looming over her head like a crown.

"How do you know which one she is?" Klara asked.

Skuntz pulled the twin into his arms and raised her up.

"Her hair," he replied. "She had cut it into this style last I saw her."

Beautiful colored flowers were strewn through her hair. She wore a long black dress, which glistened with water droplets from her container.

Sarah cupped Ellen's cheek.

"She's warm."

"Why aren't they waking up?" Skuntz stared around for an answer.

Sarah moved to the other tomb and, with Jacob's help, lifted the lid. Like Ellen, Emma rested inside. They were exactly identical aside from their hairstyles. Where Ellen had her hair growing out, Emma had cut hers short, so there was little hair on top.

But their skin was still the same beautiful brown. They were taller. Their faces and frames had thinned since Sarah last saw them.

She shook Emma. Her friend did not respond.

"Something's moving beneath us," Klara said. She looked at the ground.

"Is it the water hitting the island?" Jacob asked.

Klara shook her head. "No. It's only in this one room. Wait, I think I—"

"I hear it, too." Skuntz placed Ellen back in the water. He stepped away from his friends and peered around them.

"A hissing?" asked Klara.

He nodded. Cupping his ear, Skuntz followed the sound until he stood in the middle of the room by the well. The hissing grew louder. The water in the well sloshed.

Sarah gripped the rim. She could feel them coming, two of whatever they were. But they were moving slowly, like something was holding them back.

The dark water illuminated. The grey, worn faces of two sirens appeared.

The creatures hissed under the water, but when they touched its surface they suddenly pulled their hands back, shrinking away.

The sirens turned to one another, their heads dropping as one nursed her injured hand. Then, they looked up again, before gaping their mouths open toward the surface. The hissing ceased, replaced by a low, dreary tune.

Sarah and the others covered their ears, hoping to avoid the sirens' spell. But nothing happened.

Jacob glanced at Sarah. She shook her head.

"Their song isn't affecting us, " Klara said, staring into the well. "It's changing the water."

Splashes of what looked like black ink appeared on the water's surface. The splotches of ink danced around one another, twisting and turning until they formed words.

Two Lies,
One Truth,
You Decide,
Drink the Water and Face Them.

"They're testing us." Skuntz shot the unconscious twins a glare. He huffed and turned back to the well. "They must have set the spells up as a precaution, then put themselves to sleep."

"Do you think this is the only way to wake them?" Jacob added.

Skuntz bobbed his head with a sigh. "They never make anything easy."

"But who should drink?"

"All of us," stated Klara. "We don't know if they want all of us to drink or just one, so better not to chance it."

Sarah gulped. "Fine then."

She scooped up the water and slurped it into her mouth. A salty, bitter taste coated her tongue. Her throat felt tight. She coughed in an attempt to clear it but it only grew tighter. Then, the room became fuzzy. Her friends were frozen in place. A blackness creeped along the edges of her vision, expanding outward, slowly blinding her. Slowly erasing her friends from her sight until she saw nothing.

Sarah's heart was pounding as she closed her eyes and balled her fists at her sides. Had she been fooled? Had she lost her vision forever?

Panic made her take several rapid breaths. Her chest moved like ocean waves with the effort.

She wouldn't know unless she looked.

A shuddering inhale, then Sarah flashed her eyes open. She was standing in the market with her mother. Her small hand was clasped around Lucille's larger one.

A woman walked by them in the aisle. She smiled at Sarah.

"She's adorable!" the woman gushed.

Lucille patted Sarah's head while Sarah stared up at the woman.

"I bet she's a good little girl, too, isn't she?"

Her mother sent Sarah a slanted glance. The woman's eyes followed the quick look. She broadened her grin and returned her focus to Sarah.

Holding up a single finger, she said, "Now, remember. Good girls listen and always do what they're told. You hear me?"

The woman nodded and Sarah mimicked the movement.

But inside she revolted.

That's a lie...

The store was gone. Sarah lay on her stomach in the middle of a forest. She moved to stand but someone weighed her down.

"This is your fault!" Elaine screamed into her ear. She pulled at Sarah's red curls, creating painful tension around the roots. Tears sprung to Sarah's eyes.

"You should have stayed away from him. You're a monster."

"No one wants you here, Sarah." Elaine's friends were shouting at her in the distance. She couldn't see them.

Elaine forced Sarah's face into the soil.She tried to breathe and her mouth filled with dirt.

"No one wants the monster! No one wants you!" Their chant grew louder, filling Sarah's ears until it was the only noise she could comprehend. Her emotions welled inside her.

Sarah knew this hurt. She would never forget this memory. And she knew she hadn't been alone.

That's a lie. Tom was there. Tom wanted me to stay.

Sarah was standing in the corner of a room. The wind blew outside and the house creaked around her.

A man and woman were there, staring down at a girl strapped to the bed. Sarah's eyes rounded as she took in the sight, as she realized who the young girl was.

"You should have listened, Lucille." The woman had spoken first. "We told you stop that evil behavior."

"Aunt Catherine, please," Sarah's mother whined. "I didn't do anything. It was just pretend."

The man shook his head. "We can't have you setting a bad example for your cousins. We took you in because your parents wanted you raised right. Now, it's time we get to it."

Sarah tried to move but found she only had the one spot.

There was a lit lantern on a dresser. Another by the door. A breeze blew into the room and tickled the flames.

"This for your own good, Lucille."

While the man bowed his head and prayed, the woman—his wife, Sarah assumed—revealed a small vial in her palm.

"What is that?" Lucille asked.

"Hush!" the woman barked.

"No, no. Uncle John, Aunt Catherine, please." She pulled against the ropes. "I won't do it anymore. I won't play in the forest or talk to the trees. It was only pretend."

Her aunt Catherine emptied the vial over Lucille. Both she and John closed their eyes, then began mumbling.

A sharp gust shook the house, tossing the lanterns to the floor. A flame had caught the curtains and suddenly the room was nothing but orange and red.

Lucille shrieked.

"Get the children, John! Go!" Catherine stumbled after her husband, shouting out to her young ones. Sarah could hear them running around the house. The flames continued to spread.

A young Lucille was coughing as she struggled against the rope that held her. She tugged just right and one hand was free. She quickly untied herself and raced into the hall.

"Aunt Catherine, where are you?" Lucille wheezed. "My eyes burn. I can't see!"

"It won't move!"

"Try again, John," Catherine screamed. "Help, help!"

"Lucy, help us get out." A child's voice.

"I can't see you," Lucille replied. "Where are you?"

"Lucy, please."

"Lucy!"

The name repeated over and over again with the shrill voice of a child.

Sarah had to choose.

The voice grew louder.

She felt like she couldn't breathe. She felt her mother's heart racing inside her.

Truth. It's the truth...

Sarah jolted awake, sucking in a gasp of air. She clawed at her throat but Jacob's hand pulled hers away. She turned to him, eyes large and apprehensive.

His eyes had their own dark circles.

"It's fine, you're back."

She couldn't respond. Her chest continued to jut in and out, seemingly shrinking the rest of her body with its effect.

"Take it one breath at a time," Jacob warned. He patted her head. "One breath at a time."

Gradually, Sarah's breathing evened out. She wasn't sure she could fully move, so she let her gaze wander.

Skuntz hovered over an unconscious Klara, whispering something Sarah couldn't hear. He placed Klara's head in his lap just as she woke up.

There was the sound of sloshing water.

Sarah turned her attention forward. Ellen and Emma stood in their separate tombs, watching the scene in front of them.

"Hello," they said in unison.

Skuntz got to his feet, pulling Klara with him. "It worked. It worked!" A huge grin pulled at his lips.

"Skuntz?" Ellen and Emma both said. Their brows rose upward.

The elf's grin faltered. "I forgot how irritating that is."

The twins moved their focus across the room until it found Sarah, who tried to stand but ended up back on the floor. Jacob lifted her up and she leaned against him.

"And the fallen angel?"

They narrowed their eyes before examining the rest of the room. Their behavior was as if they were searching for someone else. Someone Sarah knew they wouldn't find.

When they realized the four in front of them were their only guests, they turned to Sarah and Skuntz.

"What's happened to Serwa?"

Sarah and the elf glanced at one another.

Skuntz sighed. "We have plenty to tell you."

CHAPTER 22

Ellen and Emma were slender silhouettes against the moonlight. They sat huddled together by the water, still wearing their thin black dresses. The water moved back and forth across the shore's edge, along their dress hems.

Sarah wore a thick cloak, long sleeves, and padded pants. She couldn't fathom how the twins were staying warm. But she understood why they were sitting alone, away from her and the others.

Ellen and Emma had lived with Serwa and Alex for nearly ten years before they left on their journey. They had seen the rise of Serwa and Alex's kingdom, unlike Sarah. Now, they were being told the same kingdom, their home, was conquered and the rulers, their teachers, missing.

It made complete sense they'd want to be alone. Still, Sarah's heart weighed in her chest., as well. Repeatedly, she had started to move toward the twins, then slumped back to the ground. They had barely said a word to her yet Sarah wished to grieve with them.

Yes, she had been gone for twelve Lyrican years.

No, she had not aided Alex and Serwa in restoring the old vampire kingdom.

But she felt the loss, too. On Earth, when she had thought of returning to Lyrica, she hadn't pictured any of the current events occuring, yet she had pushed through them. Didn't that mean she had as much a right to grieve her friends and the war in Lyrica as everyone else?

Or was she again misplaced?

She groaned.

Skuntz had taken the lead in telling them the entire tale. When he was done, both Ellen and Emma began making their way out of the tunnel, through the forest until they were by the sea.

Sarah rubbed at her eyes. She was exhausted, yet her mind was too full for her to even contemplate sleep. Her gaze traveled down the shore line.

Klara had propped her sack up and was lying against it. A slow tune poured from her, growing lazier with each hum.

At least someone was getting some rest.

Skuntz and Jacob walked beside one another. Their backs were turned to her and they were several yards away, so Sarah couldn't hear what they were saying. Still, when the elf declared he was going for a walk and Jacob offered to accompany him, Sarah thought her ears may have been clogged.

Then, she wondered if she was hallucinating when Skuntz nodded and waited for the angel to follow. What did they suddenly have in common?

She cast another glance at Klara, then the twins. It seemed everyone was occupied but her.

The boys moved farther down the beach.

"Curiosity killed the cat, Sarafina."

A frequent line from one of her mother's scolding sessions. But now, with what Sarah knew, was any of it really her mother's fault? Hadn't she been a victim like Sarah had been?

Though Sarah's heart twisted with sadness, her hands balled into fists with rage. Her mother had been a victim. In response, she made her own daughter one, too.

Did that make it right?

The boys were moving further along. She shot to her feet and followed after them. Her head was too full to sit. And if her mother's sayings held any truth, Sarah had nothing to worry about. She wasn't a cat, afterall.

Stepping behind the trees, Sarah followed after Skuntz and Jacob until they stopped their tread. She squatted down and listened.

Skuntz shook his head. "You were my truth, Jacob. The other two scenes were lies."

Jacob had cupped his chin between his thumb and forefinger. He steadily bobbed his head.

A vein pulsed in Skuntz's forehead. Sarah release a silent exhale. His pride was getting in his way again

"Skuntz, what did you see?" Jacob finally asked.

Sarah leaned in a bit more. If what Skuntz had seen, changed his mind about Jacob, she didn't want to miss one detail.

Skuntz breathed. "You were in two visions. In the second vision. I saw a younger you. And there was a lost child asking for his parents. Instead, you took him away to your realm."

"I returned that boy. I'd never—"

"I know," Skuntz interrupted him. "I want to be honest with you, though. As soon as I saw you in the vision, I thought it was a truth. But something felt wrong. You've regained Sarah's trust which made me hesitate. None of your kind have appeared to attack, which also made me reluctant."

He groaned, before crossing his arms and pivoting to fully face the angel.

"In the third, you helped the child find their way home. I had to decide. What I'm trying to say is no matter how much I wanted you to be the enemy, you've proven you're not. And...if that's the case, I can't treat you as one. And I won't."

With the words finally spoken, Skuntz flexed his shoulders, easing the last bit of anxiety from them.

Jacob chuckled.

"What's so funny?" Skuntz raised his brow.

He shrugged. "I can tell you're very proud of yourself. You don't apologize often."

Sarah's stomach growled. Both Jacob and Skuntz peered into the trees. She sunk lower to the ground, before making her way back.

As she stepped from the trees her stomach grumbled again and Sarah cursed her hunger. She didn't want to eat. There was too much to think about and her distraction was gone.

The last vision...memory she had seen was unforgettable.

Her mother strapped to a bed, her great aunt and uncle her captors.

She shivered.

Was her mother the only survivor?

Sarah scoffed, then drew her knees to her chest. Closing her eyes, she pulled at her hair. She already knew the answer. They were all screaming near the end and the flames had moved through the house. The child—

She rubbed at her eyes, not wanting to relive the memory, her mother's memory. It explained so much.

Another growl from her stomach. She groaned.

"Here." Klara stood by her, holding out a piece of dried meat. "Your stomach won't let me sleep."

"I'm sorry. I was trying to ignore it."

Klara sat beside her. "That doesn't seem to be working. We only have time now, so you should eat."

"Thank you, Klara," she said with a smile. "I was lost in my head."

The dwarf sat with her legs straight out. She rocked her head from side-to-side for a moment, letting the silence linger.

"Are you worried about what you saw?" she asked.

Sarah paused for a moment. "I'd rather not talk about it."

"Hm. You know, when Da would bring you up, he never mentioned how stubborn you are."

"I'm not stubborn, I—"

"Can handle everything on your own?" Klara gave her a long side-stare.

Sarah bristled.

None the wiser, Klara continued rocking from side-to-side. "We've only known each other for a few weeks," she admitted. "But the way Lyricans talk about you, it feels much longer for me. You're strong, I don't doubt that. But no one can do everything alone."

You don't understand. Sarah rubbed her forehead. *It's not only that.*

"Skuntz and I are not Queen Serwa and King Alexander but—"

"That has nothing to do with this," Sarah snapped, putting extra bite behind her words.

Still not looking at her, Klara paused. Finally, she turned to Sarah, a gentle look in her eyes. She was being kind and compassionate, which frustrated Sarah even more. No matter how kind the dwarf was, no matter how well she listened, no one would ever understand what it was like to have two homes that didn't need you. Or want you.

The sound of padded steps drew Sarah's attention. Ellen and Emma were walking toward her. Both she and Klara stood to meet them halfway.

Sarah reached out to console them, then drew her arms back. It had been twelve years.

The twins seemed to look through them.

Emma spoke first. "We know where Serwa is but—"

"We can't find Alexander," Ellen finished. "If what you saw is correct, Sarah, then he is in the human kingdom. But we cannot confirm where in the kingdom."

Sarah hands were trembling. "Where is she? Where's Serwa?"

In unison they said, "Beneath the river."

For a moment, Sarah thought Ree would ask to join them on their journey. She had a free, wild spirit that always seemed up for an adventure. Instead, after they had returned to the sky elves' village, Sarah and the others rested for a single day before saying goodbye.

Ree waved them on proudly, wishing them the best of luck. Though Sarah didn't think recruiting unnecessary parties into their group was the best idea, as they marched back across the mountains, she wished for Beaker and the other birds. She was certain with the birds their trip would have been shortened by less than half. To her, that was one less half of a mountain to navigate before seeing Serwa.

Since learning where the humans hid her, the witch had haunted Sarah's dreams. Almost since the beginning rescuing Serwa and Alexander had been her mission. It gave her a single objective to focus on. But now her goal was within reach and her magic tingled inside her.

Serwa was so close.

Ellen and Emma walked beside one another, taking lead of the group. They still hadn't spoken much. Sarah had so many questions, but the twins only had one goal.

Her eyes drifted to the silver circles around their ring fingers Serwa had given them. It was how they had found her, using the remnants of her energy to find her last location.

Sarah glanced down at her own finger, then quickly shook her head. Jealousy would do her no good. And it made no sense. Of course, Serwa would have given them gifts as Sarah was sure they had done for her. After all, they had been together for twelve years.

Sarah had only had a few months.

She tucked her hand into her cloak. Suddenly, it felt naked.

Klara was silent beside Sarah while Jacob and Skuntz talked amongst themselves. Their voices were too low for her to catch the full conversation. Occasionally, a "Yes" or "Agreed" would reach her ears, only for the remaining sentence to fade away.

Narrowing her eyes, Sarah glanced back at them.

What were they discussing?

"Jacob's not as bad as I thought." Klara sighed and shook her orange tresses. "I'll admit, I was suspicious of him at first."

Sarah laughed. "Was it ever a secret?"

She shrugged, sending her a sidelong stare. "No, but I like to pretend I'm more subtle than I am. He isn't like the few other angels I've met."

"What have they been like?" Sarah peeked behind her, ensuring the two young men were still lost in their own conversation.

Klara grimaced as if she had a bad taste in her mouth. "Where to begin? So arrogant. Think they know everything and that they're always right. And selfish! There's a strong sense of self-preservation among his kind."

"Seeing them is rare, isn't it? Why is that?" asked Sarah.

"The few I've met here seemed to spend their time observing us other Lyricans. Like we were their experiments."

Sarah thought of Jacob's mention of the languages he had studied. The angels must have collected textbooks of information on the other Lyricans during their visits.

The sound of gurgling water drew their attention. If Sarah remembered the map correctly, they were closer to the desert than ever before. All it would take was to cross the river, a day's travel at most, and the forests would give way to endless sand.

Lyricans believed the deserts were a wasteland. Sarah wasn't so sure. Once she had stayed after school to ask Ms. Carr more about Cleopatra. The teacher had only mentioned her briefly in a previous lesson but Sarah had taken it upon herself to learn about the woman pharaoh. Like with Queen Elizabeth, Sarah was fascinated and learned what to some was considered a wasteland was home to others.

The gurgling river came into view. Ellen and Emma came to a halt at its edge.

Turning around, Ellen found Sarah's eyes.

"Can you feel her?" she asked.

Sarah hesitated, the color rushing to her cheeks. Finally, she shook her head.

Emma bent down and placed a hand in the water. "They've concealed her in black diamond."

"What? How do you know that?" Sarah marched forward, so she was standing beside them. For a moment, she stared into the river, hoping to feel, if not see, Serwa there. But she saw nothing aside from the rushing water.

"Her energy is faint," Emma replied. "Serwa is not hiding here. There's no reason for her to conceal herself. Therefore—"

"Black Diamond is the only logical answer," Ellen finished. "It is a witch's greatest weakness. Humans know this. Please stand back, Sarah."

"Why?"

"If you don't, you may get wet," stated Emma.

"Then, you would become sick," Ellen finished. "We don't want that. It would also upset Serwa."

The bubbling irritation in Sarah's stomach evaporated. Internally chastising herself, Sarah stepped back with the others while the twins worked.

Nearly shoulder to shoulder, they began moving their arms. Their motions were fluid and exactly reflective of the other. Sarah could sense their magic in the air; she knew they were calling to water.

Skuntz took in a sharp inhale. The air whizzed and he jumped forward, catching an arrow that was a few inches from Emma's face. He snapped the arrow in half.

"Human," he growled.

Ellen and Emma continued working. They paid no mind to the armored man who appeared on the river's other side. Cupped hands holding a flame decorated his chest.

Sarah drew her sword.

"Keep your arrows to yourself, you coward!" Klara shouted. She held her axe in both hands, tapping the blade against her palm. "If not, I'll slice you open in one swing."

The man did not respond. He made eye contact with each of them but only shortly.

Skuntz peered at their surroundings. "Are you alone?"

Again, the man was silent.

Skuntz grinned. "They left you alone on guard duty."

The weapon quivered in his hands. His eyes moved from them to the river and back again. His mouth was a strained line.

He looked scared and worried but there was something else...

"Thobias." Sarah's sword remained steady as she spoke the name.

The man became rigid.

Skuntz raised his brows at her. "What?"

She nodded. "Thobias. He's—"

"How do you know my son?" He dropped his weapon to his side, his attention only on Sarah.

A dark, oval-shaped structure emerged from the river.

Sarah pulled her attention back to Thobias' father.

"Who is he?" Klara asked. "Friend or foe, Sarah?"

She eyed the man up and down. He wore the human armor, though his son was everything they hated. Thobias had told her his father had been captured. But why this?

"His name is Emry." Jacob's voice was shaking.

Klara groaned. She placed her axe on her back halter before spinning on Jacob, hands on her hips. "And who is Emry?" She cast a look at Sarah.

"Emry is...was my sister's partner," Jacob answered. "And my nephew's father." He turned to Sarah. "Whose name is Thobias. That's the name you said, isn't it?"

Everything pulled itself together. Her sight moved between Jacob and Emry.

"Where is Thobias?" Emry called from across the river. He had inched closer to its edge, leaning slightly over the rushing water. "Please, tell me where my son is."

The tears were in his voice, even though Sarah couldn't see them. She returned her sword to its sheath.

Jacob seemed on edge. His breathing had become audible and his lips were pulled back revealing gnashed teeth.

Of course, he didn't have an answer for Emry. The guilt was eating at him.

Sarah placed a hand on Jacob's arm. The tension eased and he wiped his face.

"We found him with some other children," Sarah said to Emry.

"He's safe."

Dropping to his knees, Emry released a shaking exhale. "Thank the gods. Thobias. Thobias..." He covered his eyes as fresh, deep sobs poured from him.

"We're not killing the human?"

They turned and stared at the twins.

Skuntz patted Ellen's shoulder. "Not this one."

"We couldn't sense him," Emma said. "He's hiding his presence."

"Probably with a witch stone from one of the captured," Skuntz finished.

Two crescent shadows fell over the group. Jacob had taken to the air. He landed next to the still sobbing Emry, touching his shoulder but not speaking.

Sarah turned her attention to the water between them. Could she freeze it and walk across?

Skuntz approached the diamond structure. Kneeling down, he smoothed his hand across the surface. A smile broke on his face.

"We need to get her out," he said. He turned to the twins. "How can we get her out?"

Klara smirked. "I can take care of that."

Like she had done in their previous battle, the dwarf slammed her hands into the earth. Two fists rose from the ground and began smashing Serwa's prison.

A shiver ran up Sarah's spine. Something was wrong.

Power flowed from the black diamond. It rippled through the air, pouring over Sarah, mingling with her own energy. Serwa's magic called to her and Sarah stumbled forward.

Ellen and Emma were doing the same. They were like the children and Serwa the Pied Piper.

And then the diamond's surface fell away. The last hit had destroyed it.

A searing heat shot through the air like an aimed spear racing toward its target. Sarah was pushed to the ground. Sweat had formed on her skin and her chest felt heavy.

Sarah tried to recover, only for her legs to give way.

But she was there.

The tears were burning Sarah's eyes.

The witch, her old friend, stood in what was left of her prison. Her hair hung down her back and curtained her face. But Sarah knew who she was. She knew her name.

She was Serwa.

CHAPTER 23

The moon was their spotlight. Shadows were cast from the crackling fire.

They could have been ancient statues, a treasure a wanderer comes across accidentally.

Sarah imagined the newspaper headlines. She could see the scholars and travelers all rushing to see the stone remains of the three female warriors—Serwa, Ellen, and Emma. There would be an air of mystery surrounding their origin.

And Sarah would be the only one on Earth who knew their story.

Serwa was poised and perched perfectly atop her log. She had tilted her neck back, so her face caught the moonlight. Her curls had been rolled into a sort of braid that hung all around her, trailing past her back and pooling onto the soft grass. And her eyes burned the same brilliant gold they had the first time Sarah met her, when she thought of witches as elderly women with crooked, bumped noses.

She smiled. That was long ago.

For a moment, when she had seen Serwa rise from the diamond's ashes, Sarah had become a child again. She wanted to run into the witch's arms, tell her how she had practiced her magic even on Earth, and show her how strong she had become. Tell Serwa how much she had missed her and Alex.

Sarah needed to let Serwa know she was strong enough to protect her now. Just like Ellen and Emma had done the past twelve years.

On either side of the witch were the twins. They both sat angled outward, their hands folded in their laps, their backs slightly to Serwa, and their faces were blank canvases.

Everyone else sat on the opposite side of the fire—including

Sarah.

Serwa hadn't spoken much since being set free. She had quickly looked over all who were present, then asked for Alexander and her children. Skuntz had explained what had happened since she was captured.

There was obvious relief that Bo and Kwe were safe. And obvious dread that Alexander was still somewhere in the human kingdom. Her face had contorted and her magic suddenly felt like lead spikes weighing the entire party down.

Since then, she had only eaten, drank some water, and sat on the log. Ellen and Emma had not left her side.

Sarah tried to lose her thoughts in the fire but her eyes always found their way back to her old friend.

Serwa was alive and well.

Skuntz caught her stare. He nodded to her left and she followed his gaze.

Serwa wasn't the only one who had been silent. Emry had also lost interest in speaking. After bombarding them with as many questions about Thobias as they had the knowledge to answer, he had tossed off his armor.

Skuntz glanced at Serwa, then Sarah.

Sarah gulped and gave him a quick nod. They'd have to send Emry away, and soon.

"I missed the moon," Serwa said, smiling. She looked away from the luminous stone and showed her large smile to everyone. "I couldn't feel it like this when I was in the black diamond. The damn humans were good."

She sighed. "They caught me when I was at my weakest."

"It won't happen again." Emma faced Serwa. She withdrew a dagger from her cloak.

Ellen did the same. "We're here now. Our journey is complete and we are ready to return to your side."

Serwa placed a hand on both their shoulders. "Thank you. How was your ethereal quest?"

"Amazing!" Emma replied, her hands tightening around her weapon. "Our ancestors allowed us over to speak with them. There was so much we didn't know, Serwa."

Ellen scooted a little closer. "We communed with the elements as you instructed. We saw our mother and brother, too. They're very happy in the other world."

Serwa nodded. "Your quest seems like it was a success. I'm glad to have you both back, though I wish it were under better circumstances."

Sliding her hands from their shoulders, Serwa folded them in her lap and turned to face the entire group. Her energy already had a pull but straightening her back and lifting her chin only added to the effect.

The witch had become regal since Sarah last saw her. And her magic had grown stronger.

She examined each of them, the flames flickering flecks of orange in her eyes.

"What's our next move?" Skuntz asked. He sat up, both elbows on his knees as he listened.

Stretching, Serwa rose to her feet. Her dress hem was shredded at her ankles.

"Nettle is on the battlefield. That's where we should be, as well, but I refuse to let Alexander remain with the humans." She rolled her fingers and the sound of cracking bone filled the forest.

She took in a deep breath. "This is why, Ellen and Emma, you both will travel to the human kingdom to rescue him and Charles."

"What?"

Their reaction was immediate.

"But, we only returned to you," the twins said in unison.

Serwa pressed her eyes shut. Opening them again, she composed herself.

"Yes, but my escape is only a single part of a larger plan. Many vampires are loyal to me. Many also see Alexander as their only ruler," she replied. "If the kingdom is to prosper after this war, Alexander needs to be at my side. I cannot be in two places at once."

She cleared her throat. "The kingdom must come first. It's where I'm needed, and where Alexander will call home, once you've saved him."

Ellen and Emma glanced at one another. Without another word of protest, they returned to their seats, staring at Serwa.

"Then we'll be traveling with you, Queen Serwa?" Klara asked.

"Yes, and do not call me queen, Klara. You freed me from that damn prison. Not to mention, I considered your father a friend." She paused. "Please, know you have my condolences."

She looked over Sarah. "My friend here knows how I feel about titles, don't you, Sarah?"

"Neither of us is a fan," Sarah said, chuckling. She rolled her palms over her knees and grinned at the witch. "I...we're glad to have you back, Serwa. Really glad."

"And I am glad to see you in Lyrica." Her smile softened, and Sarah felt a warmth wrap around her. She met the witch's eyes.

"We have much to discuss, Sarah," she replied, then turned to the twins. "But first, our battle plan."

"How should we enter the human kingdom?" Ellen said, grazing her dagger's tip across her clothing. Her sight found Emry, who had been sitting quietly beside Jacob. "Perhaps the human knows something."

All eyes fell on Emry. He gulped, strengthening his hold on his small mug of water.

"I...I've only been to the kingdom a few times. I can't remember much."

"You can try harder," Ellen said, staring at him over her blade. "A few times is more than enough to draw out a map."

He gawked at them.

"Or, you could let us cast a spell."

"Poke around your brain a bit." Emma smirked. "We'd only need time to find the ingredients and—"

"He is not the enemy!" Jacob shouted, flaring his wings out.

Emma tilted her head to the side and looked him up and down. "Says the traitor."

Jacob's response fell short. He smashed his mouth together but kept his eyes level.

"The angel who wanted the stone." Ellen tsked. "Did you think we forgot?"

"Stop it," Sarah said, casting a glare in the twin's directions. "We're past that now. Jacob has helped us several times since leaving the angels."

Emma kept her gaze on Jacob. "How are we certain we can trust him?"

"Angels are good liars. They may even be able to fool us," Ellen added.

Sarah narrowed her eyes. "You'll have to trust me. The same

way I trust you all!"

The fire crackled as silence descended on the group. Energy was rippling in the air.

Skuntz groaned. He fell on his side and propped his head up with one hand. The fire's light fell over his face.

"Sarah is right."

They stared at him. Sarah wasn't certain she'd heard him correctly.

"Jacob isn't like other angels we've met." He turned his attention to Jacob. "I trust him. He's an ally."

Klara raised her hand. "I do as, well. He stuck around even after I threatened to cut his wings off."

Jacob gave a small grin. "A threat I'm sure you planned to carry out if I had stepped out of line. Both you and Jacob."

Both the elf and dwarf nodded.

Sarah found Ellen and Emma again. The three gave each other direct stares.

"Fine," one finally responded. "We trust you, Sarah, and so we will trust the angel, too."

They looked at him, then gave a slight bow in his direction. "We apologize and hope you can forgive us."

Mimicking their movements, Jacob said, "Of course. I hope I can continue to prove myself."

"I think, maybe..." Emry stumbled over his words. He coughed, then took a swallow of water before starting again. "I can't draw you a map. My memory isn't that good. But, I might know where King Alexander is being kept."

Sarah's heart raced. She snapped her neck, turning to Emry. The man was weathered. He didn't look old. No, there was simply a layer of exhaustion and thinned perseverance resting over him.

"When they captured me I was taken to the kingdom for training. Everyone was chattering about the queen's new...well, they called them pets. I never heard a name but they're chained in the throne room, where the queen enjoys spending most of her time."

The delicate hand that had grabbed at Alexander's head...that was the human queen.

Sarah inhaled sharply through her nose. A layer of ice coated her palms.

"That's Alex," she said. "That's where they're keeping him and Charles."

Ellen and Emma stood.

"What should we do?" they asked, looking at Serwa.

She groaned and stretched, then met the twin's expectant stares. "Ellen and Emma, you will leave for the human kingdom. Find my boys and set them free. But, once that is done, you four should not return home just yet."

Sarah blinked. "Why? Isn't the point to get them out?"

"There's a bigger plan here," Skuntz whispered.

Serwa continued, "Once they are free, I want you to go the queen's chambers. She must be alone when you do this."

The twins nodded.

"Do you want us to keep her alive for you?" they asked.

She shook her head. "No, she'd be an easy kill. Not entertaining at all. Kill her, slowly. Make it look like a sudden illness. When she has a miraculous recovery, you will be controlling her body. She'll be your eyes and ears. Gather all you can, distort their forces. When Nettle and I arrive with our army, the humans will fall with little effort. Do you have the spell?"

They smirked. That was all the answer Serwa needed.

"We'll gather the ingredients while we travel," Emma said.

"When should we expect you?" Ellen asked.

Serwa moved her hair over one shoulder. She lifted her right arm. In the blink of any eye, it had transformed into a sword.

She sliced through her hair, leaving it swaying just above her shoulders. The remaining braids tumbled to the floor, landing with a thump.

"Two weeks." Serwa flicked at her fingernails.

"When should we leave?"

She turned to them. "Now."

The twins spun on their heels and raced into the forest. Serwa faced the remaining members of their group.

"We'll leave at daybreak to join Nettle. Emry is coming with us."

Jacob and Emry looked at one another.

"There's no other option, Jake," Klara replied, catching both their attention. "He'll have to see Thobias after the war ends. We can't risk telling him where he is. He'd either get lost on the journey or, by luck of dwarven stone, find him and be murdered."

The angel sighed.

Emry stared at everyone wide-eyed, his pinky finger tapping rapidly against the clay cup. He was like a child watching his parents fight, unsure of what to do.

"I'm sure I can find it if you give me the directions," Jacob snapped.

They all shook their heads.

"You said you trust me!" he retorted.

"You," Skuntz agreed. "Not the human. He could betray you or us as soon as the chance is given to him. There's also more than Thobias to think of. We could be putting them all in danger."

"Please, please," Emry started. "I only want to see my son. I—"

"Emry will not betray us," Serwa said. "He doesn't believe in the human's war."

Klara cleared her throat. "Serwa, with all due respect, how can you be so sure?"

Sarah was thinking the same thing.

"I may have been locked away but I didn't lose my hearing," the witch replied. Looking at the human, her face softened. She gave him a small smile. "I heard you when you prayed to Thobias, Emry. When you told him how you were happy they had assigned you to guard me, so you wouldn't become a monster like the others forced to join them."

Her lips trembled but she caught her breath and steadied.

"And I heard you as you wished you could free me because my imprisonment was cruelty. I have to say, the humans were smart posting a single guard. Of course, it would draw less attention, but I'm thankful they hadn't turned you completely, Emry."

The clay cup crashed to the floor as Emry fell forward, wrapping his arms around his middle. He rocked and sobbed, the tears streaming down his cheeks in thick drops. The fire cast shadow over his face while adding an extra shine to his blonde hair.

He shook his head; his shoulder shivered.

"I'm so sorry," he wailed. "I'm so sorry. They wanted me to kill them. I swear I didn't. I just hurt them some, so they'd think they were dead. They were so scared and I, I..."

His words were lost to his sobs.

Jacob placed an arm around him. Serwa moved to his other side and did the same.

"Do not worry, Emry." She laid her cheek against his head. "We will make them pay."

CHAPTER 24

(Ellen and Emma, Day Five)

Ellen lay perfectly still. She and her sister would not move until the moment was exactly right. Patience was key in several aspects of life, especially when planning to murder a deranged royal.

They had hidden in the woods surrounding the human kingdom until nightfall. Once it was dark enough, they had walked the wood's edge, sunk to the ground, and started crawling across the land.

The first rules of a succesful assasinaton were to neither be seen nor heard unless absolutely necessary. If one is seen, then one is dead or, worst, the mission a failure. If one is heard, then one must kill before their presence is revealed.

Their brother would be proud they still remembered the lessons.

Swords of various shapes and sizes were strapped across their bodies in positions of easy access. They had memorized the style of sword and its location on their bodies. Buying too much weaponry in any human village would arouse suspicion, so they had simply stolen them. Though illegal and morally wrong, Ellen and Emma had decided the theft was for a greater good and so it was justified. The scales were balanced.

Their cloaks were covered in long strips of pulled grass. They had tested the disguise before entering human land to ensure the possibility of detection was minimum. If they lay still enough, under the shade they blended seamlessly into the ground. Under the cover of night the human guards would never be able to see their slow procession.

And now, the back wall was only a few feet away. They would

not fail Serwa.

Emma crawled forward slowly and deliberately. Though they had hidden their presence, she could feel her sister beside her. Even as children, no matter how well they hid, the two could always sense each other. But no one else could ever find them which made hide-and-seek infuriating for the other children.

Emma's face was placed against the earth while she gazed up and under the corner of her disguise. Their visibility was limited but Emma could see the guards.

The human forces must have been strained because there were very few guards on watch. Considering what Sarah had told them about Nettle and Gan's war tactics, it was likely the humans were stretched thin.

Ellen released a slither of energy, calling her sister's attention. Emma responded in agreement.

The guards were for show more than anything else. Defeated armies resulted to such tactics when outnumbered by the enemy meaning the humans were desparate. This was good news Ellen and Emma would deliver to Serwa.

She would be pleased and, in turn, they would be pleased, as well.

There were guards on each wall. A set of five would take their station, then peer out into the night for five minutes.

Ellen had counted.

Afterwards, the next set of five would move over and the rotation would continue.

The rotations, along with the crisp air, kept the guards alert.

Ellen and Emma were certain it wouldn't be enough.

They reached the wall. Both took a breath; the guards turned to the side and began their march. Ellen and Emma got to their feet and pressed themselves against the wall.

Five minutes.

Both women reached into their bottom side pocket on the right. From there, they removed a vial, and began pouring the mixture inside it on their palms and feet. The combination of dead toad skin, honey, and magic would last them the entire night plus another week in case the kill took longer than planned.

They doubted that would be the case. Killing was easy, especially under the right cirucmstances and if rules were followed.

Many aspects of life were easy actually if procedures and guidelines were used appropiately.

Ellen and Emma first pressed their palms to the wall. Ensuring the mixture secured them, they lifted themselves from the ground before placing their bare feet against the wall, as well. Neither could hear the other's breath.

The guards continued their routine. Stare, turn, march, and rotate. Everything was a precise routine. Serwa may have even been impressed by them though their routine was going to be what led to their queen's end.

When Ellen and Emma had nearly reached the top, they moved over to the corner. Each corner rose higher than the rest of the wall, leading into alcoves which the guards passed under.

A breeze came but they had tucked their cloaks under their clothing. Nothing would go fluttering in the wind.

They began climbing the alcove gradually and would pause each time the guards moved.

Ellen could feel Emma becoming restless. She sent her soothing vibrations. Her sister's magic calmed and finally they made it over the alcove to the other side of the wall.

Only a small number of humans actually lived within the castle walls. The rest stayed in the towns and villages in the surrounding area as was custom for their kind. Humans strongly believed in class hierarchy.

At least that was what Emma had read in her mother's books.

Torches flicked along the inner wall of the castle. There was less shadow, so they had to find the perfect spot.

Ellen and Emma turned horizontally, then crawled along the wall until they found a piece of shade to step into. A set of barrels provided the perfect foundation for them to land on.

They kept their palms planted against the wall until their feet could touch the ground. Behind the barrels, they leaned on one another, taking in careful breaths. There was still much to do. They had to keep their energy flowing easily.

Ellen and Emma poured a small amount of water on their hands and feet. They sent a quick heat through the extremities to burn the potion off. They couldn't risk getting stuck anywhere with what they were about to do.

Another rule of assasination was to never be cornered,

especially by the target. Hiding or lying were to be used if an assassin was cornered but, of course, a skilled assassin was never cornered. Murdering a target earlier than planned and unnecessary killing was a last resort.

The two witches peered around the courtyard. In its center was a house that connected with patios on the left and right side of the yard. It towered slightly over the rest of the castle with large windows at its top and three doors at its base. Each window was illuminated.

We should go there.

A gust of wind blew through the yard. Ellen added her own magic to its force. The courtyard fell into darkness.

"Call a man from inside!" one guard shouted. "The wind's blown everything out. Hurry up!"

Emma followed behind Ellen, mimicking her movements. They nulled their presences, moving around the men through the darkness. It was almost like a dance, an activity Emma enjoyed doing but Ellen did not.

While the men scrambled and stumbled in the night, the twins stepped around them, spinning on their heels and tilting away from even the slightest contact. They had to listen and feel, then step around the directions of the noises and sensations.

Slow footsteps echoed in the distance and they knew their time was running short. But because failure was not an option, neither was being captured. The sisters moved faster.

Ellen and Emma were nearly to the house. There wouldn't be enough time to scale the wall and climb into the window.

"Here, take a torch and find the lanterns. Let's hurry before Queen Leonna notices," ordered a guard.

The yard began filling with light.

Ellen laid her palms flat on the door, reaching out for someone on the other side.

She didn't sense anyone. Unless a member of the humans was particularly skilled at hiding their presence, the sisters had found their opportunity.

Their small space of shadow was retreating.

The burning lanterns were gradually overtaking the shadows, and the guards were making their way toward the center house.

There was a probability the door would groan. Ellen opened it slightly to decrease the likelihood. Her sister crouched and squeezed her way through, Ellen following close behind. Together they pulled the door shut. The wooden slab closing against its frame with a low thud which was better than a creak.

Breathe.

The twins turned to one another, leaning on either side of the door's alcove. They both stared at each other while taking in silent breaths. Breaths that did not match the rapid rise and fall of their chests or their drumming heartbeats.

Rest when necessary. Never panic.

They nodded.

They had never failed before. They refused to start now.

A few more inhales.

Emma raised three fingers, dropping each one steadily. When her hand was only a fist, they stepped away from the door and made their way up the stairs. Silently but quickly they treaded the spiral staircase, unsure of when it would end.

But their goal was at the top. That they knew.

A door flung open and Ellen was knock into the opposing wall. Two guards stepped out, laughing until their sights found the twins. Their cheer disappeared. Instead, the men slanted brows and grated teeth, signs they were angry.

Ellen was in their direct path. Their eyes were trained on her and their hands flexed at their sides. Emma easily predicted the sequence of events which followed. She glanced at her sister.

The men grabbed their swords.

Emma remained at the door's edge. She didn't hesitate. Before the men could draw their weapons, she pushed them forward and slammed the door shut. Witnesses were not desired for what was about to transpire. Then, the sisters would have to kill them, too.

The less bloody an assasination, the better for cleanup and suspicion.

Ellen had sidestepped the fumbling guards. Standing two steps above, she waited for them to move. As expected one turned to her, and the other faced her sister. It was a logical response in the situation. Two enemies and two allies. However, Emma and Ellen had no plans of killing the men.

They were going to make them kill each other. Much simpler that way.

In sync, the men moved. They slashed their swords up and outward. The twins stepped back, forward, and then reached up, taking a hold of each man's wrists. They bent their wrists back, loosening their grips and maneuvering the swords, so both guards pointed at one another.

The realization Ellen and Emma weren't attacking always stalled their enemies. And in their moments of hesitation, the twins found an opportunity.

Ellen tightened her hold on the guard's arm and moved it upward, slashing his ally's face.

Emma made sure to cover his mouth as he screamed. Before he finished, she shoved his sword into his friend's stomach, just under the armor. Together they created a few more slashes and stabs, until blood pooled around the men's feet.

They placed their bodies outside the door, then reached into their satchels and poured ale down each man's throat. They left the bottle turned over on the stairs and continued on their way.

At the top the sisters slowed their steps. The stairs had turned into a hallway decorated with the human symbol: two hands cupping a burning flame.

No guards but Charles...and Alexander.

A jolt of energy ran through them. They sensed his presence; they could feel its rage and weakness.

Ellen and Emma removed their knives.

They followed the trail of Alexander's energy until they came to another door. It wasn't hunky and weathered like the others. Instead, it was painted a sky blue with foreign symbols decorating its rim.

Emma moved first, sidling through the small opening, knowing her sister was behind her.

The throne room was polished bright colors and shiny materials. Then, there were the two chained figures on either side of the throne. Both Alexander and Charles hissed at the twins. Their eyes were that scarlet shade and the veins in their muscles pushed against their slender frames. The two were not in fighting shape.

Ellen and Emma blinked at them.

"Don't waste your energy," Emma said.

"Yes, all your blood is already on the floor," Ellen added.

Both Alexander and Charles retracted their fangs. As the red faded, they leaned as close as their chains would allow. They rubbed their eyes a few times. Something changed in their stare.

"They remember us now."

Ellen and Emma spun on their heels, turning their backs to them. They examined the room again, noting the large banners on each wall. Perfect for hiding.

"Do you two hear us?" Charles whispered. "Listen, both of you."

Charles hasn't changed.

"Ellen. Emma."

They moved so they were fully facing Alexander. He narrowed his eyes at them.

"You're here to rescue us, I know that much," he said. "But where is Serwa? And where are my children?"

"Both are safe," they replied. "Serwa instructed us to come here."

"And where is she?" Charles asked.

Ellen looked at him. "Taking back our home. It's been overrun with humans."

The young man flinched. His head became slack as he took in a hard breath. Shaking himself, he rose to his feet only to fall a moment later.

Emma approached him and placed both hands on his shoulders. With limited pressure, she forced him from his knees to the floor.

"Listen to us, Charles," Ellen said. "As Serwa would say, there is no need for pride among family."

He huffed but nodded.

"What is your plan?" Alexander asked.

"No time to explain it all. We simply need to isolate the queen. Does she spend much time here?"

Charles scoffed. "We're here, so she's here as well. She's been trying to get us to feed from her. We haven't, of course."

Ellen and Emma shook their heads. "It is wise that you didn't," they said in unison.

"Her blood is certainly spoiled," Ellen added.

"And bad blood ruins a vamipre's tummy." Emma waved her finger at them.

The men gave her a blank stare. She shrugged. "Perhaps I did not say it with the right tone. It work for Serwa when Kwe becomes ravenous."

Her sister patted her shoulder. "I thought it was well executed, sister. There, there."

Alexander groaned. "Alright, listen. We're not sure what she's planning. She—"

"No time."

The twins darted behind the closest tapestries. Jumping up, they dug their short swords into the stone, urging it to give way. One more leap and they balanced on their sets of blade. Then, they waited.

Soon the room filled with humans. Strong odors came along with them that were potent and unnatural.

Ellen urged herself to breathe. She knew from her reading the scent was caused by what humans called perfume. But the mixture was different than the oil and flowers witches sometimes used.

Witch's scents were airy and fleeting. The humans' was clingy and thick.

Stale even.

Ellen pressed against the cold stone. She would remain calm and deal with the head pain later. The mission came first.

The queen took her seat.

Queen Leonna was a tall woman. She had straight, tawny hair that flowed past her waist. Her face was round and delicate, two light blue eyes gazing upon her subjects. She was much younger than either Emma or Ellen had expected. No more than twenty-two based on her features, size, and lack of wrinkles.

Yes, twenty-two was a safe guess.

A deep purple cloak hung over her shoulders but under it was a shimmering dress. The jewels glistened more than diamonds, though they weren't shaped like any gem the twins had ever seen. And they reflected the light so well...completely translucent.

The queen did not bother a glance at either vampire. She moved beside her throne. As the room filled, she positioned herself on the steps leading to the enormous chair. A smile stretched across her face and she held her head high.

"Bring him in," she called in a lithe tone.

Doors on the opposite side of the room opened. Two guards entered carrying chains. Behind them, they dragged a scrawny man wearing torn clothing. What he had on appeared to have once been a night gown, though it had changed to better resemble an old sack.

He didn't resist as they dragged him along the smooth stone.

When the guards were a few feet from the queen, they dropped the chains and stepped to the side. She approached the prisoner.

A small thimble of his energy was still there. He reached out and asked for help.

He was a witch.

They looked around the room, careful not to move too far from behind the tapestries.

Can't save him.

Queen Leonna towered over him, her purple cloak pooling around her. He looked up.

"Tell me how you escaped," she stated.

He said nothing.

"Tell me how you escaped," she repeated.

The witch tried to sit up but his effort had little affect. He became slanted on the ground, his head resting against his angled shoulder.

"I did not escape, my queen."

"Liar," she spat. "Your entire party was found murdered. Did you kill them?"

He shook his head. "No. I don't know what happened. There...was an attack."

"By who? Describe them to me."

"I didn't...I never saw them. The guards asked me to hide until they needed me," he replied.

"And?"

"When I finally came out, everyone was dead. There had been screaming and—"

"Stand up," she ordered, clasping both her hands in front of her. A stress had pulled her shoulders up. She straightened it away.

The sisters briefly turned to one another.

Royals were very good at remaining poised.

The witch sighed. Groaning, he gradually got to his feet until he stood in front of her. His knees shook and he leaned in every direction.

"Why did you come back?"

He hesitated. "To serve you, my queen."

"Tell me the truth."

The witch paused, then took in a long breath. "My brother. I wanted to see my younger brother."

"And what is his name?" Queen Leonna asked.

He shook his head.

"What is his name?"

He cast his eyes to the floor.

"Answer me, now."

"No!"

Dribbles of blood ran down the witch's body. He tilted his head up, staring at the red tip of her sword. His breathing became shaky while he gazed upon the weapon. He didn't have long though. With haste, she brought the blade down and slashed it across his throat. Splatters coated her dress.

The crowd grasped and shrunk toward the walls. Emma and Ellen slanted their heads. The queen's movements had been slow and she had missed his throat the first time. She was certaily not trained in combat.

Queen Leonna held the sword out toward all of them. She was grinning.

The scrawny witch crumpled to the floor. She stepped over his body and turned to her people.

"Let it be known this is what happens to traitors, witch or not." She drew the blade flat to her chest. "You are dismissed. Enjoy your dinner without me."

The crowd raced from the throne room. Emma and Ellen could see the humans pushing each other forward.

As the room emptied, a young girl approached the queen. They spoke in whispered tones, then the girl disappeared. Leonna took her seat on the throne.

A few moments later, the girl arrived again with a bowl of water and a cloth in hand.

"Take the sword and leave me," Leonna ordered.

The girl bowed and left the room. She shook the entire way. Finally, Leonna was alone.

The Queen moved her fingers along the arm of her chair and

took in a deep breath. She looked at Charles, then Alexander.

"Did you enjoy the show?" she asked.

He smiled. "Not very entertaining. I've seen worse."

A smirk pulled at her lips. She rose from her chair and marched to stand in front of him.

"Do you want the witch's blood?"

"Hm. Well, he does smell better than you."

The slap echoed throughout the room. Alexander's chest rose rapidly. He silently met her eyes.

"Say that to me again."

Another slap.

We're going to kill her.

Ellen dropped from where she rested on her blades, grasping onto them a moment before she fell. She and Emma landed on the floor without a sound. The queen's hand swung back-and-forth across Alexander's face.

Charles glanced between the queen and the twins.

Emma had stepped to the side, removing the items they needed, while Ellen approached head on. Just as Leonna raised her hand for another swing, Ellen grabbed her arm. She spun the royal around to face her, clamping a hand over her mouth before she could scream.

Soon the queen was on the floor. She struggled beneath Ellen's weight, her voice muffled by the witch's hand. Alexander and Charles grabbed her limbs.

While they held Leonna down, Emma lifted a vial to her nose. The queen's eyes fluttered and her fight dulled.

Ellen removed her hand.

Emma poured a pile of soil in the queen's mouth first, before removing the cap of another container. The worm squirmed to the container's rim, the left head wiggling its way out first, followed closely by the right.

Ellen took the vial from her sister and held it over Leonna's mouth. It snuggled into the moist soil, the heads releasing shallow screeches as their tail joined with the earth. Emma sliced her hands, giving the creature a few drops of her blood.

It quieted, sinking deeper into the queen until it could no longer be heard or seen.

An assassin.

The twins stared at one another. They smiled.

"Well done."

CHAPTER 25

Clotted gurgling rose from the man's throat while the sun shone down on the remnants of his comrades. He was blinking rapidly, and Sarah wasn't certain if the shocking pain or the sun was causing it.

Serwa forced her hand deeper into his chest, curving her elbow. The gurgling came to a halt as the man's eyes grew large. His gaze darted all around him.

There was a quick snap, a bloody cough, and he stilled.

Sarah wiped her sword along her pants before placing it in its sheath. "I'll start the clean up," she said.

Nodding, Serwa freed her arm and stood.

"Make sure to leave the grass this time, Sarah," the witch stated. "We don't want the humans picking up our tracks."

While Sarah went to work manipulating the earth into six graves, Skuntz and the others checked their enemies. Despite the humans having caused so much destruction, their soldiers didn't have anything of much value on them. A few didn't have swords, only daggers, and their armor looked old. Much different than the group they had encountered before meeting Ree. But these soldiers didn't wear the cupped flames on their armor.

Sarah would be glad when she never had to think about that symbol again.

"Let me help you." Serwa kneeled opposite Sarah, a single grave separating them. "You need to concentrate your magic in one place. Then, stretch it out to alter multiple areas at once. Try it."

Sarah did as she was told. She closed her eyes only to reopen them to the sound of crumbling earth. Three more graves had appeared alongside the first one.

Turning to Serwa, she grinned. The witch smirked and placed

her hand down. One after another, eight graves appeared, all the same shape and size.

She looked at Sarah and lifted her eyebrows.

"Well, you're just showing off now," Sarah huffed.

"Or perhaps you aren't showing off enough," the witch said with a chuckle. "Your magic has grown with you but you're out of practice."

Sarah groaned. "I do practice at home."

"How often?"

"Almost every morning, well, if I can sneak out without my mama finding out."

Serwa stared at her though she seemed to be looking slightly above her head. "While you were gone, Sarah, I did some research on your legend. The Chosen One. I found a few things I would like to discuss with you."

A shiver ran over Sarah's spine. There was something about Serwa's tone. It reminded Sarah of Ms. Carr when she had the unfortunate duty of informing the class Thomas was sick.

Thomas.

He had barely crossed her mind since she left Earth. She was certain he had kept his word and brought Ms. Carr to her house the next day. Except she wasn't there. She was gone. Again. What tales would her neighbors spin now?

"Sarah."

She shook herself. "Sorry. Yes. I want to know what you learned."

Jacob and Emry held out their palms, revealing a few coins.

"We didn't find much," Jacob said.

"These soldiers aren't well cared for," Emry added. "I thought there would be more of a fight the closer we came to the vampire kingdom."

"I thought the same." Klara dropped a tiny coin pouch on the ground. "This is odd. Could Nettle's forces be doing that well?"

"I wouldn't put it past her." Serwa smiled. "Fairies have their ways. We need to keep moving though. We're only a short distance from Carrington now. Let's get these bodies under the ground."

Klara, Jacob, and Skuntz dropped the bodies into their individual graves. Sarah and Serwa filled them up, ensuring the very top was a layer of grass.

They stood back and looked over their work. Someone would have to examine the ground with a magnifying glass to notice anything.

Serwa dusted off her hands, spun on her heels, and continued onward. The others followed behind her with Klara and Skuntz bringing up the rear. Sarah walked ahead some so she was standing beside the witch.

"What were you saying before? About the research you had done."

Serwa pulled at her clothes. She had taken them from the first enemy she had slain but they were a size too large.

"Yes," she replied, rolling up her sleeves. "Alexander and I built an extensive library in our home. He had developed a particular interest in messing in old ruins, forgotten cabins, the like. That's where I found the books which referenced you. Indirectly, at least."

"What do you mean?" Sarah asked.

"I mean they didn't use your name. The texts barely mentioned The Chosen One. But, there were several mentions of the girl child made from Lyrica. What would happen if you returned."

The young woman slanted her brows. Serwa stared at her pointedly but Sarah shook her head.

How could she return somewhere she had never been?

"Some old journals Alexander found were very informative. A few of the passages were missing, though." Serwa sighed, stretching her arms up. "All of this is to say, you will have to make a choice, Sarah. Lyrica or Earth. If what I read is any inclination, the longer you remain separate from Lyrica, the more your powers will dwindle."

"No." Sarah stumbled forward as the word left her mouth in haste. Serwa caught her by the elbow and straightened her up.

"No," Sarah repeated. "I...it's not like last time. My powers are..."

Her hands were quivering and her mouth had suddenly gone dry.

"Part of who you are," Serwa finished.

She looked at the witch, then bobbed her head.

Serwa rested a hand on her shoulder. "I would feel the same if I were you. Our magic is an extension of who we are."

"The books must be wrong," Sarah said. "Gan told me I would always be a part of Lyrica. I can even feel my power growing. I'm much stronger than I was last time."

"Well, you're no longer a child but a young woman, Sarah. Of course, your magic would become stronger. Your have so much potential but you aren't like other Lyricans, Sarah." Serwa sighed. "Have you ever fully used all of your magic? Just to see all you can do?"

She shook her head.

"Good. It's for your own safety. I can't be certain. I only have the bits of journals I found."

A dread settled in Sarah's stomach. Her walk had slowed into a stroll and her eyes were locked on Serwa.

The witch continued, "Everything is energy. If you were to ever fully use all your power, you'd risk returning to Lyrica as just that. Pure energy, in a constant flow. Yet, if you return to Earth, you may lose your power forever."

Sarah stopped. She positioned herself to fully face the witch, her breathing shaky and her face a pale scarlet.

"This isn't true." She shouted the words out with some bite.

"I can only tell you what I've found," Serwa replied. "Calm your hackles, child."

The others had stopped several feet away from them.

"What's wrong?" Jacob asked.

Sarah was quiet.

Without glancing at him, Serwa said, "Nothing. Sarah is a little upset."

Something's coming.

Sarah looked behind her, peering into the shadows between the trees. She moved to tell Serwa what she sensed. The witch was two steps ahead.

She glided by Sarah, patting her head. "Good girl, Sarah. I've got this one."

The trees swayed around them. A large wolf emerged from the darkness. His ears were pulled back and he showed his teeth with a growl. The strands of brown fur stood on edge.

Serwa didn't hesitate. In a few movements, she was crouched in front of the beast, looking fixedly into his brown eyes.

She smiled. The air around them cooled and the beast's eyes widened.

"Serwa?"

The witch did not respond.

Sarah stepped to the side, watching as her friend confronted the creature. Her eyes had turned a midnight black.

"Now," she hissed. "Before you approach a traveling party, hoping to scare them with a few grunts and growls, you should have some bite. Especially if I am part of that party."

She cocked her head to the side. "Do you understand?"

The beast lay on all fours. His ears turned upward, and he bowed his head.

Serwa stood, placing a hand on her hip. "Change back so you may speak with me properly."

Bones grinded against bone. Fur retracted; skin stretched and formed. And a man rose from all fours to stand on two feet.

Sarah shut her eyes, turning so her back faced the naked man. The heat flared over her entire face and her heart was ready to leap from her chest.

No warning! Not one.

"Queen Serwa," said an unfamiliar voice. "Please, forgive me. I couldn't believe it was you. You're...alive. We've been fighting but we weren't sure—"

A heavy sob. He cleared his throat.

"None of that matters now. Captain Nettle will be overjoyed to see you and your comrades."

A zap, a bit of lightning as Sarah imagined it, ran through her. They had found Nettle!

Sarah wanted to look back but kept her eyes shut. The naked man was still there.

She could hear the smile in Serwa's voice.

"I'll be glad to see her, too," the witch replied. "I'm sure we'll all be glad now that this war is about to be won."

"As the gods live and breathe, Serwa!" Nettle jumped from her table and zoomed around the witch, leaving spirals of golden dust in her wake. She finally landed on the witch's shoulder and pressed a kiss to her cheek.

Then, her eyes found Sarah and she gawked.

"Yes, seeing her surprised me, as well," said Serwa.

The fairy put both her hands on her hips and gave the girl a once-over.

Sarah grinned. "It's nice to see you, too, Nettle."

"You've grown," she chimed, then looked down at herself. "I haven't. Please, everyone come take a seat. Loren, please bring our guests some food and water."

The werewolf who escorted them bowed before stepping out of the tent. Despite Nettle likely being the smallest one fighting, it seemed she had the most authority, as well as the largest tent.

Klara sunk into a pile of cushions. She rested her axe across her lap and stretched all four and a half feet of herself out. Skuntz stood to the side of Nettle's desk, while Sarah and Serwa took the two seats in front of it.

Jacob and Emry still waited by the door.

Nettle raised a brow. "What are you two waiting for? If we wanted the human dead, we would have killed him as soon as he entered our camp."

They gulped, then found two spots separate from the others.

"Now, we have much catching up to do, don't we?" The fairy giggled. "You'll be glad to know, Serwa, you came at the best moment."

"And why is that?" the witch asked. "Does something need killing?"

She and Nettle tossed their heads back and cackled. Sarah tried to join in but the effort felt halfhearted. Apparently, cackling was not a skill she had mastered.

Skuntz found her eyes. He shook his head, a small grin playing on is lips.

Sarah rolled her eyes in response, ignoring her pounding heart and the tilt of her lips. She'd learn to cackle one day, and then she'd show him.

Aside from Serwa, they all sat quietly, watching as the two friends caught up. Skuntz or Klara would sometimes interject to add more detail or to clarify a statement.

Nettle listened to their tale with unabashed amusement.

Though fairies didn't age the way humans did, Sarah thought she could see the years on her friend's face. Nettle's hair hung down in a long braid. It was still the same lovely black shade, though its ends seemed weathered. Her eyes were still a shining blue yet a small scar decorated her right one. Even as she smiled and nodded, her actions seemed jolted.

She was tired of war.

Nettle looked over everyone in the room.

"What a tale," she finally said. "All leading you here at the perfect time."

"What do we need to do?" Skuntz asked.

"I believe we may be able to take the kingdom back. We have the numbers, the skill, and the strategy. There's only one challenge," Nettle stated. "The humans were quite clever, using the children as leverage."

Skuntz's nostrils flared and the muscles in his arms flexed. "What do you mean?"

"She's talking about Leonna's Tomb."

Everyone turned their attention to Emry. He paled.

"You're not very good at whispering." Klara snorted. "My granda probably heard that from his grave."

"What's Leonna's Tomb?" Sarah pivoted in her chair, so she faced him. "The human queen hasn't died, has she?"

He gulped.

"Tell them," Jacob said, giving Emry an encouraging nod.

Emry shivered, then sighed before finally sitting tall—at least taller than he had been—and speaking.

"I don't believe Leonna's Tomb is what the queen calls it. When I was, uh, recruited, I heard the name mentioned several times." He cleared his throat. "It's where they hold the children. The mixed race ones."

Serwa moved to her feet. "And what do they do with these children, Emry?" She towered over him.

He shook his head. "I don't know. The soldiers call it a tomb because no one ever leaves. Not the children or the guards who watch them."

"We've been trying to get them out," Nettle added. "But there are soldiers and witches forced into serving them. Leonna knows we won't abandon the children, but we can't divide our forces either. I couldn't think of any of mine who have the skill to infiltrate the building and fight off the witches. Until now."

She looked at Serwa and Sarah.

"I can lead a charge to take back your home, Serwa. My kin act as my eyes in the places I am absent. They told me the humans have sometimes pulled guards from the tomb when in need of additiona reinforcement. If my forces descend on the kingdom, Leonna's Tomb will be nearly defenseless," said Nettle. She grinned. "It could work. You and Sarah will free the children, while I draw the humans out and fight on the battlefield. I'll ensure there are no survivors."

"Are you certain we have the numbers?" Skuntz asked with a frown. "We need a better plan. As much as I hate to admit it, the humans will not take this lying down."

Nettle crossed her arms, narrowing her eyes up at him. "We have one. My soldiers can fly, burrow, and fight head on. The humans haven't been able to navigate the mountains' caves, so most of them reside in the camp they've set up. We'll make our way up the mountain, draw the few inside out when the battle starts, and then attack them all. The advantage is ours!"

He gave a reluctant nod. "You have been keeping them at bay for this long. I will trust your judgment."

"And their ships, too. I heard you sunk a few," Klara said.

"They're a rare sighting for a reason," Nettle replied. "The humans are learning we are not to be toyed with."

Serwa cracked her knuckles. "Sounds excellent to me. I also want to examine these stones the witches have made. Sarah?"

"Yes?"

"Are you going to accompany me on this mission?"

Serwa smirked and Sarah found herself doing the same.

"Wait, there's one more thing. I knew something was bothering me." Nettle fluttered her wings and flew to Sarah. She placed the tips of her toes on Sarah's nose.

Sarah smiled. "This brings back memories."

"It does," Nettle replied with a bob of her head. "It also reminds me how silly you can be. Why haven't you used your sword?"

"I have been using it." Sarah gestured toward the length of metal at her side. "What do you call that?"

The fairy chuckled. "You didn't figure it out? Didn't I tell you my gift would protect you?"

She pointed to the small sword hanging around Sarah's neck.

"Use a little magic and she'll grow as big as you need her to."

All eyes were on Sarah. The little gift she had been carrying around the last three years was making her palms sweat. It suddenly felt heavy around her neck, more like an anchor. How could she have never known?

Serwa watched Sarah. She leaned back in her chair, crossed her legs and tilted her chin. The witch's golden eyes burned with a challenge.

Sarah huffed. She pulled her shoulders back, and then reached up and snatched the sword from its chain. She held the tiny weapon in her open palm. Her skin tingled as her energy shot from her core, spreading throughout her body. Grasping it, she forced most her energy into her right, moving it along to her palm.

For a moment, nothing happened. She poured more magic into the trinket.

"Careful! Don't slice your hand." Jacob caught the blade just as it stumbled from Sarah's hand. She hadn't been prepared but managed to get a hold of the hilt.

Meeting her eyes, he removed his hands from her new weapon. It felt light in Sarah's hands and the golden handle shone without any help.

She grinned, holding the sword up and admiring the stainless blade.

"Now she's ready." Serwa grinned, staring directly at Sarah. "Let's end this war."

CHAPTER 26

"Don't fidget with it."

Sarah held in a sigh and forced her hand to the ground. When the gargoyles had flown them up the mountain, she had twisted her wrist at just the right angle. Now, two diagonal talon marks decorated the flesh.

Her cut could wait though. What they were about to do involved saving all of Lyrica and rescuing the imprisoned children—children who had been through much worse than her.

A fire brewed in her belly. She opened her eyes.

Once the gargoyles had left, Serwa and Sarah had started their way up the mountain. The human army resided primarily in the higher portions of the mountain, the land that Alex's parent's once called their domain. Leonna's Tomb, on the other hand, rested farther down the mountain, among the structures of what should have been Alexander and Serwa's new castle.

"It was supposed to be a granary," Serwa had said.

In an effort of diplomacy, Alex and Serwa had decided to relocate their capital. The jagged mountains were not only intimidating to the unfamiliar guest, but they created a level of inaccessibility.

Though Serwa hadn't said it and though it wasn't her fault, Sarah was certain the witch was regretting that decision.

The guards surrounding Leonna's Tomb all had the flaming symbol on their armor.

Sarah's eyes roamed over the land while she and Serwa hid behind a giant rock. They were several yards north of the tomb on an incline. The rock stretched up and out, providing an ideal location for spying. And the humans would have to pass by the stone when they headed in as reinforcements. There'd be no doubting their exit.

A horn blared in the distance. The soldiers stopped and turned to one another. Soon they were scrambling around the unfinished castle, decorating themselves with any available weapons. Several barked out orders, telling them to move faster and to march. With sudden coordination, they lined up in columns of four, a single soldier leading them. Chained witches marched behind them.

Sarah dimmed her energy.

As predicted, the humans and captured witches flooded from the camps in waves. Their movements were in sync but there was a deliberate speed behind them.

Serwa grinned beside Sarah. "They're scared. Good. How many are left?"

Sarah looked over the area, doing so twice to guarantee her count.

"Twenty," she replied. "Fifteen outside, and the other five must be in the tomb. Forty left."

"Hm. Nettle must have spent a considerable amount of time watching the humans. She anticipated their actions exactly."

Sarah nodded, wondering how much of that research had been voluntary or learned in the middle of battle.

Once the dust had cleared and the soldiers were no longer visible, Sarah followed Serwa down to the unfinished structure. The surrounding land was wide and open, which was why Alex had thought it ideal for their new home. This also meant there would be no cover when Serwa and Sarah attacked.

The witch looked at her young friend. Sarah raised her bow. They nodded, then Serwa rushed out.

As the witch sprinted diagonally toward the back of the tower, Sarah had already begun releasing arrows. The targets weren't moving, making them an easy kill compared to the stuffed enemies she fought back home. But many of the soldiers had found time to put on their armor.

Sarah's arrow missed, landing right beside a guard.

He looked from the arrow to her. Surprise appeared on both their faces. Serwa had slashed his mouth open before he could scream. She continued around the tower.

One-by-one Sarah eliminated the guards, and what she missed Serwa finished. By the time the last four realized what was happening, arrows were already flying toward them. They dropped like flies, and Sarah jogged over to join her friend at the front of the tower.

The front stretched out into an extended building. Almost like a barn attached to the tower, as Sarah imagined it.

The witch leaned back and looked over the tomb. She shook her head.

"What is it?" Sarah asked, copying her motions.

She tsked. "Something's wrong. That was too easy. They've also added additional rooms to the tower but what for?"

Sarah took several steps back and cupped her eyes. It was hard to make out but farther up the tower there appeared to be a tiny hovel, which hung off the side.

"I don't think the rooms are important. Prepartion is. We had a plan for a reason, Serwa," Sarah replied.

The witch pivoted, so she was facing her comrade. She crossed her arms and gave the young woman a once-over. She scoffed.

"Be confident, Sarah. Not arrogant."

Serwa moved forward and swung the front door open. A rancid smell ran from the tower. Both women, stumbling backward, gagged and covered their mouths. They slammed the door shut and took in several breaths.

It had been a combination of filth, rot, and stale air. Nothing so disgusting had ever touched Sarah's nose. The manure spreader was roses compared to what she had just experienced.

"Henry, is that you?"

The women stilled. His voice was close.

The five left inside...

Serwa ground her teeth together. She tossed the door open and grabbed the soldier. Sunlight streamed in behind her. Her blade punctured his exposed neck. Arrows flew down at her but Sarah called to the wind and tossed them away. Small lanterns decorated the tower.The remaining soldiers stepped from the shadows, drawing their swords.

If Sarah had been a child, she would have stomped her foot. Serwa chuckled beside her, then turned with a pointed look.

"Ten soldiers, Sarah. Not five. Ten."

"Fine, you were right," Sarah mumbled.

"I was," Serwa replied with a grin.

"Both of you are wrong!" barked one of the men from above. "We've got witches, too."

Serwa tossed her head back and cackled. "Oh, good. More fun."

"And now we know more about our enemy," Sarah added.

Her friend nodded. "You see, Sarah? People like him are the result of arrogance. I don't want you to turn out to be a fool like the little human."

The air in the room shifted. Both Sarah and Serwa looked up just as a human guard floated down to the tower floor. He gave them a sloppy grin and Sarah had to admit he was not a little human. He'd give the county pig back home a run for his money.

While he oozed smugness, Sarah noticed he was rubbing an item in his right hand.

"Good eye," Serwa whispered without looking at her friend.

The human had a witch stone. If he had one, Sarah felt confident the other soldiers did, as well. Then, there were the captured witches to think about. Would they fight for Serwa? Could they resist?

Serwa stepped forward. The man charged. Before he could make it across the room, the witch sent a pillar of earth speeding upward. The human soldier was slammed backward, his face crushed by the pillar. Small clinks followed his descent. Most likely his teeth.

She snatched the stone from his hand, then crushed it beneath her feet. A strong breeze shot through the tower only to quickly settle.

Air.

Sarah stepped beside her friend. Together they stared up at the remaining men.

"Next?" Sarah smirked.

Chains rattled followed by a yelp. A whistling noise pierced the air. Sarah stepped to her right while Serwa moved to the left. The dagger landed between them and eroded the earth. Smoke rose from its blade along with a steady hissing noise.

"Damn witch! I told you to send them all."

Smoking daggers rained down on them. Before Serwa could order her, Sarah pressed herself against the closest wall. She stood on the edges of her toes, wishing she could mesh with the wall to avoid the blades. There was no way she or Serwa could dodge them all.

A dagger sliced through Sarah's hair. Her red curls tumbled to the ground. She gulped, then sucked in a mouth full of smoke. While the daggers had been harmless so far, their fumes filled the room and Sarah's lungs. She coughed and waved at the smoke as it blocked her vision. Soon her breathing wheezed from her and she could see nothing.

Something heavy dragged against the ground.

"Run, miss, run!"

The witch's warning was clear. Sarah darted to the left as the human's sword scarred the stone behind where her head had been. A shrill noise followed as he moved metal against stone.

Sarah found herself spinning around blindly. The door hadn't been far from her but where was it? And where was Serwa?

Large, clumpy hands grabbed her shoulder and forced her around. Sarah unsheathed her sword, before connecting her blade with the enemy's arm. He howled yet did not release her, so she continued hacking until she was free.

She crawled backwards away from her attacker, reaching out for the door. Why couldn't she find it? Her eyes were watering. She couldn't see but Sarah could still feel. She could sense the humans if she relaxed.

A body slammed against her and Sarah found herself flattened.

"We'll finish this," the body whispered. "It's our magic they're using against you."

"What?"

The smoke froze around Sarah. It was as if air had stopped flowing. Then, it shifted away from her, twirling its way to the center of the tower. There, the smoke formed into a large ball and Sarah could finally see blurry images through her watery eyes.

A petite woman stood above her. Her hands hung at awkward angles from her wrists and she was bleeding from several wounds. Dark bruises were speckled across her body, specifically two rings around her skeleton-like wrists. Whatever chains had held her she had broken free from. Apparently she wasn't the only one.

Two other thin frames lay across the room, their tortured hands raised toward the ball of smoke. Their captors lay still on the floor including the guard who had attacked Sarah.

Suddenly the three witches collapsed. The ball of smoke shot from the room like a twister. Sarah watched its departure before turning back to the scene in front of her. With the witches help, they had killed six guards. But four remained.

The humans smiled down at her.

"And then there was one."

"Are you certain?"

The men looked up as Serwa jumped from a ledge toward them. Grabbing the wooden planks just above them, Serwa kicked two guards to the ground. She had transformed her legs into sharp blades and with them she decapitated the remaning two. Finally, she called out to Sarah.

"Those two are yours. I expect you to finish them."

Gracefully, Serwa made her way down and began tending to the three escaped witches. The last two guards had found their footing. They stood with swords raised out toward Sarah. She snatched her own up and did the same.

She could kill them.

The men rushed her together. Their two blades met her one. Sarah resisted for a moment, then let their strength push her sword away. While their momentum pushed them forward, she stepped behind them.

Sarah felt as her blade connected with the soldier's spine. She moved her blade along his spine, happily satisfied with his painful screams. His comrade realized what she had done and turned on her. He brought his sword down on the hilt of hers. However, before he could make contact, Sarah released her weapon. It protruded from the man's side as he fell to the ground.

The last soldier had inteded to cut off her hands. She had other plans for them.

Grabbing his forearm, she smashed her free elbow against his chin. As expected he became disoriented. Before he could recover, she slammed her elbow against his throat, then went to move away.

The poor man still had some fight in him. He swung his sword wildly creating a nice gash along Sarah's collarbone. The grating of bone against metal rattled her teeth but she didn't have a moment to waste.

Sarah pulled her sword from the dead human. With it, she brought the last soldier's wild swings to an end. She easily blocked his attack. His sword landed yards away. He stared up at her.

"Please," he whispered.

"No." His head landed several yards away, as well.

Sarah could feel heat dripping down her body. Only she wasn't sure if it was sweat, blood, or both. Her breaths were labored.

"You've been practicing a few things, I see."

Sarah's heart swelled. She turned, fully facing Serwa, a grin pulling at her lips.

"Do you think I've improved that much?"

She smiled. "You—"

"Hello." A child's voice.

"Is someone there?" Another.

"Sarah, I will continue tending to the three witches down here," Serwa said. "It was a risk setting them free but now I know where their loyalties lie. You start freeing the children. I'll follow behind you soon."

Ladders which led to the other levels of the tower had fallen during the battle. She forced them upright and started her ascent.

The first levels of the building were empty. Then, Sarah felt the bars. They were nearly to the very edge, leaving little room for someone to perch. No wonder more of the guards hadn't hidden in the tower. There was no space.

Behind the bars, there was only darkness. However, Sarah could just make out figures moving. She lit a flame in her palm and peered inside. Ten children huddled together. Their arms were clasped around their knees, and they all turned away from the light.

Between them and the bars, there was less than a foot of space. Dead flies were gathered in a neat pile in the corner.

Sarah's gaze moved over the odd collection and found the children once more. Each one was skin and bones. No plates, bowls, or cups were in their cells. Not even a stray bone or piece of fruit to show they had been fed.

She looked at the pile again.

Had they been eating the flies?

"It's alright now." Sarah reached for one and they all scurried away. As far as they could, at least.

"I promise, I'm not going to hurt you."

The cell had become nothing but uneven, shaky breaths.

"Do you have any food?" a tiny child whispered.

Sarah found her in the cell. "Not on me at the moment. But where you all are going, there will be plenty of food."

"We don't have to go to the healer, then?" she asked, a high pitched hope in her voice.

"There's a healer here?"

The children nodded, their eyes turning upward.

Sarah followed their gazes. Like the small hovel they had seen outside, another addition to the tower was in view, as well. And there was a light on.

She shuddered.

Looking back at the children, she said, "I'll be back. I need to...I need to see what the healer is doing."

A particular curiosity, a particular knowing clawed at Sarah.

She leapt from the ladder to the small cliff, which housed the healer's room. As she grabbed the handle, the door flew open and Sarah stumbled inside. Her chin scraped against the stone floor.

Graceful.

She was moving to rise when shuffling footsteps caught her attention. Looking up, she saw a woman cowering in the room's corner.

The woman wore a long robe. Her silver hair was cropped above her ears, and noticeable wrinkles detailed her small frame.

"Please, leave me alone," the woman pleaded.

"What? No, I'm here to—"

"I only wanted to know," she interjected. "I only took a dozen. No more than a dozen, I'm sure."

Sarah blinked. "A dozen what?"

"It was all for the good of science," she stammered. "We have to learn."

"I'm not sure what you mean but if the h—"

Sarah pulled her hands back from the woman whose own hards were covered in blood. She glanced from the crimson hands to the woman's dainty face.

For the first time, Sarah noticed a table placed in the center of the room. Rising from her knees, she peered over the items laid across the table.

The pieces. Of people.

Bile rose in her throat, which she released across the floor. All at once the rancid smell of the tower hit her again. Sarah pushed away from the table, narrowly missing the opened door and instead falling against the wall just beside it.

She tried to inhale. She tried to take in clean air, to clear away the horror she was experiencing. But there was no clean air to be had. Her head spun.

Sarah's hands moved sporadically across the wall, hoping to find something to anchor her. She grasped the edge of a shelf. Closing her eyes, she rested her forehead against the wood. When she opened them again, she had to catch the scream in her throat.

Four eyes floated in a jar, staring back at her.

Sarah moved away from the accusatory eyes, gulping hard. Peering around her, she realized they were not alone. Jars filled with fingers, hands, wings, and parts Sarah didn't recognize were all around the room, soaking in a green liquid.

Sketches with a variety of anatomy hung on the walls. "Half-breed" was written at the top of each drawing.

Sarah knew she was trembling. She didn't feel it though. She knew tears were pouring down her cheeks, yet her eyes did not burn.

"W-we had to know how to defeat our enemy," the woman, the healer, stuttered. "There were no more than a dozen. I'm sure."

Sarah drew her sword. And then she plunged it into the woman's gut.

"No, please!"

"Did they beg?" Sarah heard herself say.

She twisted the sword and watched as the emotions flashed across the healer's eyes. Her mouth moved with unspoken words.

Sarah pulled the sword free, then plunged it in again. Each time, the woman cringed, her body gasping for a relief that would be slow to come.

"Did they beg?" Sarah repeated.

The healer could only whimper.

Sarah slashed the sword across the healer's chest. Like a fish fresh out of the sea, she convulsed this way and that. Had the sudden pain jolted her senses?

Had she cared when *they* were on her operating table?

Crimson spilled from the gaping wound, along with pink,

twisted organs.

Sarah couldn't look at them. She found the healer's eyes instead.

"Sarah?"

Serwa stood at the room's edge. Her eyes filled with horror as she looked at the shelves. Then, she found Sarah.

The young woman began to breathe again. She could feel the sword in her hand, feel the burning in her eyes, feel her entire being tumbling.

The sword fell to the floor with a clank. Sarah followed after it but Serwa pulled her into her arms.

"Close your eyes," she whispered.

Sobbing, Sarah held onto her.

"I can't, Serwa," she said. "I've seen it. I've seen it all."

A warm hand moved across her face, blocking her vision. But the images were in Sarah's mind now, as if they had been done with a branding iron. As if they were a part of her now, a part she'd never be rid of.

Serwa sat comfortably atop her throne. Though the design was not at all what Sarah remembered, it was difficult not to picture Queen Isabella sitting in the very same spot. Her pulled skin and sharp features, all of the old queen looming over Sarah...but even that had been better than the healer's room.

Grabbing her stomach, she swallowed down the vomit. Everything about Sarah felt off balanced. She was still queasy, and her head was lost in a fog of the tragedy she had seen. Nothing seemed certain or stable.

She peered up at Serwa. The witch and Nettle were speaking with one another.

I need to listen. If we're going to end this war, I need to listen.

A hand lay against her lower back. She looked up, expecting to see Klara, Jacob, or Skuntz.

Emry tried to smile when she realized it was him. The effort had little result.

"You're not feeling well."

She was too tired to be stubborn, so she nodded.

"You saw inside Leonna's Tomb." He chewed on his bottom lip.

"And you lived. It's a miracle after the tales woven about that place. There was a time I thought they had Thobias there."

He added some pressure to her back.

"It was horrible, wasn't it?"

Bobbing her head, Sarah could feel herself swaying. He kept her upright.

Emry chewed on the ends of his thumbnail. "We've done ghastly things. All I wanted was to raise my son somewhere safe, somewhere where he wasn't a half-breed."

"Thobias is n—"

"I know," he interjected. "I hate that term, too."

Jacob, Skuntz, and Klara entered the room. They were freshly washed, and the scent of lavender wafted off them. Sarah had bathed as well, but she somehow still felt dirty.

Emry patted her shoulder before moving to stand beside Jacob. Serwa met each of their stares.

"What are our numbers?" she asked.

"We only lost twelve during the attack. Twenty injured," Nettle replied.

Serwa clicked her nails against the throne's armrests.

"How many children were there?" Skuntz looked between Serwa and Sarah. At the sight of Sarah, he did a double take.

The witch pulled his attention. "We found fifty. They're being cared for in the infirmary. We're not certain how many passed through the tomb."

Jacob narrowed his brows and looked at Klara.

The dwarf met his gaze, apparently having the same confusion.

"What do you mean passed through, Serwa?" she asked.

A moment.

Was Serwa blinking away tears, or was Sarah imagining it?

"Many." She coughed. "Many were killed. We're not sure the number. It was a...mess."

Sadness. Sarah could sense it rolling from the witch in waves. It smoothed and coiled around her, ensnaring her like the images in her mind.

Skuntz cast a brief glance at Serwa, then stepped out and turned to face Sarah directly. She avoided his stare.

"What did you see, Sarah?"

Don't ask. Don't ask what you don't want to know.

"Sarah."

The green liquid.

"You don't look well," Klara added.

The healer's hands were so delicate. But they were covered in blood.

"Serwa, we need to know what you saw, so we can be prepared. Or at least so I can help, Sarah."

Eyes floating in jars.

"I want to—"

"Enough, Skuntz!"

Nettle's glimmering figure huddled in front of Sarah.

"Let them rest," she stated, a warning in her tone.

Skuntz glared at the fairy. She crossed her arms, giving it right back to him.

Releasing a deep sigh, he stepped back and nodded to Serwa. "I'm sorry. I let my my emotions get the best of me."

"No need. It's been a long day," she said. "And we need to discuss our next course of action. At this point, Ellen and Emma have control over Leonna's body. Based on the low number of soldiers here, I'd say they've already started reorganizing the forces. We're next to move."

"To the human kingdom?"

She nodded. "They're expecting us in four days. We need to leave early tomorrow to start making our way. Nettle will remain here to see to our home. The rest of you will be coming with me."

"How are we going to slice them down this time, Serwa?" Klara patted the axe which hung on her back.

The witch straightened. "From the top down."

CHAPTER 27

(Queen Leonna, Day Fourteen)

"**Y**our Majesty, why are we sending so many troops east?"

"We need to find more half-breeds, don't we?" Leonna trailed her delicate fingers along the beading of her dress. The dragon tears were emmaculate against her creamy skin. "How else are we to do that if we don't send more of our own?"

The men around the table stole looks at one another.

Leoona leaned forward. "Do any of you gentlemen have a concern? If so, you may speak."

They were silent which is how she always preferred them. Subjects, even those with high rank, were to be seen, not heard except when she was demanding a response. It was a miracle her father had ever managed any of the council and an even greater miracle she had not jailed the entire entity. They dirtied her air with their aging and backwards thinking.

She pivoted in her chair, so she fully faced the withering gentlemen she had allowed in her presence. She made eye contact with each of them until they cast their gaze downward. Keeping those below her in line was a game Leonna had played since childhood. She still remembered the game even when she was not in control of her body.

"The war is won," she said. "We have the blood-sucking king, his witch bride is our prisoner, and we have conquered the north. It's time we altered our trajectory."

An old bearded man shook his head.

"Speak, Winston."

His eyes were still locked on the table.

"I said *speak*. And look at me when you do so. Do not make me repeat myself," she ordered.

The old man's brow furrowed and his mouth contorted like that of an ungrateful child. Leonna nearly gagged. Even from feet away, she could see the dry skin which decorated his face. No doubt his beard was full of dead skin, as well. How does one not care for oneself? Revolting.

"I do not wish to offend you, my queen, but you celebrate too early," he started, then scratched at his cheek. Leonna covered her mouth, not wanting t breath in any part of him.

He continued, "There are still enemies to be conquered. The half-breeds are the least of our worries at the moment." He sighed. "Your father would not approve of these juvenile tactics. Perhaps your recent illness...maybe it clouds your judgment, my queen."

There was a collective intake of breath. Winston's Adam's Apple bobbed as Leonna's gaze raked over him.

She crossed her arms and rested her elbows against the top of the table. Her generals scooted away from her.

"And where is my father now, Winston?"

His chest rose and fell quite rapidly, she noted. Leonna was certain if she scared him enough, Winston's heart would give out of its own accord. No need to call the hangman.

"He's passed on, my queen."

"And who was his only heir?" She arched her brows at each of them.

Winston's shoulders sagged. "You, of course, Queen Leonna."

"And so it is I you all will obey." She sat up in her chair, tilting her chin and gazing around at the men for any sign of defiance. "Do not forget, gentlemen. It was also my strategies, my tactics which drove us to victory thus far! How dare you question me?"

"I meant no offense, qu—"

"Yet offend me is all you have done." She waved him away. "That and waste our time. The evening grows late. I wish to be alone."

Leonna pushed back her chair and stood. Her generals mocked her movements, adding repetitious bows to her departure. She didn't bother to thank them. She didn't need to, after all. They served her.

Two guards posted at the door greeted her when she left, though they did not follow. She had made it clear over the last two weeks she wanted no one's company. After all, she didn't need any witnesses when Ellen and Emma left her body, finally allowing it to rot. Having been captured was embarrassing enough. Nonetheless, she was still a queen. Queens did not cower under any circumstances.

Yes, she had tried to fight. She wanted control over her body once more, yet it was no longer hers. She had accepted the fact with as much dignity and grace as one could. Being royal born, she had infinite amounts of both.

Ellen and Emma moved her body as they willed. The long, slender form of the worm acting as their strings.

She had nothing left to fight with. She was simply watching the days go by, almost like reading a picture book at an increased speed.

Even her consciousness lived in a limbo, but only for a few more hours.

Serwa, the witch bride, was due to arrive. What Alexander could ever see in such a heathen woman was beyond Leonna. The day would come when he would regret not accepting the offer to feed from her. Royal blood was pure blood, of course.

As Leonna turned the corner, heading toward the throne room, she flung her right arm outward. The stationed guards marched down either end of the hallway, leaving her in peace.

She closed the throne room door behind her. Then, her consciousness began fading as it always did. The retchet twins were ready to leave her. She had no choice but to let the darkness take her...

Leonna's body slumped against the wall as the twins emerged from behind the tapestries. They had wanted to hide in Leonna's personal chamber but her maids were vigilant. The women were constantly present in her chamber cleaning, fetching laundry, leaving flowers, and other servant activities. They insisted on dressing her as was custom, though Emma thought a royal's word would overturn such social expectation.

In this particular situation, a royal's word was void compared to that of persistent elderly women. It seems they had cared for Leonna since birth which gave them a matriarchial status. Emma concluded this was why their word was superior to the queen's.

It was only in the throne room the sisters had managed to find some peace.

Alexander looked over the nearly dead queen. "I have to say, that's the best I've seen her," he remarked, wiping away at the rabbit blood on his chin.

"She's accepted her fate now," Emma replied, moving across the throne room and peering out the window. Observing the guards and servants was educational for their upcoming attack. If Serwa showed mercy, the sisters would suggest who it should be granted to.

She gave the queen's body a quick look. "The human knows she will not be returning to the living."

Ellen remained by the door, glancing down at the nearly dead queen. "Her arrogance would have killed her eventually. Better to go this way. More dignity."

"When do you think Serwa will come?" Charles asked. He examined his clothing. "I'd like to get out of this filth, and get a proper meal in me."

"My wife will come, Charles. Has she ever failed us before?" Alexander gave the young vampire a pointed stare.

He shook his head. "No, she hasn't. I'm just eager to get out of this damn room."

"Patience," Alexander said. "We all have our roles to play. Ours, currently, is to wait."

Leonna's body slid from the door to the floor. It gave a satisfying thump when it landed.

Emma squatted down and stared into the dead woman's eyes. She searched for life in them. When she found none, she nodded. As predicted, their spell was working without error.

"You have the key now," she said to Charles without looking at him. Her gaze was still locked on the dead queen. "When you hear the screams, you should leave."

Emma added, "We'll be on our way now. Sister, will you stand guard while I walk her around the courtyard?"

"Of course," Ellen replied. "Our one last mercy."

Emma made her way behind the tapestry, sending tendrils of her magic out to coax the worm. As it had done several times before, the beast riggled inside the queen's corpse, gradually pumping her cold heart.

Her own heartbeat slowed to match Leonna's. Soon Emma's vision blackened around the edges, so she could only see a small patch of light...

Leonna rose from the floor and dusted off her clothing. She didn't bother meeting the witch's stare. Initially, when they had taken control of her, she had wanted to meet the eyes of her enemy. To let them know she was not afraid, that she would not cower. And she had, except neither of the women cared.

While she had forced all of her frustration and rebellion into one scolding glare, they had returned it with simple indifference.

The thought would have caused her heart to race if the worm didn't have one of its extensions wrapped around the organ. Even breathing was proving difficult as the days went on.

Leonna stood and stepped into the hallway. Then, she made her way out into the front courtyard. She knew there was a slight chill in the air, despite not being able to experience its full effects. Her senses had become limited, as well. A frustrating fact considering the courtyard was a sort of escape from the usual imbecles surrounding her. All knew when Leonna sat in the courtyard, she was not to be distrubed.

Guards bowed to her when she passed them. Emma forced her to bow, as well, despite it being out of character for her even when she had been in control.

She pursed her lips together. The witches appeared indifferent, but perhaps they enjoyed her submission more than they showed. Those in power always liked puppets, did they not?

Leonna knew she did. She had an entire kingdom of them.

Emma's magic pulled on her mouth and she was forced to smile.

Her eyes brimmed with frustrated tears but she couldn't cry. Not in her last moments. No, she would be regal as she always was.

Still, more than ever, she wished she hadn't forced the commoners to move their homes deeper into the wilderness. How had they gotten past all the villages?

Unless they'd conquered them. Her army was stretched thin; few guards had actually made a successful tour around each village before they had been called to fight. At the time, it was a brillant plan.

But none of that mattered in the present moment. The war strategy had left her home, her castle, an open target for the approaching enemies. Upon becoming queen, she had wanted to expand the castle, even add a garden.

That would never happen now.

Leonna sat on a stone bench and folded her hands in her lap. The thick tears made their way down her face despite her restraint. She tried fighting the worm thundering inside her, yet she knew she couldn't. If the damn beast wanted full control, why not prevent her tears, as well? The twin witches were truly cruel. In a way, she admired them. They would have done better work with her army than any of the old men who called themselves her generals.

While she had wished to gaze skyward, her neck was forced east, so she gazed above the wall's rim. The beast shuddered with her submission.

She was going to watch the carnage. She was going to watch her home burn.

A high-pitched whistling pierced her ears as the first boulder sailed through the sky before crushing the eastern wall. Shouts and wails surrounded her, calls of, "Find the queen!"

Emma allowed Leonna to sob, only a bit, then forced her to laugh in the next moment.

Because both she and Leonna knew their queen had already lost.

CHAPTER 28

Sarah gazed over the expanse of land in front of them. There was so much open space en route to the human kingdom, making the journey an easy one for their army. Aside from a few dispersed villages at the kingdom's northern end—all of which Serwa had sent small units to conquer—the land was theirs for the taking.

Sarah wanted to smile but found didn't have the effort for it. Until everyone who had harmed the children from Leonna's Tomb were dead, she couldn't be happy. Not after seeing what they had endured and knowing what she saw was nothing compared to the experience.

Her stomach churned. She took a deep breath, knowing she was on her way to avenge them.

Unlike her first time in Lyrica, those fighting with Sarah weren't strained for numbers. Whereas the human army was comprised primarily of humans, Nettle had brought together Lyricans from all corners of the world. Not only that, but she had the purses of many supporting their cause, including Abelard. He hadn't been able to fight, so he supplied the army with coin and weapons when he could.

Even Klara hadn't known about the expense.

Sarah looked at the dwarf as they rode side-by-side. She was certain everyone could feel it. The energy was alive in the air, the eager tension of anticipation as Serwa led them.

The witch was dressed in golden armor, immediately separating her from everyone else. She rode her horse one-handed and smoothed the other along the horse's mane. Looking over her, Sarah wondered if Serwa could feel it, too. Of all of them, she appeared the most calm while Sarah was nearly ready to jump from her skin. Confidence bubbled inside her.

She glanced at those marching behind them. The ogres were farthest from the front, so they would have enough range when they threw boulders into the castle walls. They were also responsible for pulling the catapults, weaponry Nettle had seen the humans use and mimicked.

Sarah supposed humans were forced to be innovative because they didn't have any sort of magic. As her daddy always said, *When a man's at his wit's end is when he finds the answer to his problems.*

She smiled. Her daddy was right but innovation was not going to do the humans any more good. They would lose. She, Serwa, and their entire army would be victorious.

To her left, Skuntz groaned and slumped over on his horse. Panic set in. She reached for him but a sudden nausea rolled over her.

Sarah knew Skuntz felt it before she did. He was riding beside her when his body lost all motion and he slumped forward. A cramp shot through her arm, turning her muscles into rigid rope. What felt like sharp talons dipped in ice pressed into her skin and dragged along her back.

What was happening?

"Skuntz, calm down," Klara shouted.

He shrugged her off and pulled away from the march.

Serwa whispered to a soldier who rode beside her, apparently one of Nettle's most trusted. Hopping into action, the woman charged forward with the army, while Serwa rushed to Skuntz's side. Sarah forced herself upright before ushering her horse behind them. Her stomach roiled.

The motion Skuntz had lost came back abruptly, only in slow spurts. His muscles flexed, and he took in taxed, jumpy breaths.

"Gan," he wheezed. "Someone's hurting the tree."

His eyes met Sarah's. There was a raging apprehension in his stare.

Serwa glanced between him and Sarah.

"You both will leave to help the village," she said, turning her horse forward. "I...I will remain with the army and conquer the human kingdom. Some of their troops must have found their way to the village." Her eyes were fleeting, moving from the north where the elves' village resided to the west where Leonna ruled. She pressed her eyes shut, taking a deep breath.

Skuntz had already begun turning in the direction of his home.

Sarah reached for the witch.

"Go, Sarah," the witch said, looking into the young woman's eyes. "Keep my children safe."

"We're going, too." Jacob had already freed his wings and hovered next to their horses. "Emry and I—"

"I won't go."

Jacob and Skuntz turned to him, narrowing their brows.

"Didn't you want to—I mean, we can see Thobias now, and protect him." Jacob shook his head. "Why don't you want to go?"

The human's gaze fell downward. He ran his fingers along his short sword's blade.

He said, "I've decided I can't face him, not like this. I need to atone for the things I did."

"What you were *forced* to do," Jacob corrected.

"My actions nonetheless." He sighed. "I will atone. Then, I will face my son."

"Emry!"

"The decision is his, Jacob," Klara chimed in.

Skuntz's horse neighed and kicked her feet in the air. "I'm leaving."

Without another word, the elf sped off, leaving a dust trail behind him. Sarah squeezed Serwa's hand before following after Skuntz. The breeze picked up behind her and she was glad to see Jacob at her side.

"Thank you," she said.

He nodded.

"Oy! Did you lot forget me?" Klara barged her horse between them, casting a stern glare in each of their directions. "He's my friend, too, you know."

Skuntz stared behind him.

"I don't have slow friends," he shouted. "Hurry up!"

They sped through the night. The scenery around them blurred. No one was ever supposed to go the elves' village. Everyone was supposed to be taken, so Sarah couldn't imagine how anyone had found their way. Even now, with Skuntz leading them, she swore she had seen the same landmarks several times.

The tree with a broken branch hanging from it.

The large stone with moss on its eastern side, a single flower on top.

The trail of horse hooves that she was sure they had made...

Yet Skuntz didn't seem deterred. Silently, he charged forward; silently, Sarah and the others followed behind him. Night had turned to early morning when they were close enough to see the flames.

Sarah's eyes widened in alarm.

Fire. All around them there was fire. Humans had swarmed the village like ants devouring a honeycomb. Their flames spiraled up the trees, burning the elves' homes where many of them still stood.

Wooden cages had been filled with small children. The little ones beat at their bars while the human guards swung their swords in response. Women were being dragged by their hair across the village by guards who shouted and sneered at them. And one sobbed. In the midst of the chaos, a small elf stood planted to the ground and wailed. Her long braids spilled past her waist and her face was still too round for her to be older than seven.

Skuntz covered his mouth to suppress a groan just as Sarah's vision blurred. Neither of them was in their best form, but Sarah knew they had no time for healing. She would wait for Skuntz's orders. He knew the village better than her, after all. Until then, she only needed to stay alert, focused.

She watched the wailing child, thinking of the time she had cried and her father had come to her.

"We're coming for you," she wanted to say.

The child's crying stopped. She slumped over as the soldier stood above her with the butt of his sword raised. He gave her tiny frame a small kick. When she didn't react, he lifted her up and began marching toward an open cage.

Skuntz had started to move forward but Jacob grabbed him.

"Let me go, angel," he whispered. "Didn't you see what happened? Don't you see what's happening to my home?"

"They're everywhere. We can't barge in without a plan," Jacob retorted. "You know I'm right. Think about what you're doing."

"I can't!" Tears salted his words. "My home, my family is burning. How can you ask me to think about anything but saving them?"

Something sliced the air above them. The group looked skyward.

Lines of rope crisscrossed over the village, creating a type of spider's web as their arrow ends punctured the trees. The four watched as elves ran along the ropes, dropping small packets on their human enemies

Skuntz held out his arm and began backing his horse away.

"We'll have to leave the horses here and move around the edges," he ordered.

Klara slanted her brow. "Why?"

A collective screech scratched at their ears. Whatever the elves had dropped had begun to fizzle. Long streams of smoke rose from the makeshift bombs. Coughs and wheezing could be heard from the shrouded field, while those trapped in their houses were rescued. Together the elves made their way back across the rope and disappeared into the trees with only a handful dropping into the mist, blades at the ready.

Choked gasps followed their descent.

Skuntz jumped off his horse. "Follow me. This isn't over."

Kneeling low to the ground, the group made their way around the perimeter. Sarah watched from her peripherals as the flames faded behind them. Shouts and screams still echoed around the village. Every now and again, Skuntz would stop and turn his head toward the sound before increasing his pace.

Energy moved through Sarah. She breathed deeply, taking in the essence that was the Great Spirit.

Skuntz stopped their march. He moved to face them, pressing a finger over his mouth. They nodded and walked behind him as he emerged from the trees.

Sarah knew they weren't alone. By the way Skuntz's hand glided over his sword, he knew, too.

The first human emerged from behind the tree. A long axe shook in her hand as she slowly approached them on trembling feet.

"P-please, I'm sorry." She sniffled. "I didn't take much from your tree. I couldn't even reach most of the branches."

Klara smirked and took a step back. The knife punctured the ground beside her.

The girl pressed her mouth shut and glared at them.

"Did you really think that was going fool us?" Klara laughed.

"You humans sure have your heads up your backsides."

The girl took in a sharp breath. Her entire body had become trembles as a roar erupted from her. She raised her axe in the air and began swinging it wildly. Klara rushed forward, meeting her blow for blow.

The remaining humans revealed themselves. They moved in a semi-circle from around the tree.

Sarah pressed her palm to the ground. She stretched her magic like Serwa had told her, then imagined the graves. Four appeared to their right and five humans stumbled into them.

She lifted her hand, imaging spikes raising along with it. The graves fell silent.

Her comrades had fallen into battle behind her, and Sarah joined them. She prepared to send blasts of wind at the enemy. A weight pressed down on her shoulders, and in an instant she was tossed across the field, landing on her back.

Still gripping her sword, Sarah plunged the blade into the ground and pushed to her knees. Heavy pants left her body, but the sound of crunching grass drew her attention. The man's blow landed against her side before she had a chance to look up. It had been a swift kick to the ribs and she felt its effect on her entire left side.

The cool, soft blades of grass comforted Sarah. For a moment, she considered remaining there, giving her body a bit more time to recover. It felt so nice. Yet she could see his armored boots coming toward her and she knew she had to move.

Forcing herself to her elbows, Sarah's world began to shift. The edges of her vision grew murky; the sound of her pulsing heart was deafening. Still, she could see the man coming. She wasn't certain if it was her vision or his intent. He seemed to be taking his time like he knew she was already caught.

She lifted her hand, ready to burn him if that's what it took, but she was so unsteady.

Sarah reached for her sword only to find nothing. She stared around her and realized it had been tossed several yards away. Struggling to her feet, she started toward it. Yet her world still tilted, moving her body along with it.

She stretched out her arm, her heartbeat drowned out her own breathing. She couldn't stop.

"Bring my children back."

Serwa's words propelled her forward.

She closed her eyes briefly, hoping to refocus...

"Stay away from Tom!"

Sarah flashed her eyes open and peered around her. Elaine stood in the woods behind the schoolhouse, a scowl plastered on her face. Her accomplices appeared from behind her with large rocks in their hands.

"I told you to stay away from him!"

A streak of pain moved across her forehead as the first stone hit her temple. Another was quick to follow. It spiraled toward her. Sarah turned her head and closed her eyes.

"Sarafina?" Her father's voice.

"Did you hear something?"

Sarah breathed. The sword was closer, only a few feet away when she began to fall forward...

She lay on her stomach with her cheek pressed to her bedroom floor. There was noise on the other side.

"Sarafina, if you're in there, open the door."

Mama?

"Sarah, baby?"

Daddy.

Like a child, she crawled, reaching her hand out to grasp the doorknob. Before she could, Sarah found herself in the field again. The smell of burning wood permeated the air, her friends fought around her, and screams poured over the entire elf village.

She tried for the sword again. The doorknob appeared before her.

What's happening?

Her vision moved between the two worlds like the wind flipping the pages of a novel. Only whispers of the other remained when she was tossed into one. The doorknob and sword were both so close. She just had to reach a bit more and grab one.

Extending her arm as far as it could go, Sarah gritted her teeth and spat a curse. She saw nothing but the sword and the knob, either appearing or disappearing. Her entire body felt taut, her mind indecisive. But she would have to choose.

"Damn it!" From the pit of her stomach a guttural roar erupted and shot through Sarah. It was the type of roar which would have done Abelard proud—a prolonged throat-ripping cry that rocked through Sarah.

Her throart ached from the screaming. A cutting sear ripped through her shoulder from where the arrow had pierced her those weeks ago. Her back arched outward from when Beth and Susanna had stomped on her. And her temple throbbed from when Elaine had thrown the stone.

Sarah didn't have to look to know that her body and soul were spilled blood, bumps and brusies. Yet what she desired was within reach. She only had to take hold and use the pain.

Part of her felt empty but the pain filled her. It amplified her roar, pushing her forward, closer to her decision. The doorknob and sword appeared once more.

Sarah lunged forward.

She grasped the sword.

The enemy pulled her up by her hair, snarling into her ear. Then, she felt the blade in her side, moving against her soft flesh. She swung her sword out, slashing it across his face. Blood poured and she pushed the sword into his eye socket, until the tip came through the other side. He tumbled over.

Sarah was drenched in sweat. Her hair was plastered against her skin, and crimson flowed from her wound.

Sarah's knees gave out and she fell onto them, leaning on her sword to keep her upright. The crimson was seeping across her entire armor. She cringed, then looked upward to the sky. The star were blurry shimmers but Sarah was certain. They were brighter on Lyrica than on Earth.

She took in a breath only to have it leave her in a painful gasp. Her eyelids felt heavy. Perhaps, if she closed them for a moment, she'd feel better.

"Let go of my sister!"

"Kwe, run!"

Sarah's body moved without her having to tell it to do so. The warm blood trails that flowed against her skin became an afterthought. In its place, at the forefront of her mind, were those voices. They belonged to Bo and Kwe. And they were frightened.

The sun was beginning to break across the sky, casting a warm light over the village. Yet, Sarah still felt like she was trapped in the darkness. Racing from the Great Spirit, following the terrified voices of her niece and nephew, she could only see ahead. The scenery in her peripherals had become a blank canvas to the path in front of her.

She just had to follow their voices.

Though the elves had the upper hand, the conflict in the village had not ceased. Sword clashed against sword, arrows zipped through the air, and Kwe's voice guided her.

"You're not going to get away with this. You—ah!"

Kwe's right arm already lay limp by his side. The soldier had just snapped his left one.

Her nephew's face caved in. He didn't want to cry, she could tell. He didn't want to show weakness in front of the enemy. But the pain of having two arms broken would bring many to tears.

In that moment, the world came back into view once more. Sarah's view expanded and she could see the entire hut. Gan lay motionless on the floor, like a barrier between the enemy and the small children who hid behind her. Bo was forced to the ground with a foot at her back and a noose around her neck. The rope's end was in the hand of a smirking human. And Kwe tried not to weep in the arm's of the enemy.

Then, they all looked at her.

A small voice in Sarah's mind told her to sleep, that she was hurt and needed to rest. That voice was so small though, and Sarah's rage was so much louder.

The humans had been smirking when they first saw her. Then, their breaths came out in sheets of smoke. They shivered as the ground underneath them and the hut walls were gradually covered in ice.

The three humans blinked at one another, then stared at Sarah once more.

She met the eyes of the man farther to her right before calling to the wind. His egregious bulge of a stomach convulsed and he leaned forward as if to vomit. Then, the air spiraled from his mouth like a twister. He fell to the ground with a thud.

Sarah captured the tiny storm in her right palm and met the eyes of the remaining two humans.

There was fear in them.

The woman soldier pulled on the the rope as she searched for an exit.

There would be none.

Spikes of earth pierced her abdomen and shoulder. Her body twitched like a bug who had its wings pulled off. Sarah looked her straight in her eyes until the light there dimmed, her body stilled.

Bo ripped the noose from her neck, then made quick work of the last soldier. Pulling Kwe into her arms, she hugged him and kissed his forehead.

"We're fine now, Kwe. Don't worry. Auntie Sarah is here now."

He sniffled.

"You're fine now?" Sarah asked them. The small voice inside her had grown louder.

Bo began to sob. "Thank you, Aunitie Sarah. Thank you."

They're fine now.

The leadened roars of her anger were drowned out by the small voice of exhaustion. It had raced to the forefront of her mind, pummeling her ears. Gone was the anger. In its place was the searing pain of her oozing wound, her bruised ribs, her slipping mental state.

Sarah fell. Time passed and all of her senses dulled. She only felt the heat from her blood as it left her. Her only comfort. Everything else was a void until warm arms wrapped around her.

"Hold on."

She opened her eyes. Skuntz hovered above her. He looked like a worried mother hen. Sarah was too tired to laugh.

"I can heal her." Someone else was speaking.

Skuntz moved his hand against her cheek. She leaned into him.

But she was so tired.

The world turned black.

CHAPTER 29

"**A**re you certain, Ev?"

"Yes, we're certain," the little gargoyle answered for both him and Sarah.

Jacob ignored him and turned to her instead. He had been particularly observant of her since the human attack at the elf village. Apparently, one of Leonna's generals had been plotting behind her back. He had ordered a sect of soldiers loyal to him to return to the kingdom. On their way, they found an elf child who had stumbled too far from the village and followed him back.

It was a simple mistake, and the village was recovering well, just like Sarah's body. Still, Jacob had become quite the mother hen.

He stared at her, waiting.

Holding in an exhale, she nodded. "We need to say goodbye. Everyone else has had their turn."

The angel hesitated. The door to the human's dungeons was right behind him. It was where the dragons had been kept for Leonna's dresses and where Solar was dying.

The dragon had helped Sarah travel to Lyrica during her initial journey. Yet Sarah was powerless to help her now.

People scurried around them, ripping down the human banners and tapestries. Outside, bodies were still being collected and burned on the grounds. The few humans residing in the castle were meeting with Serwa and Alex per both the royals' request. They wanted the transition be as smooth as possible. Most importantly, they wanted peace.

"At least let me escort you. I have lunch with Emry and Thobias soon but—"

"She'll be fine, Jacob. Let her be." Skuntz stood under an alcove to the room, watching them. "Plus, Ev is with her if she needs someone."

The little gargoyle sighed. He grabbed her hand and stared up at her. "Can we go?"

She looked at Jacob.

Scratching his head, he groaned and stepped to the side. Sarah sent him a thankful smile and cast one last glance at Skuntz before they descended into the dungeons.

All the cells were empty except for Solar's. The living prisoners had been set free, while those who perished were properly laid to rest. There were a number of humans either accused of sympathizing with the non-human Lyricans or who had already been found guilty.

Leonna had kept the dragons at the very bottom of her dungeon. There was a base in another region of the human kingdom where she would have her men capture them. Dragging the dragons underneath the earth, they'd travel until they reached the dungeons where the poor dragons would be imprisoned and tortured for their tears.

"Over here." They stepped off the spiraling stairs and Evley pulled her to a large cell located at their right.

Lashes were lined across Solar's body, nearly erasing her lovely blue scales with a blood red. She could only see them with her right eyes. The left had been sealed shut.

Her breaths were slow and steady. Purposeful. Still, she smiled when she saw Sarah.

"I always knew you would come back to us," Solar heaved. "You are meant to be with Lyrica after all."

Sarah stepped into the cell, then laid herself over her friend's neck. She smoothed her hands over her scars. Crying had become second nature to her, so she barely noticed when she started.

Evley stood in a corner and stared.

Solar looked at him. "Hello, there. What's your name?"

"I'm Evley. But I like Ev much more. What's your name?"

After a long, deep breath, she wheezed out her response. He nodded, then pointed to a corner in the space. Sarah looked over. Three small dragons huddled together.

Serwa had mentioned Solar had had children. Despite everyone's coaxing, the three had refused to leave their mother's side.

"Who are they?" Ev asked.

"My sons and daughter. Luma, Enro, and Solstice. I've been told there was a young gargoyle who lived with dragons for a time. Is that you?"

He bobbed his head. "Did you know Renu? She took care of me."

Solar nodded. "I did. She was my neighbor right next door."

He turned in the direction she had getsured. "How long ago did they kill her?"

"Hmm. Only a few weeks ago. She was a true dragon with a fighting spirit."

Ev stood perfectly still, staring in the direction of the cell. He scratched at his chest and sighed.

Groaning, Solar lifted her tail and ushered her children forward. They yipped and squeaked as she forced them out of the corner.

"Hush, hush now," she whispered. "Your father would be very sad to see you three whining so much. This gargoyle will take care of you now, won't you, Ev?"

"Are you sure?" he said, eyes round and hopeful.

"Babies are a big responsibility, Ev," Sarah warned.

"That's fine! I know what dragons eat. Renu taught me. And she taught about flying too, so I can help them with that." He looked over the three dragons in front of him. "Luma, Enru, and Solstice. I'll take care of you. Don't worry, Solar."

The dragon chuckled. "I'm not. This is the least worried I've felt in some time. And how are you, Sarah?"

Sarah placed a hand on her side. "I've been better but I can't complain. I wish I had...I wish I had gotten here sooner. Solar, I am—"

"No, no," she replied. "There is no point to what-ifs. I spent so much time in this dungeon wondering to myself, 'What if I hadn't gone flying that day? What if I hadn't stopped to help the human merchant stuck on the road?' No matter how many times I asked myself these questions, I was still here."

Sarah moved her hand along her cheek. "I don't want you to go," she whispered.

"And yet it's my time to go. My wounds have taken me too far," she replied. "I will be happy to see their father in the afterlife.

Abelard, as well. He'll be so proud of Klara. She's returned home to run for the head of their clan?"

"Yes. She wants to work on uniting Lyrica with Serwa and Alex."

"Good. I'm happy Lyrica will be in all of your hands. I do have a request of you, Sarah."

"Anything." Sarah pressed the words out between her lips, forcing back the ball in her throat.

Serwa sighed. "So many dragons perished in these dungeons. But I know my kin still live. Find the few of us that remain, help the gargoyle care for my children. We cannot go extinct."

"I swear it." She placed a hand over her heart. "As long as I'm around, dragons will remain part of Lyrica."

A small smile appeared across Solar's face. "Good."

Sarah scooted closer to the dragon. She positioned herself so they were cheek to cheek and both their tears spilled together.

"I know we had no choice to retaliate. The humans left us no other options." Solar breathed and her words were much slower. "Still, I wonder. When both sides lose those we care for, what reason is there to ever celebrate?"

A sob burst from Sarah. She flung her arms around Solar's neck and hugged her.

"I'm going to miss you."

A labored breath.

"And I will miss you...Sarah." Her name was carried on Solar's last breath like a leaf on the wind.

Sarah weeped a bit more, kissed her friend's cheek, then wiped her eyes and headed up the stairs. Ev and the dragons sped ahead of her, squealing and laughing. She smiled though she felt none of their joy.

When they emerged in the castle again, Skuntz was standing by the door. Ev and the dragons ran off.

He looked at her. Bandages decorated his body. He hadn't saved the elf village without a few wounds of his own, though his top and trousers did a good job of hiding most of the damage.

"Has she passed?" he asked.

Sarah bobbed her head. "She left her children to Ev to care for. He seems to have a way with dragons."

"Hm. That's true. You're not feeling well."

She scoffed. "Would you be?"

"No." Without warning, he wrapped his arms around her and pulled her to him.

Sarah sighed and fell willingingly. No matter how much she slept or rested, her fatigue would not leave her. But there was still much more to do on Lyrica.

And at some point, when she figured out how to move freely between the worlds, there would be much to do on Earth. What happened to her mother...Sarah would have to speak with her. To fix things, or at least see her father again.

She looked beyond Skuntz out into the windows where the sky was bright from the afternoon sun.

"We shouldn't waste too much time," she stated, stepping out of his embrace and moving to the window.

"You have somewhere to be?" He had moved beside her.

Sarah shook her head, gazing down at the remnants of the human war. "No, but we both have work to do."

He smiled. "Agreed."

She spun on her heels with Skuntz by her side. Together they stepped out into the grounds, prepared to rebuild their world.

THE END

ABOUT THE AUTHOR

 Natasha D. Lane is a friend of most things caffeinated, a lover of books, and a writing warrior to her core.

As a big believer in the idea that "the pen is mightier than the sword," she graduated from Juniata College in 2015 with hopes of becoming a journalist. Instead, her path took her on a different route and Natasha found herself digging up a manuscript from her childhood.

This dusty stack of papers would become "The Pariah Child & the Ever-Giving Stone." With one book under her belt, Natasha went on to release"The Woman In the Tree: The True Story of Camelot" and most recently "The Pariah Child: Sarafina's Return."

If there were a single piece of advice Natasha could give to young writers, it'd be this: Write your way through life.

To learn more about Natasha and the upcoming sequel, visit http://www.natashalanewrites.com/

To read more of her work, check her out on Amazon.

Follow her on social media here:

Twitter- @natasha_lane1 https://twitter.com/natasha_lane1

Instagram-   natashadlanewrites https://www.instagram.com/natashadlanewrites/

Facebook-   Natasha   D.   Lane   Writes https://business.facebook.com/NatashaLaneWrites/?business_id =670575196466440

Enjoyed the book? Leave a review on GoodReads (https://www.goodreads.com/book/show/47160047-sarafina-s-return) or Amazon (https://www.amazon.com/Pariah-Child-Sarafinas-Return-ebook/dp/B07T8T8GXJ/.)

www.ingramcontent.com/pod-product-compliance
Lightning Source LLC
Chambersburg PA
CBHW061321200626
46813CB00016B/2603